Also by Cara Lockwood:

Pink Slip Party

a novel

CARA LOCKWOOD

POCKET STAR BOOKS

New York   London   Toronto   Sydney

Pocket Star Books
A Division of Simon & Schuster, Inc.
1230 Avenue of the Americas
New York, NY 10020

This book is a work of fiction. Names, characters, places, and incidents either are products of the author's imagination or are used fictitiously. Any resemblance to actual events or locales or persons, living or dead, is entirely coincidental.

This Pocket Star Books paperback edition February 2010

POCKET STAR and colophon are registered trademarks of Simon & Schuster, Inc.

For information about special discounts for bulk purchases, please contact Simon & Schuster Special Sales at 1-866-506-1949 or business@simonandschuster.com.

The Simon & Schuster Speakers Bureau can bring authors to your live event. For more information or to book an event contact the Simon & Schuster Speakers Bureau at 1-866-248-3049 or visit our website at www.simonspeakers.com.

Cover design by Lisa Latwick.
Illustration by Lisa Grue.

Manufactured in the United States of America

10 9 8 7 6 5 4 3 2 1

ISBN 978-1-4391-7337-4
ISBN 978-0-7434-8883-9 (ebook)

For Daren,
for saying I can quit my day job if I want to.

Acknowledgments

I had tons of help in writing this book. I'd like to thank my parents, Jean Hass and Cary Tanamachi, for always encouraging me to do what I love to do: write. Much gratitude goes to my husband, Daren, for listening, supporting, and hiding the paper shredder. Thanks to my brother, Matt, who is, as always, my "inspiration."

A heartfelt thanks to Elizabeth Kinsella and Stephanie Elsea, two layoff survivors who shared their stories and got the last laugh. I'd also like to acknowledge the many friends who make up my honorary publicity and marketing staff, with special thanks to: Kate Kinsella, Jen Lane Lockwood, Keith Lockwood, Shannon Whitehead, Mary Chalfant, Jane Ricordati, Kate Miller, Carroll Jordan, Linda Newman, Stacey Cohen, Amy Van Etten, Kelly Ballarini, Diane Nale, Eric Bryn, Stacey Causey, Cyndi Swendner, and everyone else who convinced strangers at book stores to buy my books.

As ever, I'd like to thank my agent, Deidre Knight, and my editor, Lauren McKenna, for their hard work and invaluable insight.

Pink Slip Party

To: Jmcgregor@maximumoffice.com
From: Ferguson@maximumoffice.com
Date: February 15, 2002, 9:05 a.m.
Subject: FWD: RE: Notice of Indefinite Layoff

Jane,
Read message below.
—F

Dear [insert employee's name here],

We regret to inform you that your job at Maximum Office Supplies Incorporated has been eliminated.

We ask you to do your part to leave on good terms:

1. Clear your desk out by noon. Be considerate of coworkers who will be attempting to work this morning by doing so quietly.
2. Don't take what isn't yours! Any employee seen taking office supplies, furniture, or computer equipment from the building will be prosecuted for theft.
3. You aren't an employee anymore, don't act like one! You are no longer eligible for employee benefits, including but not limited to free coffee or soda and access to the company gym.
4. Profanity only reflects badly on you! Unruly behavior will be dealt with accordingly by our security personnel.

Let's pull together as a team to make this a great transition!

Go Team Maximum Office!
Mike Orephus
Vice President, Midwest Division
Maximum Office Supplies

1

$\mathcal{I}$ think if someone fires you, they should have the decency to do it in person. My boss, lower than vermin on the food chain, was too chicken to actually tell me. Instead, I found out via email.

It's not like I would have wanted a show of tears and prostrated apologies (although these would have been nice). I just wanted a minimum level of decency. Personally, I'd prefer a twenty-one-gun salute, but that's just me. My dad always says I have an over-inflated sense of my place in the world.

Three days ago, on the day after Valentine's Day, I was part of a massive layoff of 1,000 employees from my company (an office supplier that manufactures pink slips). The irony here is not lost on me. Technically, we print office supplies—your blue phone-message pads, your Post-it notes. I worked in design and development on such riveting projects as redesigning "While You Were Out" notes and writing instructions for the backs of correction fluid jars.

On my last day of work, my boss (is it wrong that I wake up and hope daily he's reincarnated one day as toe fungus?), a bald, corpulent, *smelly* man with a shiny, greasy-streaked ring of hair around his ears and down the back of his neck, blinked his black, beady eyes at me and said, "Your severance package would be greater, but you've used up all your sick days."

I suppose I should have been glad. Some people got laid off via voicemail. And others got the news scrolling across the screens on their BlackBerry pagers.

The worst thing about being laid off is that it completely nixes your dream of storming into your boss's office, telling him what he can do with his status reports, and quitting to internal audience applause.

"Does Mike know about this?" I asked my boss. Mike Orephus was the vice president of the Midwest Division, and just happened to be the same man I'd been dating for seven months.

"He knows," my boss said. "He's the one who signed your pink slip."

The pink slip wasn't actually pink at all. It wasn't even a slip. It was just a regular piece of paper, white, with large even margins and a form filled out in Helvetica font, point size 12.

"Listen, we both know this isn't working out," Mike said, when I went into his office that same day. He couldn't look me in the eye. He fixed his gaze on the framed picture of his chocolate Lab, Buddy, sitting on his desk. I didn't know whether he meant my job performance or our relationship or both.

"You're firing me *and* breaking up with me?" I squeaked. I thought he'd show me a little pity. I didn't take him for the type who'd run me down with his car, and then throw it into reverse for good measure.

"Jane, come on, you know that the layoffs are not my decision. They come from above me." He sighed. "And, you had to see that our little fling was over. I mean, I didn't call you for almost a week. You had to see this coming."

I'd believed it when he told me he couldn't talk, that he was swamped at work.

"I thought you were just busy," I said.

"Don't be ridiculous," he said. He used that annoyed snappish tone. The one that all men use when they're breaking up with you and feel bad about doing it, so they try to make it somehow all your fault.

"But, I thought . . ." Now would not be a good time to tell him I'd been thinking we were headed somewhere. That I'd been secretly flipping through *Martha Stewart Weddings* magazines on the newsstands—not because I expected us to get married, but when you reach seven months, *anything* could happen. "I thought you loved me," I finished.

Mike just shook his head at me, looking annoyed.

"Are you going to cry?" he asked me, squinting.

I didn't cry. I'm not a crier. I've never cried in a movie theater, not even when I saw *The Joy Luck Club*. My ex-boyfriend Ron says I've got a heart of granite, but he was a geology major, so who knows what he really meant. There are events that make me teary—plucking my eyebrows and looking at my MasterCard bill are two that come to mind. I'm just not overly sentimental. I worked for two years designing Post-its and while-you-were-out notes. It's hardly the sort of work that encourages romantic dreams.

Besides, I've lost better jobs and boyfriends. At least, I think I have.

I've been laid off three times now, and I'm only twenty-eight. My dad always tells me that I should be sure to make a niche for myself in the market. "You see a need, you fill it," is what he would say.

I've made a career out of being disposable. I'm always the first one to go.

When I told my mother about the layoff, she told me, "Well, dear, look on the bright side. This will give you more time to date."

I'm skinny, but don't hate me. You try going through grade school being called a skeleton. It's not at all fun.

Sure, now I'm reaping the benefits, now that I'm an adult and still sometimes dream of a bully named Sheila who would body-slam me into the jungle gym bars and call me Toothpick. As far as I'm concerned, I deserve to be able to fit into boy jeans.

Besides, the downside of being skinny is that I have no boobs. I should invest in Miracle Bras, but I think that would just be false advertising. There are men who have more cleavage than I do.

I've got honey blond hair, but not naturally so, which I usually keep up at the nape of my neck in a messy knot. When I'm lounging around the house, I wear glasses, which are thick and boxy and I think they make me look like Lisa Loeb, but my friend Steph says I look more like Elvis Costello.

I am not normally what you'd call a go-getter. But, I did try hard at Maximum Office. More than tried, *really* put forth an effort, my best work. I wanted to impress Mike, naturally. Mike, the youngest VP in the company at age thirty-five. Mike who looked thirty, who would listen to my ideas in department meetings and congratulate me on them, like a doting professor. I worked fifty hours a week almost every week. Now, I see that as time wasted. Hours I could've spent happily watching *The E! True Hollywood Story.*

Here's my life in a nutshell:

I'm unemployed. I am currently living in a gigantic, two-bedroom apartment that I can't afford. And instead of saving three months' salary, like every fiscally responsible person should in these uncertain economic times of two weeks' severance pay, I blow three months' salary repeatedly and often and carry roughly that and then some spread out over three credit cards. You could say I'm financially dyslexic.

My mother wishes I'd date more.

My dad feels like I should get married and have babies and stop trying to prove I can handle a career.

I made the colossal mistake of sleeping with an executive who dumped me and was kind enough to spare me the awkward run-ins at the water cooler by firing me.

There. You now have the vital statistics. My life isn't so bad, really. The one perk about being unemployed is that you have the perfect reason to lie around in your flannel pajamas and sulk. It's nice to have a real reason to mope. It's nice to be able to frown at family gatherings and have people whisper: "The job market is getting to her, poor thing," instead of "She's twenty-eight and single, poor thing." At a cousin's couples shower yesterday, my aunt and uncle stuck a couple of $100 bills in my purse. Personally, I'm not above pity as long as it takes the form of cash.

"Tell me what Star Jones is wearing," says my good friend Steph, calling as she does every day around ten. Steph works at Maximum Office and was spared during the last round of layoffs. This does not make her happy, as she's never been laid off, and she feels like she's missing out. Not to mention, now that she's a layoff survivor, she has to do the work of the five other people they let go in the public relations department.

"Let me just say that probably fifty polyester stuffed leopards had to die for her outfit," I answer.

"Has she started shouting yet?" Steph asks me.

"Not yet," I say. I have an irrational dislike of Star Jones and everyone on *The View*. When I had a job, I liked *The View*. It was a guilty pleasure to watch when I called in sick. Now that daytime television is my only intellectual stimulus and social outlet of the day, I find I have no patience.

I wonder why they have jobs and I don't. I could shout. And be opinionated on subjects I know nothing about. And badger celebrities with dumb questions. Watching daytime television always sinks my morale, but I simply can't help it. It's one of those self-destructive desires like craving cheese fries or nicotine.

"Be glad you aren't here," Steph breathes to me.

"What's happening? Has anyone quit?" I ask, hopeful. I like to imagine that after I was laid off, hundreds of other workers took to the parking lot with lighted torches, flipping executives' cars and demanding their fellow coworkers be reinstated.

"God, no," Steph says. "Everyone's scared shitless. Plus, there's no time to quit, not with the work we have to do. Did I tell you I have to write marketing proposals for eight new clients? And that's just what I'm supposed to do today. I haven't left the office before nine anytime this week."

"That does sound rotten," I say.

"Worse, Mike's been talking about having a weekend retreat," Steph says. "As if we aren't giving enough blood to the company, they want our Saturdays and Sundays, too."

"Well, it could be worse. You could be held captive in front of *The View* like I am," I say.

"Considering I have a stack of work on my desk taller than the Sears Tower, that doesn't sound so bad," Steph says. "Shit, here comes the boss. I think he's going to tell me I have to stay late again tonight. Let me call you back later."

Two minutes after I put the phone down, it rings again. It's my brother Todd.

"Jane, you promised you'd look for jobs today," he says. He's older and put together and doesn't like the idea of his tax dollars supporting my extended hiatus. He can't stand the idea of anyone not being a slave to the same institutions he is. He can't bear the thought of someone else living a free life outside the box.

"I am looking," I lie. The classifieds are open and they're sitting on the other end of the couch. If I stretch my neck to the right and squint hard enough I could probably make out one or two of them.

"If you were really looking, you'd be online, and the phone line would be busy. Have you at least *made a plan*?"

Todd feels planning is essential. Like showering. His

idea of spontaneity is to use free hand calculations instead of an Excel spreadsheet.

"I was thinking of checking out the profession of dereliction," I say. "I'm more than qualified for it."

"Jane. Be serious."

"I am serious. I'm not a picky eater. I could eat out of trash cans."

"I hardly think that counts as a valuable skill," he says.

"Maybe I could test out new Nabisco products," I say.

"Have you sent out your resume?" Todd is nothing if not relentless. I know that this is just his way of showing he cares.

"I've sent out twenty resumes, and I got one call-back from a man who informed me the fax number I was dialing was out of service," I say.

"Well, maybe we should update your resume," Todd says.

"Todd—don't you have tax returns to do?"

"Look, I don't mean to be an asshole, I'm just saying, you should think about what you're going to do next," he says. "You should take this time to reevaluate your life goals."

It's hard to reevaluate your life goals when you've just lost a job you didn't even much like. It's hard to plan for your future when you are beginning to suspect that everything you touch turns to crap. I don't exactly have the confidence at the moment to engineer my next brilliant career move, since my Fall-in-Love-With-an-Executive plan didn't work out.

Todd is still talking.

"You should take this opportunity to really ask yourself: What do I want to be?"

"Todd, have you been reading *Who Moved My Cheese?* again?"

When I was in college, I had dreams of becoming the next Andy Warhol, except that after three art classes I discovered that my talent landed somewhere between Walt Disney and Sherwin-Williams. Not to mention, when you graduate as an art major, you don't, as popularly believed, get a gallery showing handed to you along with a big fat check from the National Endowment for the Arts.

"Have you at least gone down to the unemployment office?" Todd asks me.

"I thought you didn't believe in government handouts," I say.

"Well, you've more than paid for it in taxes. If you don't go apply, then you're letting Uncle Sam steal more of what's rightfully yours."

"I'll go, Todd," I say.

"When?"

"Today, all right?"

"That's my girl," he says and hangs up. Todd and I have your typical older brother/younger sister sibling relationship: He tells me what to do and I largely ignore him.

· · ·

Because I'd rather do almost anything than change out of my pajamas, I sit down at my computer and scroll through job listings for awhile. There are no new creative or graphic design positions posted. They are the same five that have been listed for the last week. Three of these are from now-defunct dot-coms (having tried emailing them, I know) and two are at companies currently going through a hiring freeze (it is cheaper to leave a posting online than to take it down).

Since there are no jobs posted that I'm qualified for, I apply for a few I'm not, including Zoo Assistant. I make up a wild story in my cover letter about my fictitious exploits in India, where I grew up and learned how to train elephants by watching Biki, our family's servant, care for the animals.

I like to think that somewhere, there is a human resources employee with a sense of humor. I have faith that one must exist. Like life on other planets.

While I am already in a foul mood, I decide now is as good a time as any to go to the unemployment office. I have been putting off this activity for too long. I do not want to admit to the state that I have, indeed, lost another job. It feels like admitting to your friends that the boyfriend you told them was planning to propose has run off with your downstairs neighbor. Dumped. Again.

· · ·

The unemployment office is a dingy horrible place with army posters on the walls and horrifically artificial fluorescent lighting. All state buildings, I think, are required to have very unflattering lighting. It's part of an elaborate plot to make state employees look even more disheveled and bored.

When I arrive, around two in the afternoon, there is already a line of degenerates behind a coiled rope, much like a ride at Disney World, except there's no sunshine and no overpriced soda stands. I am tempted, however, to raise up my arms and shout, as if I am sitting in the front car of a roller coaster. Ahead of me, there's a woman in a business suit who looks like she only just got fired today (she's clinging desperately to a potted plant). Ahead of her is a man with a full beard who has drawn swastikas on his shirt. At the very front, I can hear two unemployment office employees arguing.

"That's not my job, Lucinda," one of them is shouting. "Why don't you stop being so *damn lazy*."

"Mmm-hmmm, I know you didn't just talk to me like that, *biatch*."

"Who are you calling a bitch?"

"Well, you's the only one here, so I guess I be talking to you. *Biatch*."

"You want to go right now? Let's go."

"Oh, I'm ready to. Anytime you wanna go. I'm ready."

Somewhere, at the head of the line, a few of the lower dregs of society start cheering.

"Ironic, isn't it?" says the woman in front of me with the potted plant.

"That they have jobs and we don't?" I say.

"Exactly," she says and sighs.

A tall, sloped-shouldered man in a white short-sleeved collared shirt and a tie, the uniform of a lower midlevel supervisor, pulls the two workers apart. He tells them to "Take five" just like my middle-school gym coach.

"Wind knocked out of you, eh, McGregor? Take five. Put your arms over your head and breathe deep."

I hated gym. Every time we played a sport involving a ball, I always got hit in the stomach with it. It was like there was a tracking device inside. Ooof. Every time. It's no wonder then that my Pavlovian Response to physical exertion is acute stomach pain and difficulty breathing.

"Come on people, let's move," the reedy man up front is saying. He has quite an overbite. "Everyone that's just been laid off, go to the right. Everyone who's been fired, left."

I go to the right. The low-level manager with the buck teeth eyes me suspiciously. Perhaps I look like I've been fired. Maybe I look guilty.

I fill out more forms than are necessary to donate a kidney.

I am jostled from window to window, like a nerdy party guest no one wants to talk to. The clerks have stickers instead of stamps, and fingernails longer than mechanical pencils. They smack gum irreverently as they glare at the back of their supervisor.

I look at the floor and try not to make eye contact.

"You need the *blue* form," says the grandmotherly woman behind counter number two.

"I have the blue form," I say.

"Not *that* blue form. This blue form," she says holding up a form that looks exactly the same.

"But isn't that the same?"

"Look, miss, would you hurry it up?" says a man who smells like onions standing behind me.

"Step out of line," commands the woman behind the glass partition.

Just like that, I am bumped out of line, and back to the table with the forms at the back.

It is almost five before I am finally, officially, registered for unemployment. They say it may be two weeks before I get my first check. I ask the woman behind the glass if this includes pay for the three hours I've stood in line. She doesn't think this is funny and frowns at me.

When I was fourteen, my mom thought I should audition for *Saturday Night Live*. She'd said so when I was younger and I'd make her laugh by sticking Pixie Stix up my nose and pretending to be a walrus. She thought I was a natural comedian. Then I went out into the real world and found that *lots* of people have mothers who think they should be on *Saturday Night Live*.

It was the same feeling going into the working world. Discovering that you are not special, even if your mother thinks you are. You are expendable. Your worth is calculated by hourly rates and vacation time. You are not a person. You are no more than a series of numbers. A cell in a spreadsheet. A glint in a beancounter's eye. Your whole existence fits into a neat series of ones and zeros.

As I'm leaving the unemployment office, I nearly bump into a girl coming in. She's wearing entirely black, with silver eye shadow and a ring through her nose. Her hair is tied in two blond knots on either side of her head, and her T-shirt has a ☺ face, not a smiley and not a frown, either—indifference, and so I peg her as a techie. There's something about her that looks vaguely familiar, and then it hits me: She used to work at Maximum Office.

"Maximum Office, right?" I ask her.

The girl nods. "Yeah, I worked there," she says. "I was the system administrator before the cocksuckers laid me off last week." She studies me, then extends her hand. "I'm Missy."

"And I'm Jane," I say.

"You're the one who was sleeping with the Midwest Division VP," Missy blurts.

I turn bright red. I think everyone in the office knew. It's why I couldn't pass a watercooler without hearing hushed whispers and giggling.

"Look, I'd better get going," I say.

"Hey, don't take offense," Missy adds quickly, putting up her hands. "I didn't mean anything by it."

Missy is very small. She is literally half my size. Her feet look like children's feet.

"So, where do you live?" Missy asks me, deliberately ignoring my "this conversation is over" vibe. She's also blocking my way out the door.

"Lakeview," I say, trying to avoid giving an actual street address.

"Me too," Missy says. "Where?"

"Uh, near Sheffield's," I say, being deliberately vague.

"Me too!" she says. "What street?"

It's impossible now to avoid it. "Kenmore," I say.

"Cool," she says.

Missy is eyeing the Tiffany charm bracelet on my left arm (a college graduation gift from my maternal grandparents) with interest. I tuck it into my sleeve.

"One bedroom or . . . ? " she trails off.

"Two bedrooms," I say.

"Got your own washer/dryer?"

Missy is beginning to sound like a real estate agent.

"Yes, as a matter of fact, I do," I say.

"Hardwood floors? Exposed brick?"

"Look, I'm renting the apartment, I'm not selling it," I say.

"Touchy," Missy says, holding up her hands.

I think for sure this conversation is over. But because Missy, like so many techies, is unfazed by deliberate rudeness, she continues. "I'm just asking because I'm looking for a place to live. I'm house-sitting but that gig is up in a couple of weeks."

"I'm not looking for a roommate," I spit, quickly. No use in giving her false hope.

"Oh," she says, shrugging. "Well, if you change your mind, here's where you can reach me."

She gives me one of her old Maximum Office business cards. Most of the information is scratched out, except for a handwritten number at the bottom. She's drawn devil horns on the *o* in "Office." I put it in my purse, as if I intend to keep it, when I plan to throw it out at the next available opportunity. Only a mentally deranged person would shop for a roommate at the unemployment office.

I arrive back in my apartment and immediately take a shower to wash off the stale smell of government work and the recirculated air of lowered expectations.

I change into a set of clean pajamas and feel like I never left home. I feel like there's something I ought to be doing, and when I realize that that something is paying the rent because it's due today, I sigh. I have next to no money in my checking account. I blame the financial advisors on CNN who claim that the only way to get out of credit card debt is to pay for everything with cash. I did that at the beginning of the month (including some extravagances like seven cab rides, a pair of Prada shoes that were on sale, and a pair of cashmere gloves). And now I have no cash to pay my rent. How does that make any sense?

I'd been spending like crazy (in part because I'm an art major and math and budgets are foreign concepts to me, and in part because I thought I was falling for Mike and wanted him to fall for me, too, and so I bought a new wardrobe of borderline professional, borderline sexy, kittenish outfits for work). Honestly, it never occurred to me that I would be laid off—again. Something about third time being the charm, that while layoffs could happen twice, three times seemed a bit of a stretch, even for a person with my kind of persecution complex.

Plus, I had insurance: my relationship with Mike. Not that I consciously counted on that, as it was a consensual relationship, but I felt protected. Little did I know that Mike was plotting to discard me like Kleenex.

The next day, I get my last check from the Evil Pink Slip Company, and I deposit it into my bank account and, for a full afternoon, soak in the illusion of being rich. It is a double paycheck (the extent of my meager severance), and it feels like I've won the lottery. I go and buy five full bags of groceries with luxury items like olives and salad dressing and brand name cereal that comes in a box. I buy organic vegetables and double-ply toilet paper and quilted paper towels. I feel like skipping down the street and handing out fives.

Of course, this is willfully ignoring the fact that after paying off my minimum credit card balances for the month, and my utility bills (including my $480 gas bill for the record-breaking freeze in February), I will not quite have enough for the rent. Still, I allow myself to feel a little optimism. My mom always encouraged me to use my imagination. She never dreamed it would pave the way for my huge capacity for denial.

To: jane@coolchick.com
From: Headhunters Central
Date: March 4, 2002, 10:30 A.M.
Subject: RE: Your Resume

Dear Jane,

We have received multiple copies of your resume today via email and fax and feel compelled to tell you that changing your middle initial in no way disguises your resume.

We will contact you should we find anything suitable for your needs. And we do not appreciate you asking, even in jest, if we include escort services in our job placement list.

Please stop faxing us.

Sincerely,
Lucas Cohen
Headhunters Central

2

Like all ill-fated work relationships, Mike and I got together at the company holiday party. The party, normally held in November, was moved up to early September because we were celebrating a good fiscal year. The party was at Blackbird, one of those upscale places that serves a single prawn on a plate of baby greens and calls it an entrée. Everyone was celebrating bonuses. Even I'd gotten an extra $300 in my paycheck that week, and my salary wasn't usually tied to profits.

I was sitting at the bar smoking a cigarette, because even if you quit like I had, company functions of any kind are exceptions. Everyone knows this.

I was watching Dave Nedles from accounting swig down two cranberry martinis in succession, while he tried pathetically to pick up the cute, leggy cocktail waitress. Dave was smacking his lips, puckering them up like a big, wet fish. I hated Dave. He was the sort of guy who took off his wedding ring when he went out to bars. He thought nobody knew this about him. He thought he was sly.

It was about this time that my boss's boss, Mike, emerged from the smoke and shadows. Mike, boyishly handsome, was noticed by every woman in the office. The secretaries had fights over which one would take him his mail.

He said, "You don't look like you're having much fun."

And I said, "I didn't think it was possible to have fun at these things."

He'd laughed, and leaned in. He had that way of making you feel like every conversation was a shared private joke.

"I probably shouldn't tell you this, but I will because I've had four drinks to work up the courage to do it," he said. "I think you're incredibly sexy. But I'm sure you have a boyfriend, right? Girls like you always have boyfriends."

That was all it took, really. I was that easy to pick up.

We had drunk sex, blurry, would-be-embarrassing, clumsy sex, the kind you pretend didn't happen. But he called me two days later and asked me out on a proper date. For the next seven months, we hardly ever separated. He said he loved me. I said I loved him. Then he fired me. That's the short version.

I feel like I have single-handedly pushed the feminist movement back thirty years. When a vice president had the hots for a secretary in 1972, she got promoted. In 2002, she gets fired. It's about that simple. You can't advance when you're a liability.

Mike left four things at my apartment: a toothbrush, a disposable razor, a pair of Halloween boxers, and a Gap T-shirt. This is all that's left of a seven-month relationship. It's all the proof that he was ever here at all.

I lay out his things, one by one, across my living room floor and study them. I smoke several cigarettes in succession, stubbing out the last one into one of the jack-o'-lanterns on his boxers.

A toothbrush. A razor. A pair of boxers. A shirt.

If I can figure out why he tired of these things, then maybe I'll figure out why he tired of me.

He used to call me a Live Wire. He used to say I was exciting, thrilling, sexy. He used to not let me even get into my apartment before he had his hands up my skirt. He couldn't get enough of me. He'd call me every night, insist on seeing me, drink me up with his eyes.

Now, I'm just one more thing that's disposable. Like his toothbrush or razor.

Part of me hopes he'll call me for them. But I know better. He's left things here he's not attached to. He's left things here he's willing to lose. It's like he planned a quick escape from the beginning.

I realize that it's over, and yet, I still haven't stopped expecting him to call.

"You're better off without him," Steph assures me on the phone.

"I don't feel better off," I say.

"For one thing, he's got a funny walk."

"He does not," I say.

"He *does*. He sort of walks like a duck."

"He does not walk like a duck."

"Jane, you're just in that 'he's perfect because I can't have him' stage. Trust me, he walks like a duck."

"I liked the way he walks," I say.

"In three more months it would've driven you crazy. You'd see him walking down the street, and you'd be thinking to yourself 'why am I with a guy who walks like a duck?'"

"I'm not that superficial," I say.

"It's not being superficial, it's being genetically practical. Do you want your kids to walk like ducks?"

I sigh. There's no arguing with Steph, especially when she's off on a tangent.

"So, what does that say about me if a guy who walks like a duck doesn't want me?"

"Oh, you've got it bad," Steph says, exhaling loudly.

"Tell me about it," I say.

"Can't we just skip the part where you obsess about Mike and what you did to push him away when it's obvious it has nothing to do with you because he's the asshole?"

"I wish we could," I say. "But I'm afraid I'm going to have to wallow a bit."

"OK, but just humor me, all right? Tell me one thing that doesn't have anything to do with Mike."

I think about this for a moment. "I ran into Missy the system administrator at the unemployment office," I say.

"You mean the same Missy who is rumored to have stolen two laptops, a stapler, and an executive's ergonomic chair?"

"Really?" I exclaim. If I'd known of her Maximum Office terrorist activities, maybe I wouldn't have been so eager to give her the brush-off.

"Well, that's the rumor. But you know how these things get started. She probably just took the stapler."

"She's looking for a roommate, believe it or not," I say. "Now can we talk more about Mike?"

"No," Steph says, emphatically. "Tell me what's happening on *The View.*"

Star Jones is having a shoe confession. She has too many of them apparently (as if anyone could ever have too many shoes—the mere thought is preposterous).

"Star Jones says she has too many shoes," I tell Steph.

"Ridiculous!" Steph says. "That's practically sacrilegious. You could do her job. Have you thought of applying?"

"I've got oily skin," I say. "They'd need my weight in powder to get the shine off my forehead."

Everyone on *The View* has very matte make-up. I've

abandoned make-up temporarily. It doesn't go with flannel pajamas. And it's just something else I have to wash off at night, when I'm rinsing off the stink of failure. These days, showering in general has become a low priority. I don't see the need, and I am secretly wondering how long it will take before I start smelling like a sophisticated European.

"So what are you going to do today? Besides burning Mike's likeness in effigy?"

"I'm going to do something more constructive. I'm going to wish myself some rent money."

"Can you wish me a smaller ass while you're at it?"

"I'll give it a try," I say. "By the way, do you know what the tenant laws are in Illinois? How long can you technically go without paying your rent before your landlord can have you forcibly removed?"

"If you need a loan, you know I'm happy to give you a loan."

I'm tempted, but I can't take Steph's money. She's got as much credit card debt as I do.

"No, that's OK," I say. "I'm just going to squat."

My landlord is a Frenchman named Bob whose thickly accented English makes it sound like he is spitting rather than talking. He also yells, which can be frightening and intimidating, except that once, after he'd drunk quite a lot of vodka, he told me that he only did that because he hates being asked to repeat himself. Bob wears his bathrobe at all times, and showers about once a quarter. He has a perpetual five-o'clock shadow, even in midmorning, and he used to have a soft spot for my former roommate Karen, who moved out four months ago to live with her Almost-Fiancé, leaving me high and dry with rent to pay.

Bob lives in the top floor apartment, and, as he's averse to exercise, he rarely comes downstairs. I'm counting on his laziness to allow me a few days extra before he starts coming to look for his rent.

The afternoon passes in a series of talk shows, starting with the high-end ones with B-list actors as guests, like *The View,* and ending with your low-grade circuses like *Montel Williams.*

I realize that it's been hours since I've left my couch, and I wonder how long it takes to develop sores, or for muscles to atrophy so completely that I won't be able to walk to the bathroom unassisted. After that, I could be a guest on *Maury Povich*—the Sloth Girl—crippled from aggressive, reckless laziness.

Maybe that's my career calling—talk show guest. I imagine a line of T-shirts with Sloth Girl logos on them, a tell-all best seller about my downward spiral into catatonic laziness. I can see my brother Todd being interviewed on the *Today* show: "I tried to tell her to get a job but she wouldn't listen—and now look at her—confined to her couch for life."

Because I realize that *Maury Povich* should not be my highest aspiration, I decide that it's about time I do something constructive and deal with the bills from last month. I have sorted them into three piles: 1) bills I won't ever pay; 2) bills I would pay if I had the money; and 3) bills that I am going to pretend I never got.

I'm going to spend the entire day canceling services. This does not make me happy. This makes me feel poor.

Digital cable. *InStyle* magazine. Cell phone. *People* magazine. I say goodbye to them all.

Digital cable is the worst. I wait online for a half hour to talk to a real person about disconnecting service.

It's insulting, really. They assume poor people have plenty of time to sit around listening to "Baby Got Back"—the Muzak flute version. Poor people's time is not valuable. People of means wouldn't sit on hold for twenty-eight minutes, waiting for their service to be disconnected. It's what the companies count on.

While I am on hold, I stare out my front window. I watch the old lady who lives on the first floor come out with her dog, a white, fluffy thing that's about the size of a grapefruit. I've never formally introduced myself, but her mailbox says "Slatter." She doesn't pick up the dog's poop like she's supposed to. I've seen her kick dirty snow over it and move on.

I watch as she makes her way straight over several big ice patches on the sidewalk. I guess that's the kind of confidence you have when your health insurance is covered by Medicare.

While still on hold, I tear myself away from the window and head to my refrigerator. I never thought of myself as a pig, but I've run through my gourmet groceries at a rapid clip. There are a few Diet Cokes, some wilted vegetables that I never cooked, some Brie, well-past-due milk, and two jars of expensive olives.

The cable representative finally comes on the line. He sounds bored. I wonder how much he makes. I imagine myself sitting in a drab, gray cubicle, wearing a headset, and reading customer service speeches off a laminated index card. If I had that job, I'd be tempted to put on a thick Hungarian accent, or pretend not to know English.

The customer service representative I talk to doesn't have that kind of creativity. He tells me that even if I offered sexual favors, he wouldn't be able to let me keep my cable free of charge. I've never run into a cable guy who was willing to be bribed. I've been spectacularly unlucky.

I get teary over losing HBO, but he doesn't seem to care. I'm sure he gets that a lot—people crying over lost cable.

"Thank you for calling," he says, but he sounds like he doesn't mean it.

The cable goes out almost instantaneously, and I have to go back in my closet and dig out the antenna for my television. I hook it up, and find the television awash in static. I can receive four channels—CBS, NBC, ABC, and public broadcasting—but only if I attach a frightening amount of tin foil to the edges of the antenna. I mold it into the shape of Gerald Ford, but there's still a double picture and passing moments of static. I vow, in Scarlett

O'Hara fashion, that once I find a job, I will never be without cable again. As I'm waving my fist in the air, the phone rings.

It's Todd.

"I've emailed you a notice of a job fair. Did you get it? Are you going to go?"

On the Todd Spaz-o-meter, a scale of one to ten, the tightness and urgency in his voice only really ranks as a three.

"Are they going to have clowns there? And cotton candy?"

Todd does not laugh. He is missing the humor gene. He doesn't know what's funny. When he's at the movies, or in a business meeting, he hangs back and waits for other people to laugh and then he joins in. It's very sad.

"No, *Jane*. They have recruiters and HR professionals there."

He seriously thinks I'm unfamiliar with what a job fair is.

"Sounds like as much fun as an undertakers' convention."

"Jane. Come on. Go. You can meet me for lunch. Come on, I'll buy."

I pretend I'm choking from shock. "You'll buy? Is this the seventh sign of the apocalypse?"

Todd is notoriously cheap, like my dad. When the bill comes he's always struck by a sudden case of alligator arms. They're always too short to reach the bill.

"Very funny," Todd says.

This is good. I am giddy. Any time I get an excuse to leave the apartment, I feel like celebrating.

"But," Todd says, rather sternly into the phone. "I'll only pay if you update your resume."

"Todd," I cry, my exuberance for seeing the outside world tempered by the fact that I have to do work to earn lunch. "That's extortion."

"I know you won't do it unless you're bribed."

That much is true.

"I've already updated my resume," I lie.

"I don't mean copying someone's resume from Monster and passing it off as your own."

Damn that Todd. Smarter than he looks.

So. The resume.

The resume is difficult because it requires a lot of imagination, creativity, and a propensity for outrageous, ambitious lies. The bigger they are, the more believable they are. Small ones are noticed right away.

I boot up my computer, and pull up my resume. My last job description, before Maximum Office, was technically "part-time graphic designer who answered phones." On my resume, however, I put "Director of Graphic Marketing and Chief Communications Coordinator, Midwest Division."

I stare at my resume and wonder what I should say about Maximum Office. My official title was Design Specialist.

This sounds impressive, but "specialist" means "cheap labor with little experience." They might as well have called me Pawn. Or Plebe. Or Indentured Servant. Or, most accurate, Acceptable Loss.

So. What. Am. I. To. Write.
   I like,

> Imperial Grand Duchess, Ruler of World, Worth
> Far More Than She Has Ever Been Paid, Supreme
> Being of Supernatural Intelligence and Artistic
> Creativity, Destined For Great Fame and Riches.

This might be too much.

I delete "Worth Far More Than She Has Ever Been Paid"—this sounds like I've settled for less than I deserve. CEOs and royalty never settle. Neither shall I.

I spend another half hour before I am sucked back into the temptation of daytime television. Maury is having yet another round of Paternity Tests. I think he is trying to single-handedly subsidize the nation's DNA labs.
   Those tests are a waste of time.
   The father is never the clean-cut guy with the regular paycheck, the khakis, and superior dental hygiene. It's always the pimp with missing teeth who grabs his crotch and taunts the audience.
   It's like watching a bad sitcom.

The ending is always the same.

As always, watching television sucks in time like a black hole. Everything in its immediate grip moves very slowly. Everything outside moves very, very fast. I like to think if I never left my couch, I'd live forever. I could watch everyone grow old outside my window. I'd stay exactly the same and wouldn't age, like Dick Clark and Twinkies.

When I look up again from the crotch-grabbing Neanderthal, I find that I have run out of time to shower (not that I would have had the motivation to do it even if I did have time).

It is only Todd.

And a career fair.

I throw on a bandanna to cover my grease-slicked hair, and put on a moderately clean pair of crumpled pants I find in a heap on my closet floor.

"What the hell are you wearing?" is the greeting I get from my brother Todd. Todd, predictably, has not come to lunch alone. He is with his sidekick, Kyle Burton. Kyle, who grew up next door, has known me since the days I used to run around wearing only the bottoms of my Wonder Woman Underoos. Not that I won't still do that, but these days it requires quite a significant amount of alcohol.

"I can't afford drycleaning," I say, by way of defense. I notice, rather belatedly, there is quite a large dust ball clinging to the hem of my pants.

"Nice bandanna," Kyle says, pointing to my head. "Going for the urban look?"

"I'm thinking of forming my own gang," I say.

"The Packin' Power Puff Girls?" he suggests.

"That, or Barbie's Bitches."

"Jane," sighs Todd, who is shaking his head slowly back and forth. "Jane, you can't go to the job fair looking like that."

"Todd, it's not your problem," I say, beginning to wonder if a free meal is worth all this hassle. A waiter plunks a menu in front of me, and I realize I've survived the day eating only olives.

Kyle is smirking at me.

"What?" I say, shooting him a dirty look.

"Er, well," Kyle says, clearly trying to hide a smile. "Your, uh, bandanna is crooked. It's leaning quite dangerously to the left."

I reach up and give it a tug.

"Your other left," he says.

I let Kyle's insolence slide.

Kyle—successful corporate attorney Kyle—recently suffered a serious relationship mishap, and therefore wins the Sympathy Vote.

A year ago, Kyle was in a long-term, when-are-they-going-to-get-married relationship with a woman named Caroline who I never cared for, but could see her obvious attractions (the most obvious of which was that she looked like Catherine Zeta-Jones). One day, however, Caroline decided she'd rather live in Sydney. Without

Kyle. Since then, he's been on permanent rebound, taking up with Todd in pursuing fake blondes half his age.

Kyle, being steadfastly good-looking, too smart for his own good, and the owner of a black BMW, has been wildly successful in this quest for women with IQs in the two-digit range.

I take satisfaction in the fact that I am one of only two people who know that when Kyle was nine, he once stuffed eleven Cheerios up his nose on a dare.

"So?" Todd says, hand out palm up.

I slap it, giving him five.

"Your *resume,*" he grunts, rolling his eyes.

Kyle, in the meantime, snatches it out of my other hand.

"Hey," I protest, weakly. I am trying to figure out if it would be bad if I had a two-martini lunch.

"Since when did you graduate from Harvard?" Kyle asks me.

"Can we order?" I ask, hiding behind my menu.

I spend the entire lunch answering Todd's rapid-fire career questions—and Kyle and he have quite a laugh at my expense reading over my resume. They don't appreciate creative art, and I dismiss them.

"I'm thinking I won't get a new job. Do you know how much I can sell a kidney for?" I ask Todd.

"Maybe $250,000 on the black market," he says, seriously. Todd, being an actuary, is always putting values on things. He doesn't see the joke in it.

"You can't be contemplating organ-selling already,"

Kyle says. "You've only been laid off for a couple of weeks."

"You're saying that because you think I'm fiscally responsible?"

"Remember, Kyle, this is the girl who, when she was twenty-two, didn't open her mailbox for six weeks for fear of seeing her MasterCard bill," Todd says.

"I was not *afraid* of my bill," I say. "I was shooting for plausible deniability."

"Right, you thought if you didn't see the bill you wouldn't have to pay it," Todd says. Todd gives me an affectionate shove as he says this.

"I don't know what's so crazy about that plan," I say. "And, if I don't get my unemployment check soon, I'll have to put the Bill Avoidance plan into effect again."

"What about your Mystery Boyfriend? I bet he'd give you a loan," Kyle says.

Mystery Boyfriend is what Kyle and Todd call Mike because I refused to introduce them to him. For one thing, I knew they'd disapprove. It was a relationship that has *Jerry Springer* written all over it. If Todd knew about it, he'd feel the need to have a family intervention to talk about sexual harassment and the laundry list of reasons you shouldn't date coworkers, especially when they're in management. Todd is very overprotective, which is nice when you're nine and being chased by a 150-pound-sixth grade bully. It's not so nice when you're twenty-eight and trying to have sex more than once a decade.

"The Mystery Boyfriend dumped me," I say, "so no, I'm not going to tell you about him."

"Ouch," Todd says.

"Sorry," Kyle adds.

"It's OK," I say. "I figure, if you're going to lose your job, why not your boyfriend, too? Get all the sucker punches out of the way at once."

The bill comes, and Kyle reaches for it. Naturally, Todd—like Dad would—lets him pay without any protest.

Todd does, however, do me the good service of drinking half my vodka martini on the grounds that I shouldn't smell like booze at the job fair.

I am not very marketable. I do not need anyone to tell me this. I am a creative person with an art degree who has worked at a number of thankless jobs, and even in the best of times, the art staff is expendable. I went to a headhunter's office last week, and she had the audacity to snigger at my resume *as she read it.* The three most deadly words in the English language to a recruiter are Art Major and Unemployed.

Todd and Kyle insist on taking me directly to the career fair. They know me too well. They know I plan to run home as soon as they leave me.

The career fair is dingy and depressing, with cardboard booths and a sea of bored-looking human resources people wearing uniforms of beige.

"I'm leaving," I say, turning around. Todd and Kyle grab my arms and pull me back to the fair.

"Let's explore," Kyle says, tugging on my arm, taking me in the direction of the Kentucky Fried Chicken booth.

"Are you interested in management opportunities?" says a man wearing a beige tie.

"I hate you," I say to Kyle, who coughs loudly to cover the fact that he is laughing.

We move along, and I am accosted by a man with his hair parted down the middle and a bushy mustache.

"You look like you're someone who knows her mind," says the man. He's the only one at the fair not wearing beige. He's wearing a black business suit and red tie. He's overdressed. "What's your background?"

"Design. Creative work," I say.

"We're looking for people like you," he says, nodding.

I don't think anyone is looking for people like me. I look over at Kyle, who shrugs.

"We have some great opportunities for people with your skill set."

"Really?"

I am beginning to perk up. People don't usually refer to my employment experience as a "skill set."

"Have you thought about transitioning into finance?"

Finance? Huh?

"I'm with AmeriVision," he says, handing me a card.

His name is Andy Organ. I am having a hard time not snickering.

Kyle is tugging at my arm. He's trying to pull me away.

"Why don't you come to one of our meetings? They're the first of every month," Mr. Organ shouts after us, as Kyle drags me to another booth.

"That's the best prospect I've had all day," I say, even though it sounds like a cult.

"It's a scam," Kyle tells me. "You might as well join Amway."

"I'm thinking more along the lines of Mary Kay."

Kyle snorts. I try not to take this personally.

By the end of it, I have shaken fifteen hands, dropped down twenty resumes, and am more sure than ever that my job search will be hopeless and that I'll end up working on an assembly line stuffing vacuum bags into plastic wrappers.

"Cheer up," Todd says, seeing me look depressed. He gives me a big brother squeeze, a one-armed hug. He's in an unusually cheerful mood, probably because he's finally successfully corralled me into doing something constructive in my job search. "You'll find something."

I give him a weak smile.

The next morning, I decide I am going to do something constructive with my day. I clean. I restack the dishes in my kitchen cabinets, and then I decide to clean my floorboards. And dust. And vacuum. And sweep. After two hours of scrubbing and disinfecting and sorting, I take to the couch to watch the local news and think how everyone else with a real job is commuting home from work.

When I finish, I notice that my apartment smells funny. It does. There's something in the air. I check my trash cans, but they're all empty (I used to be too busy to empty them, and they'd always been overflowing with empty Diet Coke cans and crumpled up paper towels but now, I have all the time in the world). I empty the trash when there are only two things in it. I make four trips to the Dumpster a day. I think of it as added exercise.

It could be a gas leak. I check my pilot lights, which look OK.

It takes me four hours to realize that it's just Pine-Sol. My apartment, for once, smells *clean*.

There's a knock on my apartment door. I freeze.

I creep over to the peephole, and glance through and see Bob, my landlord, wearing his ratty pink terrycloth robe. In a panic, I fling myself on the floor and hope he hasn't heard me. Rule number one in squatting: Avoid landlords at all cost.

"JANE, I KNOW YOU IN ZERE, EH? I CAN HEAR YOU BREATHING."

Damn my building's poor insulation and cardboard walls.

I open the door.

"Bob! I didn't realize it was you," I say. "I thought you

might be an ex-boyfriend I've put a restraining order on."

"I DON'T UNDERSTAND A WORD YOU SAY," Bob shouts at me, shaking his head. "I'M HERE FOR RENT, EH?"

"It's not due until tomorrow," I say.

"It was due five days ago," he says.

"It was?" I ask innocently.

"JANEZ, PLEAZ. I HAVE BILLS TOO, YES?"

"I'm just waiting for my unemployment check to come and then you'll be the first one I pay," I tell him.

"HOW DO YOU SAY, ER, 'BOOKIE'? I LOST BIG ON THE BLACK HAWKS, YES? I'M GOING TO NEED THIS MONTH'S RENT AND THE DEPOSIT ON YOUR APARTMENT, TOO."

"Bob—that's TWO months' rent," I exclaim, and roughly $3,300. "You can't do that."

"LOOK IN LEASE, EH? ZAYS NOTZING ABOUT WAIVING DEPOSIT."

"But you told me I didn't have to pay it," I say.

"NOTZING IN WRITING," Landlord Bob says, playing his trump card.

Technically, all I have is a verbal agreement. You don't have to be a tenant law expert to know I probably have no grounds.

Giving up my apartment is not an option, either. It's more home to me than my parents' house is, having outlasted two pets, three boyfriends, and two roommates. The thought of moving makes me feel light-headed.

"I just don't have that kind of cash," I plead.

"JANEZ, I HATE TO EVICT YOU, YOU KNOW? YOU GOOD TENANT. BUT IF I DON'T HAVE RENT MONEY BY TOMORROW, SAY BYE BYE, OKAYS?" he says, because he thinks "Okay" is plural. "I RENT APARTMENT TO MY COUSIN WHO PAY ME IN ADVANCE."

"You're going to evict me for being four days late with the rent? Bob, come on, I've been a good tenant. I've never been late before."

"JANEZ, NOT MY PROBLEM. I WANT TO KEEP MY LEGS UNBROKEN, YES? RENT IN THREE DAYS, OKAYS?"

To: jane@coolchick.com
From: HR@maximumoffice.com
Subject: Your Old Job
Date: March 6, 2002, 3:15 P.M.

Dear Jane,

We received your request for your old job back, and we are sorry to inform you that it is not within our power to reinstate you into your old position. While it has been several weeks, the company has not made large enough strides financially to begin re-hiring.

We are very sorry that you are in danger of losing your apartment and becoming, as you put it, "a smelly vagrant," but there is simply nothing we can do. We are not, as you assume "cold, heartless spawns of the devil" bent on your "personal destruction." We are just trying to do our jobs. We hope you understand.

Best of luck,
Duckett White
Assistant Human Resources Director
Maximum Office Supplies

P.S. We're afraid we cannot retroactively approve increases in severance packages. And because you are no longer an employee, we cannot offer you an advance on a forthcoming paycheck.

I spend all morning waiting to speak to a customer service representative at the unemployment office. I need my check. Landlord Bob is going to evict me if I don't get him his money, and last time I checked, I think I had $300 in my checking account. What I need is $3,300.

When I finally get a representative on the line, she tells me there's nothing they can do about advancing me my unemployment check money. "Didn't you read the brochure? It will take ten *business* days."

"But it's been more than twelve business days," I say.

"Ten business days is the *minimum* time it could take," the woman tells me.

"What's the maximum?" I ask.

"Six weeks," she says.

"I can't wait that long. I'm going to lose my apartment," I say.

"Ma'am, there's nothing I can do. All I can suggest is that you call back next week," she says.

"Next week, I'll be kicked out of my apartment and won't have a phone to call you from," I say.

"Just try back next week," she says. "Thank you for calling Social Services. Goodbye."

In frustration, I slam down the phone. This calls for a raid on my emergency stash of cigarettes, which I keep in the back of my closet. Technically, I quit smoking eight months ago, but if the unemployment office won't drive you to nicotine use, I don't know what will. Besides, smoking will help me think.

I light up a cigarette and lean out of my bedroom window, blowing smoke into the frigid Chicago air. I haven't taken two puffs before I see a familiar figure walking along the alley. Ron, my ex-boyfriend from college, looks like a displaced surfer. Bleached blond hair, tightly beaded necklace choker around his neck, a grungy Free Castro shirt, and a fraying jean jacket. He has managed to hold onto some of his boyish charm even though he's grown a thready goatee and looks a bit like Shaggy with his slouchy, sloped-back walk. He sees me and waves. Tentatively, I wave back, and before I can stop him, he's climbing up my fire escape.

Ron comes from an embarrassing time in my romantic history—late college—when my standards for boyfriend material were at an all-time low: if they had moderately scruffy good looks and played an instrument (even poorly), then I was all over them. This is a time that I don't like to revisit, and every time Ron comes around, I have to remember how I used to loan him money and write his papers for him because I thought he might one day be the new Kurt Cobain. I also have to remember that I slept with him, not once, but repeatedly, even though he is practically a walking warning advertisement for the adverse effects of pot.

Ron, who has never held a job longer than three months, and still—at thirty-one—plays bass in a struggling cover band, heard about my layoff through a mutual friend. Since then, he's been plaguing me. He thinks being unemployed has brought us back together. Secretly, I think he's hoping for a Fuck for Old Time's Sake. But revisiting a relationship with Ron would be regressing to the point of no return. I'm mature enough now to know that living in the back of a van for a summer is not fun—no matter how much he says it will be.

"I'm busy, Ron," I say, as he clambers up my fire escape and in through my bedroom window. He rarely uses doors.

"You don't have to put up a front for me, Jane," Ron says, smiling. He's chipped another tooth since the last time I saw him. That makes three. He has a habit of getting very stoned and then trying to take out his recycled newspapers down one flight of his narrow, circular, and half-detached fire escape. He always loses his footing and ends up landing on his face. Even if he had money, he says he wouldn't get them fixed. He doesn't believe in dentists.

If I squint hard enough, Ron can look like Brad Pitt in *True Romance*. If I don't squint, he still looks like Shaggy.

"Ron, seriously, I'm busy. I've got to think about where I'm going to come up with rent money."

"I know what will help," he says, holding up a fat joint. Ron is always offering me drugs. This lends more credence to the theory that he's only trying to get me into bed. I refuse it.

"Come on, you can't just lie around here like this," Ron says. "Especially not sober. If you're going to lie around, at the very least you should be high."

"No thanks," I say. "I'm just saying no to drugs."

Ron rolls eyes. Any references to the Reagan Administration annoy him.

"Do you have anything to eat?" he says, but he's already on his way to my refrigerator. He opens the door and leans in. He stays so long in that position—his bony butt in the air—that I think he might have fallen asleep. The thought of him drooling on my lettuce makes me shout at him.

"Ron!"

"Hmph?" he mumbles. His mouth is already full of something. I hate to even think what. Recently, I found a chunk of cheddar cheese with bite marks in it. Clearly Ron's doing.

"Get out of my refrigerator."

"Don't you have *anything* organic in here?" he shouts from behind the open door.

"You've eaten it all," I say.

He straightens, and I see he's drinking out of my milk carton. He has the decency to finish it off. Ron burps loudly.

"That milk was past due," I inform him.

He shrugs.

"It's the hormones that will kill you. Not the bacteria."

Ron plops down on my couch, wiping off his milk-mustache with the back of his sleeve.

"Dude," he says, tossing me a crumpled flier from one of his cavernous front pockets. "I've got a freelance gig for you."

"Does it pay?" I ask skeptically, squinting at the moist flier, which is for his band, Sink Gunk.

"YES," he says. "I even have a down payment to give you." Ron slumps on the couch so he can reach down to the bottom corner of his pocket. He retrieves a twenty, balls it up, and arcs it at me.

"Thanks," I say. "What's the job?"

"Design our CD cover," he says.

"You have a CD?" I ask, amazed. Sink Gunk usually only plays lame cover songs for tips at local bars. There was a time, back in college, when I thought even lame cover bands were cool. Back then, I'd relish wearing Sink Gunk T-shirts. Now, they're just another local band that probably won't ever make it.

"Not yet, but Dan's working on it," Ron says.

Dan is Sink Gunk's "visionary," the front man who is always claiming he knows someone who knows a record producer, and who can sing on key only when he's high. Ron is the group's bassist, and two other guys, Russ and Joe, play guitar and drums, respectively.

"You don't happen to have three thousand more where that came from, do you?" I ask.

Ron scoffs. "I hardly think so," he says. "Twenty now, three hundred later. All in cash, tax free."

"It's a start," I say. "And I like the sound of tax free."

Freelancers don't get unemployment benefits. In one of the many ironies of our public benefits systems, it is in my best interest to turn down freelance jobs and not work, rather than risk losing benefits. As far as I can see, the unemployment benefit system, like most welfare, is designed to lower self-esteem and create dependence.

My goodwill toward Ron evaporates almost immediately after he sticks his hand down in the waistband of his pants and lets out a long, low-pitched fart.

"OK, that's it, Ron, got to go," I say. "I've got to figure out how I'm going to get my unemployment check."

"Wait, are you going to Social Services? I can *totally* help," he says.

"I don't think so," I say.

"Come on, dude, I have *connections*," he says, flashing me his chipped-tooth grin.

•   •   •

As it turns out, Ron is very helpful when it comes to the unemployment office. Even though he's never held a steady job for as long as I've known him, he seems to be intimately acquainted with everyone at the state building. For example, he calls the guard at the door Bob and asks about his kids.

I take my place in the coiled-rope line behind a man muttering obscenities under his breath and tugging obsessively at his tie.

"Lucinda!" I hear one of the employees shouting. "LOU-SIN-DAH!" Somebody behind the counter, invisible to the people in line, shouts, "She's on break."

"Oh, she better not have left me with this *line*," the woman sniffs.

"Cheryl, just tend to the people, all right?" says the buck-toothed manager. His tie is askew, and his hair is oily.

"Why does *she* get to take three breaks. I don't get to take *three* breaks." She's shouting.

"We're in the wrong line," Ron tells me.

"But this says 'new beneficiaries' and that's me," I say.

"Trust me, dude, we have to go upstairs."

Reluctantly, I head to the elevators. Ron trails behind me, his Birkenstocks making loud sucking sounds against the tiled floor.

On the fifth floor, there is another line, and it is twice as long as the line on the third floor. I am suddenly possessed by an urgent need for a cigarette.

"Do you have any smokes?" I ask Ron, who digs in his ample pocket and retrieves a joint.

"Not that kind," I say, cross. I only abuse legalized substances. I have standards.

"You know nicotine is *terrible* for your lungs, right?" Ron scratches his weedy goatee. "You know how many impurities are in cigarettes?"

"This from a guy with a six-joint a day habit," I say.

"At least the pot isn't laced with arsenic and formaldehyde." He taps the joint. "This is one *hundred* percent cannabis, babe."

I snort.

"OK, OK." He puts the joint back in his pocket. "Hang on a second," he says, digging down further. Ron is skinny, a trait amplified by the fact that he insists on wearing extraordinarily baggy clothing. He could fit a full roast inside one of his front jeans pockets. After several long seconds of digging, he pulls out a small piece of folded paper. Inside are two single white pills. E, probably. Ron is a fixture in the clubbing scene.

"This will make you happy," he says, smiling his chip-toothed grin. I slap his hand away.

"Dude, no need for violence," he says, carefully wrapping up the pills and putting them back in his pocket.

Nearly a half hour passes, and my craving for a cigarette has become nearly unbearable.

"You need to *chill*," Ron tells me as he tries to rub my shoulders in line. I slap at his hands and he withdraws.

"I was just trying to help," he says, sullen. "You're so freakin' tense."

"Next!" barks the woman behind the third window. The man in front of me, who's been bouncing from one foot to another, as if preparing to sprint, bolts from his stationary spot and nearly collides with the window. He needs adult Ritalin. I need a smoke.

I glance over at the other unemployment window. There's a small man with thick glasses sitting there behind a computer. He's not calling anyone forward, but he doesn't appear to be helping anyone, either. He's not on the phone. He's not eating his lunch. He's just typing on his computer in short, controlled bursts. I decide he's playing a video game. Maybe some 1980s games like Space Invaders or Centipede. I want a job where I can play video games. And take long lunches. And not show up for long stretches at a time.

I sigh.

"Next!" barks the woman at the first window. The guy playing Tetris is still intent on his computer screen.

"Hi," I say as I walk over to the woman's window. I smile to show I'm friendly and not insane, and that she should help me because I can be cute and perky when I'm not clinically depressed. The woman isn't buying it. She's frowning at me, and clearly unhappy in her job.

"I need my check," I say.

"ID?" she says.

I scrounge around in my pocket and produce a battered Illinois driver's license. I look fourteen in the picture, even though I was twenty-two. My hair was short then and spiky, and a mismatch of colors because I didn't go regularly to a salon. Now it's long and has deliberate highlights, and I usually wear it up in a messy, haphazard way. My brother Todd says I look like an ostrich, because my hair sticks up and I have a long neck.

I take off my Buddy Holly glasses so the woman can get a good look at me. I smile again to show that there's no hard feelings about her curt manner.

"This doesn't look like you," she says, squinting at it and holding it up against the glass to get it closer to my face.

"It's an old license," I say, smiling brighter. I'm sending her "please like me, I'm perky" vibes.

"You have another form of identification?" the woman asks, coldly indifferent to my overtures of false friendship.

I reach into my purse and retrieve a gas card, but this is not enough, apparently. Ron then steps up beside me and says, "Oh, I can vouch for her, Deena. She's OK." Ron puts his arm around my shoulder. Visibly, I flinch.

"Ron? Is that you?" cries the woman behind the counter.

"In the *flesh*," Ron answers, showing his chipped front teeth. Ron is the sort of person who uses lines like "in the flesh." He also, on occasion, will say "you rang?" in an exaggerated Scottish brogue.

She rolls her chair backwards and calls to some of the invisible people in the cubicles behind her. "Girls! It's Ron, come back to pay us a visit."

Immediately, two rather large ladies lumber up to the front window.

"Ron!" they cackle. They look like a small herd of yaks wearing Kathie Lee Gifford dresses and Payless faux-leather shoes.

"You got any more sugar for us, honey?" one of them asks.

Carefully, Ron looks one way and then the other, and puts his finger to his lips. Then, stealthily, he takes the small white packet containing the pills and pushes it under the glass.

In one swift motion, almost so I don't see it, the woman behind the counter grabs the packet, shoves it into her pocket, and hands a slip of paper to me. It's a check with my name handwritten on it and the amount of my meager unemployment: $1,035.

"Is this for one week?" I ask, hopeful.

"One month," corrects the woman behind the counter. "It's forty percent of your regular salary, minus taxes."

"Taxes?" I shout. "I have to pay income taxes on my unemployment?"

"I didn't make the rules," the woman says. "I just hand out the checks."

"Wow, that's a *lot*, dude," Ron chirps. "Last time I was here, my check was only $203."

The unemployment check, plus the money already in my account, means that I have $1,330, and even though I was an art major and stink at math, I know this means I'm almost two thousand short of the rent. I am so royally screwed.

Human Resources Dept.
Barnum & Bailey Circus
8607 Westwood Center Dr.
Vienna, VA 22182

Jane McGregor
3335 Kenmore Ave.
Chicago, IL 60657

March 7, 2002

Dear Ms. McGregor,

Thank you for your interest in employment with the Barnum & Bailey circus. Unfortunately, we do not have any openings for you at this time.

While we appreciate that you have a natural sense of balance and have always dreamed of walking on a tightrope, we must inform you that we only hire trained specialists to do all of our acrobatic acts. A two-week gymnastics camp during the summer of your 8th grade year, we're afraid, does not qualify as adequate training.

Thank you for thinking of Barnum & Bailey Circus.

Sincerely,
Kate Ricordati
Co-director, Human Resources Dept.
Barnum & Bailey Circus

4

I have emptied out my closet hoping to find something worth $2,000 to sell on Ebay. The only things I find as salvageable, sellable merchandise are:

a) **one radio alarm clock** (I no longer have use for this. It is simply a curiosity item).
b) **the sweater Grandma gave me last Christmas** (it's pink and four sizes too small. Grandma still thinks I am ten).
c) **my old roommate's set of electric hair curlers.**

Call me crazy, but I think I'm going to be a few dollars shy of the rent. I'm going to have to do what any self-sufficient modern girl would do in my situation: sell my eggs. Since I'm not getting any action these days, maybe I should let my eggs have a go.

I go online to research egg donation and discover three things in rapid succession: 1) it pays $7,000; 2) there is a screening process; and 3) it requires minor surgery and something scary called transvaginal ultrasound. "Trans" and "vaginal" are two words that don't belong together in any context other than *Jerry Springer*.

But, the pink and blue fertility site assures me I'll "have a great sense of fulfillment from helping an infertile couple fulfill their dream of parenthood."

Fulfillment is less tempting than the seven grand.

I consider this, and while I'm doing so I'm suddenly struck by the horrible thought of my life turning into a bad sitcom where I end up dating my own son or running into my daughter at the gym—complete with garish laugh soundtrack.

Still. It is seven *thousand* dollars. I could pay Landlord Bob what he's asking and still have more than a month's worth of expenses paid for. All in cash.

No. That's crazy. I don't want them to accidentally take my only healthy eggs, since I probably only have five or six of them. The last time I checked, smoking, not exercising, and eating your weight in high cholesterol foods does nothing for reproductive health. Besides, egg harvesting takes at least two months, and I don't have that kind of time.

My thoughts are interrupted by a hard knock on my door.

I jump, fearing it's Landlord Bob, but when I get to the peephole I see Mrs. Slatter, my downstairs neighbor. As she's never even made sustained eye contact with me before now, I am curious as to what she wants.

I open the door cautiously.

"You're too loud," she says to me, right off. "I can hear you all stomping around up here like a herd of elephants."

"It's just me in here," I say.

She looks past my shoulder into my apartment.

"You sure you're the only one in there?" she croaks.

"Sorry, it's just me."

"Well, I'm going to Bingo, but when I get back, I think you should tell your *friends* to go on home. I've gotten a new hearing aid, and I don't mind telling you that things up here are loud."

"Mrs. Slatter, honest, there's no one in here but . . ." Did she say Bingo? "You're going to play Bingo?" I ask her.

"Every Wednesday at the Y."

"Can I come?"

Mrs. Slatter looks at me like I'm about to hit her over the head with a metal pipe and take her purse.

"Why?" she asks.

"I need rent money," I say.

She considers me a moment. "Young people. Always spending what they don't have," she sniffs. "Well, if you pay my way, I'll let you come along for the ride."

"Deal," I say.

• • •

Bingo is in the basement of the local Y, about four blocks away from our apartment. There's a healthy showing of seniors, and by seniors, I mean stooped women with blue hair and smudged red lipstick. It's wall-to-wall over-sized pearl earrings and leisure suits.

"Don't embarrass me," Mrs. Slatter hisses at me when I balk over the $35 she wants me to dish out for her set of Bingo cards. Reluctantly, I hand over the last of my MasterCard cash advance, and we take our bingo cards and sit at one of the long tables.

The Bingo sheets are practically poster size with gigantic letters and numbers on them, I guess for the hard of seeing. Across the table from us there are two women with ten sheets in front of them and giant markers made exclusively for Bingo.

"Show-offs," Mrs. Slatter mumbles.

The banner at the front basement wall reads BINGO FOR CHARITY but it doesn't say which charity. There's an overwhelming smell of gym shoes and moth balls in the basement, and my allergies are threatening to attack me. I rub my nose and try to concentrate.

The announcer, a middle-aged man with a shiny bald head wearing salmon-colored polyester pants and a too-small golf shirt, approaches the microphone to announce the start of the game and the feedback is deafening to me, but none of the other women in the room seem to hear it.

"Let's get started with round one," Mr. Salmon Pants says, sounding like an over-enthusiastic game show host. "Today's jackpot is $5,000."

One woman lets out an "ooooh" from the back.

"Ah, shut it," Mrs. Slatter grumbles, taking out a round highlighter from her purse and hunching over her score sheet.

There's a bent wire cage with balls in it up front, which looks like someone has kicked and stomped on it, because it's completely caved in on one side and is leaning dangerously to the left.

"B-1. The first number is B-1. Did everyone hear that? B-1 is our first number. That is B as in boy, and one as in the number one," says the announcer in salmon pants. His voice is breathy in the microphone and he sounds like he's really trying to get into Bingo announcing, as if he were a radio DJ.

"Bingo!" a woman cries.

"Simmer down now, simmer down!" Mr. Salmon Pants cautions. "There can't be a Bingo after just one draw." He laughs a staccato laugh. "Now *that* would be really something. Wouldn't it? Wouldn't it folks?"

No one answers him.

"Again, our first number is B-1. That's B as in Bingo. Ha. Ha. And one as in the number one."

There's a thwack, thwack, thwack sound as Mr. Salmon Pants turns the wire cage over and pulls out another ball.

The women in front of us with the multiple Bingo

sheets are poised over them with two highlighters in each hand.

"N-32. The next number is N-32. N as in Nancy. Thirty-two as in Thirty. Two."

"Bingo!" shouts the same woman.

"Alzheimer's patients," Mrs. Slatter mutters under her breath.

"Will someone get her out of here?" someone else shouts.

This could be my future. Right here. Bingo playing. Every Wednesday.

This thought, or the mold in the basement, I'm not sure which, causes me to sneeze. Not once, but three times in a row.

This reminds me that should some horrible medical condition befall me—like the sudden onset of asthma—I would not be covered with health insurance. I couldn't go to a hospital for treatment. I couldn't even go to my primary care doctor, the one that takes four weeks to see. I couldn't, sadly, even get to a vet's office. I feel worse than a fugitive. I feel like a leper. No treatment anywhere, except for self-induced exile. I don't know what happens exactly for people who don't have health insurance, but I'm pretty sure that once the paramedics find out, they just dump your body on the side of the road. And if you manage to actually sneak into a hospital, then, in exchange for treatment, the government extracts all your eggs and fertilizes them with alien DNA like on *The X-Files*.

I could, of course, apply for Cobra. But I don't have $350 a month to spare. If I pay for Cobra, then when I'm evicted and living on the street and get sent to the emergency room for starvation and exposure, my medical expenses will be eighty percent covered. Sure, sign me up.

"Oh-75. That's O as in orange. And seventy-five as in Seven. Five."

"Bingo!" the same woman yells again.

I decide that if I'm ever diagnosed with a life-threatening illness and want to make sure that every last minute of my life is stretched to its fullest capacity, I will come here. Two hours feels like twenty years.

I look around at other people's tickets. Everyone has more squares blotted out than I do.

It's going to be a long afternoon.

Clearly, Bingo is not the proper gambling outlet for me. I should have tried slots, or better yet, the lottery.

If I ever won the lottery, I'd set up a special charity fund specifically for people like me. Lazy people. People without clear career goals. I'd set them up for a year—a full year—doing absolutely nothing. I would call it "A Year of *The View*" or "Pop Culture Sabbatical"—something like that. The laziest person wins. No type-A personalities. No essay questions. Any hint of motivation or actual ambition would disqualify you from my fund. It would be like welfare for the uninspired.

Ron says if he wins the lottery, he will charter a cruise ship, fill it up with his closest friends, and sail around the world for a year. It would be stocked with the best drugs money could buy. "In international waters, drug laws don't apply," he says. "Plus, I'd be fucking rich, so I'd hire the very best doctors to be on board in case of massive overdose." Thank goodness Ron doesn't actually play the lottery. I shudder to think about what a boat of 1,000 stoned and terminally high people would do for a year. Not to mention, he'd no doubt ask me to go. And if I didn't have a job by then, I know I'd be tempted to say yes, if only for the free healthcare. Then, I'd spend the next 365 days regretting my moment of weakness. It's a lot like my whole relationship with Ron: eight months of sexual relations, a lifetime of regret.

"Bingo!" someone yells, and I realize it's not the demented woman, but Mrs. Slatter, who's sitting next to me. She jumps up and pumps one wizened fist in the air. "In your face, you old biddies!" she cries. "I'm going to Vegas!" She does a little victory dance, as much as her arthritic hip will allow.

I fail to convince Mrs. Slatter to split her winnings with me, even though I technically bought her Bingo cards. She double-bolts the door even as I'm talking, and less than an hour later I see her dragging a suitcase down our stoop along with her little white fluff dog in a carrying case.

Because I still have Landlord Bob's rent money to fetch, I'm left with Plan C: Get a loan.

I dig out a legal pad and make a list of the possible candidates. Let's see.

There's **Steph.** She's broke, like me. And I suspect, like me, she has limits on the cash advances on her MasterCard.

Ron. Also broke.

Todd. Out of the question. If I asked him for a loan, I would be handing over a "Lord This Over My Head for Eternity" card. When I was twelve, I borrowed twenty bucks from him to buy New Kids on the Block tickets, and he's never let me live it down. For years afterward, he'd introduce me as his "little sister who borrowed money to go to New Kids" even when I was sixteen and listened only to The Smiths and The Cure.

Kyle. Even worse than Todd because technically he's not a blood relative, but because he's Todd's best friend he'd feel the need to tell Todd, who would naturally lord it over my head anyway, even though he didn't actually loan me the money.

That leaves **my parents.**

My parents lead simple lives, a rare thing on the North Shore in Evanston. My dad works in insurance, and my mother is a housewife. They are both industrious people who cling to the outdated dream that working hard will actually get you somewhere. Dad spent a lot of time grooming Todd for a career and Todd is now an actuary at an insurance company with nice offices downtown, but Dad didn't spend a lot of time on me. He just assumed Mom would teach me how to bake and I'd go off to college and find a nice husband, and my husband and

Todd and Dad could stand around the barbecue pit in July and complain about the humidity and the Cubs. This is the life Dad envisioned for me. The worst contingency he ever foresaw was me marrying a White Sox fan, and even under those circumstances, Dad had planned to be open-minded and magnanimous.

I disappointed him by not meeting Mr. Accountant in college and by dating boys with no ambition and no money and odd piercings. And then I graduated college with an art degree (something Todd was forbidden to do, but was all right for me since Dad never planned on seeing me single at twenty-eight and really just humored me while I was studying at college). I found a job, only to be laid off six months later. I've never moved back home with my parents, so maybe that will win me good favor and the $2,000 I need.

Plus, I have something even better than the I'm-Your-Daughter-Please-Help-Me card to play. Tomorrow is my twenty-ninth birthday.

"Happy Birthday!" cries Steph into my phone line the next day. She's bubbly and happy as is only possible when it isn't your birthday and when you have a job. She's calling from an office supply convention in New York, where her boss has sent her to stay until Friday.

"As soon as I get back, we're going out, understand?"

"Sure," I say.

"You want me to come back early, I'll be on the next plane. Just say the word."

"No, no," I say. "I promised Mom I'd come home for dinner tonight."

"OK, but Friday, we're tying one on, OK?"

I suspect by then, when I'm evicted, I'll be in dire need of a drink.

I barely hang up before Todd calls.

"First, Happy Birthday. Second—interviews? Resumes? What's the score?" If Todd wasn't a well-meaning relative, he might just fall into the category of stalker. "Have you written to any of the people you met at the career fair like I told you to?"

"Todd, it's my birthday. I am not sending out resumes on my birthday."

"Jane!" he scolds. He's more stressed about me being out of work than I am.

"*Todd*," I scold back.

"You can't just sit back in this economy and think employers are going to come court you," he says.

When I don't say anything, he adds, "You have to take this job hunt seriously."

"I am, Todd. Believe me, I am."

"OK, then, how many resumes have you sent out?"

"Fifty," I say, which is true. I don't mention that this number includes the resumes I sent to the Barnum & Bailey Circus, Hershey's Chocolate factory, and NASA.

"Well," Todd says, momentarily taken aback by my efficiency. "Maybe you need to network more. You know that 99 percent of jobs are never advertised."

"You've mentioned that before." Only about a hundred times. "Todd, maybe you want to be looking for another job."

"What?"

"Well, you seem so consumed with my job search, maybe subconsciously you want to be looking for a job."

"Me? No. I've got my own office with a door. If I went to work somewhere else, I'd have to start at the bottom, all over again."

The thought of this, I can tell, makes my older brother shiver with fear. He's always walked a straight line in one direction. In life, he never developed a reverse gear. Me, on the other hand, I spend half my time driving backward.

"So I'll see you tonight?" Todd says. "I can't pick you up, because I've got to work late."

Todd is always so industrious. He's always working late.

"Todd, don't even pretend that you're going to be late," I say. Todd is physically incapable of getting anywhere late. He simply cannot do it. It's like trying to make someone with an obsessive-compulsive disorder step on a crack in the sidewalk. If you held Todd and made him late, he'd start foaming at the mouth.

"Jane, if you really need a ride," he says, relenting a bit.

"No, no, I don't need your charity," I joke.

"Jane, I'll pick you up, all right?" Todd says. "I've just got to pick up Deena first."

"Deena?"

"My girlfriend," Todd says.

"Girlfriend—that sounds serious," I say. Todd usually doesn't add "friend" to the word "girl." He generally just refers to the women he's slept with as Girls. That girl, or this girl. "I went out last night with this girl," he'll say. He rarely even uses first names.

"Don't even start," Todd says.

"Forget about the ride. I'll take the train."

I don't begrudge Todd's attempts at helping me walk the straight and narrow path to financial solvency. I understand he's doing it because he thinks it's a good way to show he cares, and because he thinks he can run my life better than I can. I appreciate this, and see it for what it is, a show of brotherly affection. It is better than my dad, whose stoic, stubborn silence on the issue of my joblessness is proof of his disapproval. He hasn't once asked me about the job search, except to drop heavy hints that I should move into a smaller apartment.

I call my parents, trying to get a vibe about how open they'd be to me asking for a loan.

Dad's first response is not a positive one.

"So, are you eating lunch at your grand dining-room table? Must be a lot of echoes in that mansion of yours," Dad says when I call that afternoon.

"I'm not eating lunch, Dad, it's three in the afternoon," I say.

"Well, since you don't really have a schedule to keep, I figured you'd be eating at odd hours."

"I eat at regular times," I say.

Dad and I have nothing to say to each other, which is why Mom insists that we speak. She's the one who's always dragging Dad away from his Barcalounger and demanding that he "speak to his daughter." It's the same thing she used to do when I was a kid, and she'd demand that Dad spend quality time with Todd and me on Sundays. After enough nagging, Dad would take us into the office with him, so he could catch up on work, and we could run around making paperclip ropes.

"You really ought to get a smaller apartment," he says. This has been his sole piece of advice since he saw the place four years ago.

"I'll think about it, Dad," I say. It's impossible to explain to Dad the difficulty of finding a decent roach-free apartment outside the known Chicago move-in months of October and April.

After a small silence, Dad clears his throat and says, "Well, I'll put your mom on the line."

"Oh, hi honey," she says, coming on to the line, sounding breathless. "I've got your favorites—cherry pie and strawberry cheesecake."

This is the great thing about Mom. She's like a walking Rolodex of all my favorite recipes.

"I've got pot roast and mashed potates—the kind you like with sour cream and cheese. Todd's coming and he's bringing a girlfriend, and I thought if you wanted to bring someone special you could."

"Er, I don't have anyone special right now." Ron, I

know, would come if I asked, but I think I would rather have someone punch me in the throat.

"Oh, well, Kyle is coming," Mom says quickly. I can tell she's worried that she may have brought up a sore subject. Mom is under the mistaken impression that I have a crush on Kyle. That I am pining for him. This is based on the fact that when I was three and he was seven, I said I wanted him to be my boyfriend. Explaining to Mom that you can't be held accountable for things you did or said when you were three (like eating Play-Doh or announcing that you are the smartest person in the world) is an exercise in futility.

"I don't want to micromanage your dating life. All I'm saying is that Kyle would be a *fool* not to want to date you. You're perfect for each other. Not that I'm saying you *should* like Kyle."

"Mom—Kyle doesn't like me. I don't like him, OK?"

"OK, OK. I didn't mean to pry."

Mom is always very concerned about being a bad mom—about falling into the trap so many of her friends do by pressuring their children and making them miserable. Mom feels like the best approach to getting what she wants is to let us believe we've chosen it for ourselves.

"Oh—and, honey—I've got some news, just so you're prepared."

"What news?"

"Well, I'll tell you at dinner."

"Mom—what news?" I persist. Now she's got me curious. She's being all secretive.

"Oh, it's nothing, really. And I'd rather tell everyone at once."

"Mom . . ." I start, thinking I should test the waters about the loan.

"Yes, dear?"

"Well, it's just, uh . . ." I'm having a hard time forming the words "I need money." My tongue feels sticky. I suddenly am struck by the idea that it will be better to ask in person, when I can gauge her real-time reaction.

"Nothing, Mom. I'll talk to you about it later."

"OK, sweetie. See you in a bit."

I suppose there's a reason they call pride a sin. It gets in the way of you doing practical things like asking your parents for money.

I open the door to leave, and find Landlord Bob standing on my welcome mat.

I cringe because I doubt he is here to give me a birthday present.

"OKAYS," he says. "TOMORROW YOU HAVE MY MONEY, YES?"

"I'm going to get it," I say. Why is it that Bob is the one with the gambling problem, but I feel like the one being shaken down for money?

"OKAYS, BUT IF YOU DON'T HAVE IT TO-MORROW, YOU'RE OUT, OKAYS?"

City of Chicago
Parking Enforcement Division
P.O. Box 88292
Chicago, IL 60680-1292

Jane McGregor
3335 Kenmore Ave.
Chicago, IL 60657

March 8, 2002

Dear Ms. McGregor,

We feel the need to tell you that your resume does not meet our qualifications for a parking enforcement officer. While we are sure that you would be "willfully indifferent to the pleas of civilians" who let their parking meters run out, there is more to being a parking authority officer than being "a trained monkey in polyester pants."

At the City of Chicago, we pride ourselves on the fair and judicious enforcement of the law, and seek to hire only the best candidates for our positions.

Sincerely,
Marc Seiler
Human Resources Professional

5

The train ride to my parents' house is long and I'm squashed between smart-looking commuters in pin-stripes and black wool. I'm wearing the furry pink V-neck cashmere sweater and black skirt Mom gave me last Christmas, along with the silver earrings Dad gave me the year before, in an obvious brownnosing ploy. I put on my kitten-heeled knee-high boots just because they make me feel confident and capable, two traits I'm going to need when I plead my case to the Bank of Parental Control.

I almost look like one of the Employed, lacking only a briefcase and the tired look of someone who's been sitting under fluorescent lights all day.

My parents' stop takes forever to reach, and I read every single advertisement in the train car ten or twelve times—including the get-out-of-debt ones in Spanish.

As I step off the train at the Dempster stop, I notice everything but the adjacent bank is pitch black. Evanston, for all its fine houses, invests nothing in streetlights. It's a good thing there aren't too many violent crimes on the North Shore, or the city might be liable. I nearly trip over a large, gaping crack in the sidewalk which would have been illuminated had the streetlight above me been working. I wonder if I break my ankle, if Mom could get Dad to spring for a doctor's visit.

I get to Mom and Dad's house around ten after seven, but Todd has already been there for fifteen minutes. Kyle is also there, as well as Todd's new girlfriend, Deena, who has herself half-draped over Todd's shoulder.

Kyle is sitting on the couch drinking Harp from a bottle and looking immensely pleased with himself. This is probably because he is.

"Happy Birthday, Jane," Kyle says from the couch.

"Thanks," I say, but I am distracted by Deena, who is wearing too much makeup and not enough sweater. It clings to her, leaving nothing to the imagination, and I can tell Mom is uncomfortable because she avoids looking at the corner of the room where the girlfriend is sitting. Dad, however, seems to like the girlfriend quite a lot and keeps asking her if she wants anything to drink when she already has a glass of water in her hand.

Kyle, I notice, is taking in the scene with some amusement. I almost think he hangs out with Todd and my nuclear family for the sheer entertainment value.

"Jane!" cries Mom, distracting me as she throws her arms around my shoulders. "Happy, Happy Birthday!" she shouts, taking a silver cone hat from nowhere and placing it atop my head. The elastic strap snaps against my chin and stings. Kyle hides a smile under his hand.

"Thanks, Mom," I say. I suspect I look like a total dork. Now would probably not be the best time to ask for money. I want to go for the "I'm responsible and will pay you back" look, not the "I've got the fiscal IQ of a four-year-old and can't handle my own checking account" look.

Dad still hasn't looked up. I fear he is in a trance, unable to stop staring at Todd's girlfriend's tight-fitting sweater. Todd waves at me and says, almost grudgingly, "Happy Birthday."

I am sure he is thinking that people without jobs should not be allowed to celebrate birthdays. Either that, or he is still disappointed in my lackluster job search.

It is the latter, because not two minutes pass before he blurts out this fact.

"Jane's not even trying to find a job," he says. I cannot tell if he's trying to scare me straight, or if he's succumbed to his youthful impulse to tattle.

"I am so trying," I say.

This, however, rouses Dad out of his tight-sweater stupor.

"Jane! You know you can't expect someone to just hand you a job." Dad sounds like a parrot on Todd's shoulder. "And that apartment!" he declares.

I snort, and I don't think he appreciates this.

"I just don't know when you're going to accept the fact you're living beyond your means. I mean Todd tells us you could be getting by just fine in a smaller apartment. I don't know why you insist on living there."

I send Todd a McGregor Look of Death, a skill that I've inherited from my mother, who has the ability to drop a charging rhino in its tracks at a hundred paces with one severe look. I wish Todd a sudden onset of laryngitis. He's mucking up my plot to ask for a loan. If he gets Dad in a frenzy about my apartment, there's no way I can make a case for rent money.

"I am not moving," I say, trying to keep my voice level. I refuse to be the first one to shout this time.

"Well, it's your life, if you want to throw it away," Dad grumbles, peering at me over his reading glasses. I am possessed by the desire to poke him in the eyes, Three Stooges style, but I doubt that would win me a loan.

"Dad . . ." I say, my voice close to shouting level.

"I mean, it's just such a waste. Girl of your brains," he says. He's speaking as if I'm fifteen and pregnant. Not as if I'm twenty-eight—er, twenty-nine—now, and living in a bigger-than-average apartment. I find myself wishing I was there now.

"I don't see that my apartment is anyone's business," I feel the need to say. Dad, I can tell, will be hopeless. I can't ask him for a loan. I'm going to have to start working on Mom.

"We're just trying to help," Dad sighs. He throws up his hands.

"Yeah, Jane, we *care*," Todd says. His gift, I see, noticing his empty hands, is an intervention.

"Dinner's ready," chimes Mom happily from the kitchen.

The spread on the dining-room table is impressive. There's a giant pot roast in the middle that looks like it came straight from a grocery-store circular. Half a dozen plates of vegetables and side dishes—including two casseroles and a giant plate of creamy mashed potatoes. A huge, homemade white rose and tulip topiary centerpiece. Martha Stewart couldn't have done better.

I wonder why I don't invite myself over to my parents more often. My stomach, shrunken on a strict ketchup-and-mustard sandwich diet, rumbles and I realize it's been days—if not weeks—since I last ingested animal protein or green vegetables. It's a wonder my hair hasn't started falling out.

Mom insists Dad say grace, which is ironic because since I was nine, Dad has made a regular habit of falling asleep during Sunday service. This does not stop him, however, from confidently addressing the Lord.

"Lord, bless this grub," Dad says with bowed head and his usual eloquence. "Now let's eat."

I load up on everything, and I feel like a sailor who's been out to sea and forced to eat a diet of dried fish and crackers. I inhale my food.

Deena, Todd's girlfriend, picks at hers, and keeps

sending furtive glances at the mashed potatoes, as if worried that they might leap off the plate and attach themselves to her hips when she isn't looking. I have a second helping of them, and she looks at me as if I'm about to bungee jump off the top of the Sears Tower.

"Don't choke," whispers Kyle, who has been strategically placed next to me (no doubt by Matchmaking Mom), so that I might not be able to enjoy a single moment of my own birthday.

"Thanks for the tip," I mumble, mouth full.

Mom waits until we have dessert in front of us, the cherry pie and the cheesecake, before dropping the bomb.

"I have news," Mom says, glancing around the table. She's nervous, I can tell, because she's licking her lips.

Dad does not stop eating. Few things, short of a gunshot or the announcement of the NBA draft, can interrupt his shoveling of food into his esophagus. He is even worse than I am. He eats at such an alarming rate that I think he bypasses his tongue and teeth altogether. While Dad is attempting to eat a whole piece of pie in one bite, the rest of us look at Mom expectantly. She takes a deep breath and presses her hands into her lap.

"I have been thinking about a change," she said. "And, well, you know I've always been interested in cooking." She pauses and takes a shaky breath. Dad doesn't even stop chewing.

"Oh, I'll just come out and say it."

We're all (except Dad) waiting.

"I got a job," Mom squeals, clapping her hands together.

The table sits in stunned silence, until Dad drops his
fork on his plate. The stainless steel makes a high-pitched
plunking sound on Mom's good china.

"What?" Dad says, shocked as the rest of us.

"I got a job," Mom repeats, this time more softly. She
looks as if she's losing her nerve.

Kyle rallies first.

"Hey—that's great, Mrs. M. Really great."

Mom gives Kyle a grateful look.

Meanwhile, the rest of the table is too stunned to say
anything.

My mom never had a job, not while I was alive. Todd
told me that she'd tried going to cooking school to be a
pastry chef before I was born, but Dad complained about
having to watch Todd in the afternoons (after preschool), and how he made enough money for Mom to
stay home, and why did she want to cook for perfect
strangers when the people who would appreciate her
cooking the most would be forced to eat frozen TV din-
ners and be neglected while she was off at some fancy
cooking school? Besides, Dad was not a big believer in
education. He thought people who went to school to
learn how to decorate their living rooms or paint were
people too dumb to figure out how to do it themselves.

He also subscribed to the theory that most of the professors at the community colleges were scam artists, out to make a quick buck.

Mom eventually did drop out of the pastry classes when it was clear she was pregnant with me, and she said the morning sickness combined with the smell of dough was too much to take all at once. She had me nine months later, and settled into the habits of a resigned housewife. She never did give up her interest in cooking and baking, and was always threatening to open up her own catering business or go back to cooking school. Dad had not expressly forbidden it, but he has been known to make sexist remarks on occasion, like "my wife's place is doing my laundry." Mom always said he was kidding, but I was never sure.

Mom looks to me for support. I am not sure I can give it to her—I am just too taken aback to think about anything except the fact that my mother—a fifty-five-year-old with no discernable job skills and only half her college credits—has gotten a job, while I am languishing in the unemployment lines.

"Where?" I squeak.

"Well, it's one of those Web places."

"You mean dot-coms?" Todd says, speaking for the first time.

If possible, Dad's jaw drops a bit further.

"You don't even know how to work a computer, Doris," says my dad.

"I do so know how to work a computer," Mom says. "I send email all the time."

This quiets Dad. In fact, it quiets the whole table.

"That's cool," says Todd's girlfriend Deena. "I worked for a dot-com. They're a lot of fun."

"I'm very excited," admits Mom to Deena. The two share a girlish giggle.

Meanwhile, Dad is turning purple.

"Don't even start, Dennis," Mom warns Dad. His head looks as if it might, seriously, explode. The vessels are popping out of the sides of his temples. "You know we need the money."

Dad pounds a fist on the table, causing the salt shaker to jump and then topple.

"I thought we *agreed* not to discuss that."

"You *agreed*. I said that if we don't do something, we're going to lose the house."

"Mom," whines Todd, who has always been deeply affected by arguments between my parents. For a full five years, from age ten to fifteen, he was certain they'd get divorced.

"Todd, this has nothing to do with you. It is between your mother and me," says Dad.

Todd appears in danger of whimpering. I look at him through squinted eyes.

"The truth is, kids," Mom says, "Dad's been reduced to working part time. We didn't want to tell you because we know you have enough to worry about."

Mom looks at me when she says this.

"Anyhow, your dad's being forced out."

"I am not," Dad protests, but I can see it's just for show.

"They asked you to take the early retirement package," Mom says to Dad, who seems to have suddenly lost his appetite. He shoves a bite of piecrust to one side of his plate with the tip of his fork.

I stare at him, unbelieving. Dad, the man who my whole life has been spouting Republican propaganda about how all you have to do in this country to get ahead is work hard and hope no one elects a bleeding-heart president, is suddenly looking sheepish and small. The same man who argued with me that "corporate welfare" is liberal labeling, and that a company's first priority should rightly be to its shareholders, is now sitting at the head of his table unable to look anyone in the eye.

I can't believe it. It doesn't seem possible.

He's too old to adjust to the cold, hard reality of modern corporate America—he entered it when it was full of promise—like a new suburb built in the '50s. Now, it's been reduced to drab strip malls, chain restaurants, and drive-by shootings.

I feel suddenly selfish and petty. Here I am thinking I'd borrow money from them, when they might actually need to borrow money from me.

"When?" sputters Todd. "When did this happen?"

"Last week," Dad says.

"Four months ago," Mom says at the same time.

I look from Dad to Mom and back again.

"Four months," Dad admits, after a pause.

"And you kept this from us?" Todd asks, the look of betrayal and childish angst on his face. Leave it to Todd to blow things out of proportion. He sounds as if he's just discovered that Santa Claus doesn't exist.

"Well, we didn't want to worry you," Mom says. "We didn't want to be a burden."

I feel about the size of an ant.

"But we have a right to know," Todd says. I am not sure what rights he's asserting here. "I mean, what other secrets are you keeping from us? Is one of you dying from cancer?"

"Todd," I scold.

"Well, Jane, I mean, seriously—doesn't this upset you? I hate secrets. This family is always keeping goddamned secrets!"

Todd, unfortunately, is prone to fits of paranoia and conspiracy theories. He, like Dad, believes there is a secret government ruling the world made up of billionaires who decide the fate of nations based on high-stake poker games. He also thinks global warming is a fiction devised by liberals.

"Watch the language!" Mom commands.

Todd throws his napkin on the table.

"Todd, shut up," Dad shouts. "This isn't any of your damn business."

I snicker. I can't help it. Todd so rarely gets any negative criticism from the parents. Dad and Todd usually tag-team me, so it's two against one (with Mom always acting as Switzerland).

Todd can't believe Dad's told him to shut up, and his bottom lip starts to quiver slightly as if he might cry. Instead, he slams back his chair with a screech and declares, "I'm going to the bathroom."

"I don't want you working, Doris," Dad says, ignoring Todd as he stomps out of the dining room. "I'm still working part time. You don't need to work."

"Honestly, Dennis. You're being ridiculous. Let's face facts. We can't live on your reduced salary."

"I'm not the one being ridiculous, here," Dad says, throwing down his butter knife. "Just what are you going to do for them? Bake cookies?"

A hush falls on the table. Mom's mouth draws itself into a thin line. She doesn't turn to me like she usually does to say, "Your father is just joking." Her eyes get that steely look of determination, the one usually reserved for PTA meetings and Tupperware parties.

"For your information, I am going to write about cooking," she says, teeth clenched. She is trying hard not to raise her voice. She is trying not to let the strain show. "They are going to pay me for my expertise."

Dad laughs. He really shouldn't have. As it is, I doubt he will see the inside of the bedroom for weeks.

"Well, that doesn't matter," he says. "The fact is that you don't have to work. I mean, if Jane paid us back those loans she owed us from college . . ."

Now, it is my turn to drop my utensils. Those are not loans that any child is supposed to reasonably be asked to pay back. Everyone knows that. I look to Mom, hoping for a vigorous denial, but she is still studying Dad, saying nothing.

"Mom," I protest. She doesn't turn.

"I mean," Dad continues, seizing upon her silence as encouragement, "we still have $18,000 on one of her loans, and if we calculate all her spending money from age sixteen to twenty-one, that would put us right around $80,000."

"Dad!" I shout, in a panic.

He can't be serious. This is in direct violation of the parent-child contract that allows for youthful spending and irresponsibility during college without fear of future financial reprisals. I mean what's the fun of being a poor student if you've got to worry about paying your parents back for all those hundreds of 2:00 A.M. pizza runs?

Upon hearing the panic in my voice, Todd returns, presumably to gloat.

"And if we ask Todd to pay us . . ."

"Todd already paid us back for his school loans," Mom says, her voice eerily calm.

I stare at Todd. He shrugs.

"Oh, you're right," Dad concedes. "Well, if Jane pays us the near hundred grand she owes us, then we'd be all set."

Mom actually considers this a moment. I feel like I'm in the middle of a parental Savings and Loan Scandal.

Kyle's head is bobbing back and forth like he's got a front-row seat at Wimbledon.

"Mom, don't listen to Dad," I say, desperate. "He's just trying to convince you not to work. He feels threatened."

"But even so, it isn't enough. I'm taking this job. And that's that." She slams her flat palm on the table, causing everyone to jump. Mom rarely raises her voice and never, except behind the scenes, disobeys my father. An argument of this magnitude is rare enough—but having my mother win a public fight? Unheard of.

They have a traditional relationship, one based on outdated gender roles and a mutual fear of confrontation.

"But, Doris . . ." Dad starts.

"No more," Mom says, and her eyes flash a warning, her hands curling around the handle of her steak knife. "I've taken the job. I'm starting tomorrow."

"Doris . . ."

"Don't say another word, Dennis. Not another word." Mom's teeth are clenched, and a small blue vein in her temple is throbbing.

After a pause she adds in a pleasant, high-pitched hostess voice, "Would anyone like seconds on dessert?"

Todd drives me home, and I am sandwiched in the backseat next to Kyle. Deena, naturally, gets the front seat. Todd hasn't even pulled out of the driveway before he brings up the obvious.

"Mom got a job, Jane—MOM."

"I know," I sigh. I can't help but feel slightly jealous

that Mom has a job and I don't. Not that she isn't deserving of one, but how did her resume get through when mine didn't?

"I think it's cool she got a job at her age," says Deena. "What is she? Fifty?"

We all ignore her.

"Mom doesn't even have any dot-com experience," Todd says.

"I *know*," I say.

"I don't know what the hell is up with this job market," Todd says, for once not telling me that it's my fault I'm unemployed. "I just don't get it. And Dad . . ." he trails off. "Do you remember when Dad used to take us to his office?"

Todd looks at me in the rear-view mirror. I look back, and for a second, I think we share a moment.

"Yeah, and we used to play cops and robbers, and you were always the cop," I say.

"That was a lot better than playing Wonder Woman with you and that damn paper clip lasso."

"You played Wonder Woman?" Kyle laughs.

"I didn't play Wonder Woman," Todd clarifies. "Jane was Wonder Woman. I was Spider-Man."

"Spider-Man and Wonder Woman didn't work together," Kyle says. "They were totally separate comics."

"Spider-Man was in the Justice League," Todd says.

"He definitely wasn't," I say.

"Whatever," Todd says, rolling his eyes and sighing. "I just liked Spider-Man, OK?"

"I can't imagine Dad without his job, can you?" I ask Todd.

Todd shakes his head. "Nope, I can't imagine it."

"I still think it's cool your mom got a job," Deena says. "That's what I call girl power."

We stare at her until she says, "What?"

Todd pulls up in front of my apartment and Kyle hops out behind me. I am almost to my front door by the time he catches me.

"Wait, Jane," Kyle says, touching my shoulder. He's holding a small, wrapped box in his right hand.

"Happy Birthday," he says, giving it to me. He has already turned and is jogging back to Todd's car before I can say anything.

Inside my apartment, I open Kyle's present. In the box, there's a sterling-silver, flat skipping stone. On one side is carved the single word, *hope*.

Kyle's gift hits me hard, like a dodge ball to the stomach.

I don't deserve it. This act of kindness.

Then, for no reason, I start to cry. For the first time since I can't remember when, I cry.

Hard.

I cry so much that I fall asleep in the fetal position, hiccuping.

Citibank Financial Offices
Customer Service
Wilmington, Delaware 19801

Jane McGregor
3335 Kenmore Ave.
Chicago, IL 60657

March 9, 2002

Dear Ms. McGregor,

While we are glad to see that you are getting use out of your free Balance Transfer checks we sent you in February, we cannot accept one of these for your minimum balance payment of $524.32, which you included with your March statement for your Citibank Platinum MasterCard.

Please call your customer service representative at 1-800-PAY-NOW2, and arrange a payment of your outstanding minimum balance immediately in order to maintain your credit rating.

Sincerely,
Andrew Causey
Citibank Customer Service Manager

P.S. We have also received your request to raise your credit limit to $54,000. We are afraid that in light of your late payment status, we cannot approve such a credit line increase.

6

I dream that I am at the center of an action movie, where I must defuse a nuclear bomb to save all the members of my former company. They are all shouting at me to cut the wire.

A persistent and annoying ringing wakes me up in the middle of the night and it takes me several long dreamscape seconds to figure out it's my phone. It is pitch black in my bedroom, and I think it must be 3:00 A.M. I snap on my bedside lamp, blink back the agonizing brightness, and reach for the cordless on my nightstand.

"Hello?" I croak, only half awake, my throat sore from crying.

"Jane? Jane did I wake you?" It's my mother, and she sounds anxious.

"Mom, of course you woke me, it's the middle of the night," I say, yawning.

"It's seven in the morning," Mom clarifies.

"Right, the middle of the night," I say. What's the point of being depressed and unemployed if you can't sleep half the day away? Sleep is one of the only free activities (next to daytime television) that I have to look forward to. The longer I'm awake, the more time I have to contemplate my bleak finances and seemingly worthless job skills. While indulging in a moment of self pity, a thought occurs to me. "Is everything all right? Did Dad have a heart attack?"

"No, no, no," Mom says. "Nothing like that. Maybe I should let you sleep."

She pauses on the line, and I know she feels obligated to give me a way out, but that she doesn't actually *want* to let me sleep.

"Mom," I say.

"Yes?" she says.

"What's the problem?"

"You're sure? You're *sure* I'm not bothering you?" Again, the expectant pause.

"I'm sure."

"I could call back later . . ." She lets her voice drift off.

"Really. I'm awake."

"You're sure."

"Mom!" I cry, starting to get annoyed. "What do you want?"

"Well, I sort of have, a, er, issue."

"Yes."

"It's about work, you see. I start today, and I'm not exactly sure . . ." Her voice drops and I can tell she's trying to keep Dad from hearing. ". . . what to wear." She says the last part quickly, almost as if she's embarrassed.

"You don't know what to wear?" I echo.

"Yes, that's right." She sounds guilty, as if she's admitting to shoplifting Miracle Bras. "They told me casual, but I'm not sure what they mean by 'casual.' Can I wear slacks? Is that appropriate? Or do you think I should wear a dress and hose?"

Mom uses words like *slacks* and *hose* despite my reminders that they make her sound older than she actually is.

"Mom, when you went there for an interview, what were people wearing?"

She thinks about this a moment.

"Well, I don't exactly remember. I think, though, the receptionist was wearing sneakers. And, maybe I saw a couple of maintenance workers. They wore blue jeans."

"How do you know they were maintenance workers?"

"Well, surely, the people who work there don't wear blue jeans? I mean, it *is* a respectable office."

"Mom," I say. "Dot-coms usually don't have dress codes, so jeans are probably fine."

"Blue jeans!" Mom cries, sounding offended. Mom

uses the word "blue" to describe jeans, even if they are another color like "white blue jeans" or "pink blue jeans."

"Well, why don't you just wear some khakis and a regular shirt."

"You mean like a beige skirt?"

"No, pants. I mean like regular pants and a regular shirt."

"A pants suit?"

"No. Like a pair of black pants, and like a shirt."

"A blouse?"

I hate that word almost as much as I hate the word *slacks*.

"Sure. That," I say.

"What color?"

"Whatever color you want, Mom."

"Well, I was reading in *McCall's* that color makes an important statement about your personality."

"Trust me, no one in the office is going to be reading too much into your outfits. Not unless you wear spandex and go-go boots."

"Jane!" Mom sputters. She is so easy to shock, I almost can't help it.

"Mom, you'll do fine," I say.

"Do I sound nervous?" she asks.

"Petrified," I say.

"Rats. I thought I could fool you."

"Never." I hear her laugh softly on the other end of the line.

"Well, I'd better run if I'm going to catch the train."
She pauses.

"Mom," I say. "You'll do great. Really. You'll knock
'em dead. Remember, you make Martha Stewart look
like an amateur."

"Thanks, sweetheart," she says, and it sounds like
she's teary.

There's a pounding on my door, and shouting, and I realize it's Landlord Bob.

I sigh, and throw the covers over my head.

"JANEZ, I HAVE A KEY, NO? OPEN ZEE
DOOR!"

I jam on my jeans, and throw a T-shirt over my head,
and I am fishing around for my glasses when I hear Landlord Bob's key in my lock. I am halfway out the window
when he bursts into my bedroom.

"GOING SOMEWHERES, EH?"

"I'm taking out the garbage," I say.

"WHERE GARBAJ? I SEE NO GARBAJ."

I am still weighing the risks of fleeing down the fire
escape. Landlord Bob is distracted. He is looking around
my bedroom, assessing the value of my second-hand
Ikea furniture and Target knick-knacks. I could still flee.
It's not too late. I lean a bit further out of my window,
and Landlord Bob comes alive.

"COME DOWN FROM ZERE," he says. "WHERE
IZ MY MONEY? MY COUSIN CAN MOVE IN TO-
MORROW, IF ZOO DON'T HAVE IT."

"Bob, give me until this afternoon, all right? I'll have it for you then," I say.

"OKAYS, BUT ZAT'S IT. IF ZOO DON'T HAVE THE MONEY ZIS AFTERNOON, YOU OUT, YES?"

I have eight dollars in my wallet and wonder if I should use the money to buy cigarettes or lotto tickets. As I'm digging through my purse, hoping that somehow I'll find something of value (like a new credit card or a misplaced old bonus check from Maximum Office), I run across Missy's business card.

I need advice. I call Steph's cell phone. I get a half ring, before I'm instantly kicked over to her voicemail. She's still in New York, and knowing Steph, she's probably forgotten her cell phone charger.

There's nothing more to do.

I call the handwritten number on the card.

"I TOLD you I didn't touch your fucking stereo," Missy shouts into the phone.

"Uh, hello?" I ask tentatively.

"Huh? Who the hell is this?" Missy asks.

"It's Jane. From Maximum Office. We met the other day . . ."

"Jane?"

"I've got the two-bedroom apartment in Lakeview."

"Oh, right. Sorry, I thought you were my boyfriend calling."

"Listen, I know this sounds weird, but are you still looking for a place to live?"

"Am I ever. My house-sitting gig is over today. Do you have any idea how hard it is to find a decent place to rent in March?"

"How do you feel about paying for a couple of months' rent in advance?"

Missy, it turns out, has cash to spare. She says she saved most of her inflated techie salary, and says she's more than willing to pay cash up front if the apartment is in good shape, and she can have the bigger bedroom. She agrees to come by this afternoon to take a look at the place.

Two hours later, there's a hard rapping on my bedroom window. Since Ron never knocks, I know it can't be him. When I pull up the blinds, I see Missy looking in with a cigarette hanging out of her mouth.

"Are you going to just stand there?" she barks.

I open the window, and she clambers through it and onto my bed, dropping ash in her wake.

"I have a front door," I inform her.

"Nice place," she says, ignoring me. She scans my bedroom and walks into the hallway, checking out the living room, kitchen, and bathroom.

"Looks good," she says. "I'll take it."

"OK, great . . ." I say as she heads back out my bedroom window. Seconds later, she's back again, with a heavy Samsonite suitcase.

"You're moving in *now*?" I ask her, perplexed.

"No time like the present," Missy says.

Missy is wearing cut-off jeans, her hair is in knots on the top of her head. She looks like she left her house-sitting assignment in a hurry. She does not look like a Rich Techie. She looks like a Bill Evader. She looks like the sort of person who regularly skips out on restaurant checks.

I have a bad feeling about this.

Besides, she could be a serial killer, even if she is half my size.

"Missy, maybe we should talk about this," I start.

Missy clomps through my apartment, her muddy boots making track marks along my floor. "This is my room," she says, coming back to my bedroom and bouncing once on my bed. "I can use your furniture, right?"

"Maybe we should reconsider this arrangement," I say, as she sits down on my comforter.

"Here's the $2,000 you asked for—that's for three months' rent, right?" Missy says, handing over a thick manila envelope, like a blackmailer. Inside, there are crisp $100 bills.

"Cash?" I squeak.

"I hope that's OK," Missy says.

Looking at the bills, I decide instantly she isn't a serial killer, and that maybe she should have my room, after all.

Missy snaps down my blinds, and peers out of them as if she's afraid someone's following her.

"Thanks, roomie—would you mind getting the rest

of my things? They're in the alley," she says, still looking out of the blinds. "I'd get them, but I have a bad back."

My smart-ass comeback is silenced by the thick envelope full of money in my hand. I suppose we all have a price. Mine is $2,000.

There are four more boxes in the alley, and what looks suspiciously like a Maximum Office desk chair. I do a few rolling twirls in the chair before I carry it up. The boxes are next, and they're filled with a mix of clothes, shoes, and serious electronic equipment—a DVD player, a stereo speaker, and what looks like a Sony PlayStation. I lift up one of the wires, and underneath is a man's wallet, a man's gold watch, and a set of house keys. I tap the box and the wallet falls open—there's one edge of a $20 bill sticking out and the corner of a driver's license with a man's face on the front.

Hmmmm.

I don't think I want to know.

By the time I've put the boxes and chair in my bedroom, I'm sweating. I haven't had this much physical exertion in weeks.

I take the cash and run it upstairs to Landlord Bob. I give him the envelope along with my check for most of what's left in my bank account.

"SANK ZOO!" Landlord Bob exclaims. "MY LEGS SANK ZOO, TOO." He's in his rumpled pink bathrobe and I see his hairy shins. For a second, I think Landlord

Bob might cry tears of relief. He makes a move to give me a hug, but I put my hand up.

"That's OK, Bob," I say. "Stay away from the bookies, OK?"

"YES. BOOKIES BAD," Landlord Bob agrees, nodding his head emphatically.

When I get back to my apartment, I see Missy has taken up a position on my couch, and is flipping through my three channels and the snow that makes up the rest of them.

"You don't have cable?" she exclaims, shocked, as if she's just discovered that I'm a cannibal.

"No," I say.

"I wish you'd told me this *before* I moved in," she says.

"You mean before I moved you in," I correct.

"Whatever. Look, do you know where your cable box is?"

I shrug.

In amazement, I watch as Missy follows my cable cord out the window. She grabs a pair of pliers from one of her open boxes and scrambles up the fire escape and onto the roof. Within minutes, the cable is back on. And not just any cable, there's HBO, Cinemax, and Showtime.

Missy comes back into the apartment knocking roof dust off her pants.

"My ex-boyfriend was a cable guy," she says, by way of explanation.

I am silenced by the bootlegged cable. I feel at once

very lucky and very anxious. Just who is this girl I just let move in with me?

The entire afternoon, Missy doesn't move an inch, except to ask me to fetch her Diet Cokes from the refrigerator. If I didn't know better, I'd say she is nesting. When I get too close, she starts squawking like a blue jay.

My phone rings, and Missy, who is sitting on the cordless phone as if it might hatch, answers first.

"Hello? Jane? Nobody named Jane lives—" I hear her say, before I can snatch the phone away from her.

"I'm Jane," I hiss.

"Jane? I thought you were *Jan.*" She shrugs.

I grab the phone.

It's Steph. The connection on her mobile phone is terrible, like she's standing in the middle of a crowded bar. I can barely hear her.

"Bike has a Beyoncé Single," is what it sounds like she says.

I say "What?" over and over again, but I still can't understand a word Steph is saying.

"Steph, I can't hear you, can I call you back?"

I hang up, and try to call her back, but all I get is her voicemail.

The phone rings again. I snatch it up.

But it isn't Steph. It's Kyle.

"How are you?" he asks me. I wonder, for a minute, if Todd has asked him to check up on me.

I sigh.

"If you insist on knowing, I'm doing fine. I narrowly avoided eviction by getting a roommate."

"Very industrious of you," Kyle says. "I hope you can keep this one longer than six months."

"What is that supposed to mean?"

"Your track record with roommates is terrible," Kyle says. "One of them almost sued you in People's Court."

"That's a blatant exaggeration," I say. "That was Mandy, and she wasn't going to take me to People's Court, she was going to take me to small claims court for breaking her VCR."

"Right. And Karen?"

"Karen was psychotic, that's not fair," I say.

"But was she a diagnosed manic-depressive *before* she moved in with you?" Kyle asks me.

"Don't even start," I say. "Now why did you really call?"

"I thought you might like a field trip," Kyle says.

"A field trip?" I ask, skeptical.

"To the Art Institute," he says. "I know how you love the Art Institute."

It's true. I could spend hours there, days even, except on my reduced salary I can't afford the "suggested dona-tion" cost of admission.

"My law firm is having a cocktail party tonight with the Impressionists," he says.

"Cocktails and art, my two favorite things in the

world," I say, starting to perk up at the prospect of leaving my apartment.

"Who knows you best?" Kyle says.

Kyle comes to my door wearing a black suit and one of his trademark Burberry ties. He is carrying white roses and his wide, lawyer's smile.

"Do you ever go a day without wearing plaid?" I ask.

"Well, good evening to you, too, Ms. McGregor," Kyle says, ignoring my comment. "My, but you do look good when you shower. I appreciate you washing your hair. I feel special."

I stick my tongue out at him.

I am, actually, looking the best I've looked in weeks. I did shower, and not only washed my hair but blow dried and styled it, too. And, miracle of miracles, I've actually put on makeup. And high heels. And an above-the-knee red cocktail dress. I look less like an unemployed degenerate and more like a lady of leisure.

"Who's the fucking stiff?" Missy cries from her perch on my couch.

"Kyle, I'd like you to meet my roommate, Missy. Missy, this is Kyle."

"Is that Burberry?" she asks him.

"I'm afraid so," he says.

"He's a keeper," Missy tells me.

"Thanks for the advice," I say.

"You're fucking welcome," she says.

Kyle raises his eyebrows, and I suspect this whole

field trip ruse might have been just an excuse for him to get a glimpse of my roommate.

"These are for you," Kyle says, giving me what are, objectively, very pretty white roses.

"Does this mean I'm your date?" I ask him.

He laughs. "If you'd like," he says.

"Don't steal anything while I'm gone," I tell Missy before I walk out the door. "My dad's a cop."

This is a lie, but Missy doesn't know that.

"Fucking great," Missy says.

To my surprise, despite all my attempts at baiting him, Kyle doesn't insult me, or belittle me, or make jokes at my expense. He behaves like, well, a *great guy.* He is being so nice and considerate that I fail to detect a single trace of sarcasm anywhere. In fact, he is acting suspiciously like Mr. Dream Date.

I expect Kyle to abandon me once we step foot at the party, which is located in the foyer between the Monet and Van Gogh exhibits, but he stays close to me.

The room is full of lawyers prowling around in sharp-cornered tuxedos and severe black evening gowns. Even the women have shoulder pads that could cut glass.

I try focusing on the art, but I am the only one who appears interested in what's on the walls. Everyone else is more concerned about drinking and exchanging business cards.

To entertain myself, I pretend I am narrating a National Geographic documentary.

"Observing the rare Legalese tribe in its natural habitat is something only a select few scientists have the opportunity to do," I whisper into my glass of champagne, which I use as a makeshift microphone. "Notice how bottom feeders tend to rely on networking for survival. See the tribe's gravitation toward black outerwear, making them harder to be singled out by predators."

Kyle, who is probably the only lawyer in the room with a sense of humor, laughs.

"Kyle!" cries a stout, barrel-chested, blond man in his mid-forties who lumbers straight into my commentary without a pause. He thrusts out a hand and begins shaking Kyle's vigorously. "I wanted to congratulate you on the Kinsella case. Excellent work. Excellent!"

"Thanks, Gary," Kyle says. "Jane, I'd like you to meet Gary Godheim, one of the senior partners in the firm."

"Nice to meet you," he says, taking my hand and shaking it delicately, as if it is the tiny paw of a trained poodle. "What do you do?"

"Recreational skydiving," I lie.

"Really?" Gary says, momentarily interested. Kyle is delicately squeezing my arm.

"Actually, that's just a hobby," I say, smiling my most charming, best-behavior smile. "I'm in between jobs at the moment."

Gary becomes instantly disinterested.

I read somewhere that when Americans meet someone, their first question is always "What do you do?" In Europe, where they take six weeks vacation, they don't ask this question first, or second, or even third. Because in Europe, what you *do* isn't who you *are*. These are two very separate things, unlike here, where your worth, your identity, can be boiled down to the job title on your business card.

"What field?" he asks me.

"State correctional facilities," I say. Gary looks stricken. I pause just long enough for Kyle to cut off the circulation in my arm.

"Just kidding," I tell Gary.

"Looks like you've got quite the live wire here, Burton," Gary says, a gleam in his eye. At the mention of "live wire," I immediately think of Mike. Gary sends me an approving smile. I'm sure he is imagining me in a women's prison getting frisky with blond, buxom inmates in the group shower.

"No doubt about that," Kyle says, taking a measured sip of red wine.

"Have you met my wife, Michelle?" Gary asks, looking for his wife in the crowd.

The partners' wives are standing together in the corner. They are all wearing expensive jewelry, low-cut dresses, and are an equal mix of women in their fifties (the first wives) and women in their twenties (second or third wives). Together, they have more carat weight on their fingers than the Hope Diamond.

Kyle and Gary have drifted off to have their own conversation, leaving me alone with Michelle.

"Pleased to meet you," Michelle says, but doesn't

shake my hand. I am just young enough and skinny enough to be mildly threatening. I find this funny. She wouldn't think I was threatening if she could've seen me this morning, wearing my Lisa Loeb glasses and my unwashed, stained flannel pajamas.

"Have we met before?" she asks me.

"I don't think so," I say.

"Do you ride?"

"Ride?" I echo.

"Horses."

"Not if I can help it," I say.

"Oh. I thought maybe I'd met you at the stable."

"Will you excuse me?" I say.

I pluck off a glass of champagne from a roving waiter, swallow it in three gulps, and set it down on a table beside a swan-shaped ice statue.

I make my way to the *American Gothic* painting. The farmer with the pitchfork and his wife look like they've just been laid off. I feel their pain.

I see Kyle across the room talking to a leggy brunette who's smiling brightly at him and lightly touching his forearm, clearly flirting. This happens with Kyle a lot. It's why he can go through more girlfriends in a year than I go through jars of peanut butter.

Kyle catches my eye, and I make a smoochy, makeout face to him, because I am not above juvenile behavior. To my surprise, Kyle excuses himself from the leggy brunette and makes his way to me.

"Very funny," he says.

"I try," I say.

We both look at the painting.

"They look like they just got the news that they have to abandon their farm and come work in a cube," Kyle says.

I grunt a laugh.

"Did I ever tell you I was laid off once?" he asks me.

"You?" I say, surprised. I can't imagine Burberry Tie Kyle ever in the unemployment line.

"It was my first job out of college. In New York."

"Really?"

"It took me six months to find another job."

"What did you do for all that time?"

"I watched reruns of *Green Acres* and *Days of Our Lives*."

I laugh, because I think he's kidding.

"That Stefano is one bad-ass dude," he says, straight-faced.

This makes me laugh.

"You have a good laugh," he tells me.

"What is that supposed to mean?"

"It's supposed to mean you have a good laugh."

I study him. Wondering if he's trying anything funny.

"Relax, Jane. Have a bit of fun, will you?" he tells me. "Remember when you used to have fun?"

"I'm trying," I say.

I don't know if it's the champagne at work, or if I'm actually enjoying myself. It's hard to say exactly when I stop wondering why Kyle is being nice to me. At the end of the evening, he insists on parking, which in my neighborhood is anything but easy.

At my door, there's an electrical charge in the air, and I can't decide if it's the champagne I ingested, or the fact that Kyle is flashing me one of his deliberately charming smiles. I've seen him use The Smile countless times on unsuspecting women. He reels them in with a smile, and then when he gives them the "it's not you, it's me" speech six weeks later, they never know what hit them.

"Aren't you going to invite me up for coffee?" Kyle asks me, still smiling.

It occurs to me that Kyle actually is quite good-looking, if you go for cookie-cutter types. He looks like he'd be right at home in a Ralph Lauren ad.

"That's pathetic," I tell him. "You're so used to girls fawning all over you that you aren't even trying to come up with good lines anymore."

"I have no idea what you're talking about," he says, pretending innocence.

"You know very well that most women, God knows why, find you attractive," I say.

"Hmmmm," he says, pretending to contemplate this concept. "Perhaps it's my boyish good looks," he jokes. He pauses. "So why is it that . . . you know."

I smile, amused. "No, I don't know."

"That you never . . ."

"Yes?"

"Well . . ." He's squirming. ". . . wanted to date me?"

I laugh.

"Your ego is entirely out of control," I tell him. "You really think every woman should fall at your feet?"

"Only the really, really hot ones," he says, flashing me his smile again.

I laugh harder, and give him a playful shove, which causes him to flail his arms in an exaggerated windmill and pretend he's going to fall over.

"Good night," I say, slipping through my door.

Illinois Department of Health and Human Services Office
Springfield, IL 62781

Jane McGregor
3335 Kenmore Ave.
Chicago, IL 60657

March 12, 2002

Dear Ms. McGregor,

We received your request for food stamps and are afraid that you do not qualify for them, despite, as you wrote, "being a single mother to your two-bedroom apartment's appliances." We appreciate the fact that should you receive food stamps you would not use them to buy "booze or drugs."

However, with your unemployment benefits being what they are, and your lack of (human) dependents (we're afraid roommates, no matter how annoying, don't count), we have no choice but to reject your application for food stamps. Should you have further questions on this matter, or would like more information, please feel free to contact us.

Best,
Jane Miller
Associate Social Worker
Illinois Department of Health and Human Services

7

 am flat-out broke.

I have less than $10 in my bank account, which means that I can't effectively get it out of any ATM, and because my bank charges me $5 to see a teller, I'd be essentially halving my meager savings if I go in person to collect it.

These are desperate times. I have two minimum credit card payments due and the electric company just sent me a bill in a pink envelope.

"Do you have any money I can borrow?" I ask Missy. She snorts at me.

"Do I look like Bank of America to you?" she hisses at me, not looking up from my television set. My couch has a permanent imprint of her butt in it, which is only one of the many drawbacks of living with Missy.

Another happens to be that Missy claims to have severe allergies to dishwashing liquid. This is her reasoning for not touching the dirty dishes in the sink. Or her laundry piling up in the hallway. Detergents of any kind, she claims, cause her to break out in life-threatening hives.

Oddly, this does not prevent her from using my Bed-Head shampoo.

"I'm going out," I say.

"Whatever," Missy calls back.

I pack up thirty of my CDs and take them around the corner to the used CD shop, where I get $10. Apparently, Oingo Boingo and Duran Duran aren't the hot items they used to be.

It is a sad day when ten bucks doubles my total net worth. On the bright side, I can now deposit this $10 into an ATM and retrieve a full $20 out.

My next stop is the blood bank around the corner, where I have to answer a list of a hundred questions, including "Have you ever sold sex for money or drugs?" and "Have you ever taken intravenous drugs or had sex with a person who's taken intravenous drugs?" I pause on the question: "Have you had sex with an ape/monkey/or any species of primate since 1980?" I almost check yes to this, thinking Mike might count, but decide that he's less of a monkey and more of a pig.

I sit in a chair while a young nurse pokes me eighteen times with a needle before she finds the vein she calls "slippery." When the bag fills up in a matter of seconds, the nurse tells me I've got big veins, which makes me a fast bleeder.

At least I'm good at something. It's nice to know if I'm ever in a major car accident, I'll bleed to death in eight point two seconds.

It's only after they take enough blood from me for a major transplant operation that I discover they no longer pay people for blood donation. For my trouble, I get a juice box and a small pouch of Oreo cookies.

When I get back to my apartment, Missy is nowhere to be seen. I check my valuables—a pearl necklace from Grandma and my television and DVD player, but nothing seems to be missing. Plus, Missy's boxes are still here, as well as her boyfriend's cash-stuffed wallet. I assume she's coming back.

I take advantage of the silence to get started on Ron's CD project, which is the first fun thing I get to do all day. For me, there's nothing better than concept art, and having no constraints except what you can draw. In a half hour, I have a rough sketch of a giant sink stopper, which I fill in with some deliberately oversized brush-strokes. If I had a job that just allowed me to do this all day, I think I could be happy. I just want a job that requires more creativity than designing office supply catalogs.

I decide it's time to try looking at job listings. Looking through online classifieds is boring and self-defeating, and by the time I've scrolled through hundreds of job result screens, my eyes feel red and strained, and I am filled with self-loathing. I resent my parents, who did not have the ingenuity to invent something really marketable, like the beer hat or Liquid Paper. I resent the people who stumble into fortunes by inheriting the buildings around Wrigley Field, where you can rent out your roof to a Budweiser ad and happily sustain a lifetime of excess by simply allowing a beer company to paint the top of your building. And where's my benefactor? Where's my check from the National Endowment for the Arts? Where's my corporate welfare?

It all seems so hopeless.

In desperation, I start firing off resumes to things I'm overqualified for, including: Gap sales representative, theater usher, and dog walker.

I apply for those as well as thirty other jobs that I'm underqualified for (including CFO of Chrysler). Like Todd says, how do you know you won't get the job unless you throw your hat into the ring?

The benefit of having lots of time is you have the rare luxury of being able to waste other people's.

My front door opens with a bang and Missy walks in, wearing a wool suit, complete with heels.

"You had an interview," I accuse, pointing at her fitted black blazer. I feel like I've walked in on a boyfriend having sex with my best friend. I've not even had a telephone interview, much less one that required business attire.

"It was a wash," Missy says. "They're only paying seventy. It would be a step down."

"Seventy *thousand dollars*?" I spit.

Missy shrugs. "It's beneath me," she says.

The phone rings.

"Are you ready to get plastered? I am," Steph declares on the phone. "My mobile phone died on me. My plane was late. The conference was a mess, and, well, I've got some serious news to tell you, but I think I should do it in person."

I have $20. I try to tell myself this is enough for a night out on the town, like back in college when I managed to get the change in the couch cushions to support a night of pitchers and cheese fries.

"I've got news, too," I say. "Missy's moved in."

"What? Are you *joking*?" Steph coughs. "You let the klepto into your apartment?"

"I sort of didn't have a choice, and besides, you said you didn't even think those rumors were true," I say.

"OK, well, what the hell. I'm feeling generous. She can come along if she likes."

"She might have to. Of the two of us, she's the one with cash."

We all gather at the bar at Red Light, because Missy won't be seen in one of our "local dives" and she insists that she'll pay for our ten-dollar mango martinis rather than be seen in an Irish pub sucking down Harp.

"So? What's the news?" I ask Steph.

"Well . . . Ferguson has lost weight," she says.

Ferguson was my old supervisor at Maximum Office. Everyone called him Fat Ferguson with no sense of irony. He was probably nearly three hundred pounds, and because of this, Fat Ferguson had a sweating problem. He carried a ring of sweat around his armpits and a spot on his belly even on the coldest of days. I never saw him without his sweatbands. I kept thinking that perhaps they meant something, like the rings in a tree, but I never found any correlation. They were just there. Pit stains.

"You don't know pain until you have to work on that man's computer," Missy says. "Do you know he once got an entire French fry stuck in his keyboard? Don't ask me how he did it."

Steph laughs.

"So how much weight has he lost?" Missy asks. Fat Ferguson had already started the Subway diet well before I left, and was already less of Fat Ferguson and more like the Incredibly Shrinking Ferguson. His pants always seemed in danger of falling down.

"You wouldn't even recognize him. He looks almost normal. He's lost fifty more pounds," Steph says.

"Are you stalling?" I ask Steph. "Surely your big news isn't that Fat Ferguson is still on his diet."

"OK, well, do you want the bad news or the good news first?"

"Good," I say, without hesitation. Missy snorts.

"I quit my job!" Steph beams, looking proud.

I drop my cigarette. Missy pats Steph on the back. "Nice work," Missy says.

"You quit! Do you have any idea how crazy that is?" I can't believe Steph would willingly embrace a life of squatting, bill-evading, and bad credit. It doesn't seem possible.

"I'd taken all I was going to take," Steph says. "I quit on the last day of the convention, after I'd not slept for nearly three days."

"But, Steph, maybe you could still get your job back," I start. "You don't know what it's like out there. The job market is terrible."

"I'm not too worried. I'm going to freelance," Steph says.

My mouth drops open. "Freelance? Are you crazy?"

"Don't listen to Jane. You don't need those cocksuckers," Missy says, tapping out some ash into my empty martini glass.

"Steph, I think you need to think this through," I say. I am beginning to sound like Todd.

"Too late. I told Mike that he was a low-life asshole and Ferguson that he smelled like Vienna sausages."

"You told Fat Ferguson he smelled?" I know I should find this funny, but since I am channeling Todd, I seem to have misplaced my sense of humor.

"Worse, I told him he should check out the new modern invention called deodorant," Steph says.

Missy starts laughing. "Now that is the funniest damn thing I've heard all night."

"At least someone appreciates it," Steph says, sending me a look.

"It's funny," I say, but I'm not laughing. Selfishly, all I can think is that most of my friends are now unemployed. My only free beers will have to come from Todd or Kyle. "You're sure you can't get your old job back?" I ask, hopeful.

"I wouldn't take it if they offered it to me at twice the salary," Steph declares.

"Amen, sister," Missy echoes, holding up her martini and clinking it against Steph's glass.

"So if your quitting is the good news, I hate to even hear about the bad news," I say.

"Right," Steph says. "Well, I'm not sure how to say this, so I'm just going to come right out and say it."

I wait, expectantly.

"OK, well, the thing is—" Steph pauses and gives me a worried look.

"Just *say* it," I say.

"Right. OK. Well, it has to do with Mike."

"OK," I say, cautiously, trying not to hope too hard that he's been fired, or that something awful happened to him like he somehow contracted leprosy.

"Well, it seems that, Mike, sort of, well . . ." Steph coughs. "Mike has a fiancée."

"No shit," Missy exclaims.

I can't seem to speak. I have lost all feeling in my tongue, and my ears are ringing like I've just come back from a Metallica concert.

"What do you mean, he has a fiancée?" I manage to say, slowly and carefully, pronouncing each syllable deliberately, so that I don't start shouting.

"Well, she was there. In New York. She lives there, or she did until a couple of weeks ago when she relocated to Chicago." Steph pauses and coughs. "And, she told me that they've been engaged for more than a year, dating for three."

Missy is slapping her knee. "Son of a bitch," she breathes. "I *knew* he was an asshole, but damn."

I feel like I'm turning three shades paler than white. He has a *fiancée.* Of course. It all makes sense now. The fact that we always sat in the darkest corners of restaurants. How he never gave me his home number, just his mobile. How he kept making unexpected trips to New York. How he never suggested that I meet his family, or his friends, or anyone who might be able to expose his double life. It's no wonder he was so quick to end things with me. His fiancée was moving to town.

I am the dumbest girl alive.

"This calls for another round of drinks," Missy says.

"I second that," Steph shouts.

The bartender plops down three more martini glasses. My hand is shaking, but I manage to pick up my drink and down it in one long swig.

It is only by some miracle that I do not drunk dial Mike.

Steph stops me at the bar by locking her mobile phone and refusing to give me the pass code. Both Steph and Missy stop me from using the pay phone in the bath-room.

Missy and Steph bond over this, and they both shake their heads at me when I'm too drunk to actually walk myself up my own stoop. I don't know if it's Missy or Steph, but somebody hides all the phone cords in the apartment, so that when I try to pick up a phone at 3:00 A.M., I get no dial tone.

I wake up the next morning feeling like sometime during the night someone hit my head with something hard and flat. Repeatedly. I sit up and groan, rubbing my eyes and pushing back the mat of hair that has formed into the consistency of a Brillo pad sometime during the night. My tongue feels furry and sour.

I stumble into the bathroom, my ears a roar of white noise. I drop my toothbrush several times in the sink, my coordination gone along with all ability to concentrate on anything for more than two minutes at a time.

It is then that I realize that Steph has spent the night. She and Missy are drinking coffee in my living room.

"Look," Missy shouts from the living room, "Fat Fer-guson!" She's pointing to a picture of a man on *Ricki Lake* who's confined to his bedroom and can't get out because of his excessive weight.

"Don't you just love this girl?" Steph asks me.

"There she is, the queen of martinis," Missy says when I enter the room.

I groan and head to the kitchen to pour myself a much needed cup of coffee. My head is splitting.

I notice that Steph and Missy act as if they've known each other all their lives, instead of only for twenty-four hours. Steph didn't even really know Missy, except by reputation, before last night. Now, they act as if they've always been the best of friends.

"I want to kill Mike, the smug bastard," Steph sighs.

"Me too," Missy says.

The two pause, staring at the television screen.

"I want to break into Maximum Office's computer system," Missy says, after a moment. "It wouldn't be that hard. Take down email."

"Could you do that?" Steph asks.

"Yeah, I was the system administrator, so I can do just about anything," she says.

"You could?" I can see the wheels in Steph's head turning.

"All I need is a keycard to get into the building," she says, her nose ring catching the light. "I wouldn't be able to do it remotely. I'd have to be in the cage."

"The cage?" I ask.

Missy snorts and rolls her eyes, as some techies do when dealing with lay people.

"The *server* room," she sighs.

"Oh," Steph and I both say at once.

I look at Steph, but she doesn't catch my eye. She's seriously considering Missy's proposition, whereas I think it confirms my fears that she's crazy.

"You can't be serious."

"What else could you do?" Steph asks Missy.

"I could send out emails to upper management saying they're fired. I could probably even freeze their paychecks for a month or two."

"You can't do that," I say.

Missy snorts and shrugs.

"What else?" Steph asks, eyes bright.

"Lots of stuff," Missy says.

"You guys are insane," I say.

"OK, somebody is crying out for attention," Steph sighs at me. "Give us a status report. Are you OK? About Mike?"

I shrug. "I can't do much about it, can I? Missy's hidden the phone cords. I can't even send him a Fuck You email."

"It was for your own good," Missy says. "Besides, I put back the phone cords this morning."

"If you want to talk about it we'll listen," Steph offers.

Missy grunts and rolls her eyes.

"No thanks," I say.

Talking about it will only make me want to cry, and that's the last thing I need to do, cry over Mike.

Besides, how can I explain that Mike was special because he was the first guy I dated who had matching furniture? He had more square-footage in his Hancock Observatory condo than my parents had in their house. He had a full-service bar, complete with matching mixer and martini glasses. He was in all senses a grown up. He was a man who would never be thrown by the sudden appearance of a cocktail fork at his place setting or a French wine list. He knew how to cook. He had a full set of pots and pans and a cabinet full of herbs I'd never heard of. He took me to the best restaurants. He ordered in French.

And he had a fiancée. I'm not sure why I should be surprised. You can't assume smooth, sophisticated men go around telling the truth.

My phone rings.

It's Mom. She has a sixth sense about me, I think. Like she knows when her offspring are in trouble.

"Is this a bad time?" she asks.

"You have no idea," I say. I want to tell her about Mike, but instead, I just say, "I found out an old boyfriend cheated on me."

"Which one?" she asks me.

"I'd rather not say," I say.

"Was it Ron? I never really trusted him," she says.

"No, but it's OK."

"Well, what are you going to do about men, anyway?" she sighs. Mom's voice wavers, and it sounds like she's going to abandon her official "phone voice"—a high sing-song bursting with goodwill.

"What's wrong?"

"Why do you think anything is wrong?"

"Mom, what's going on?"

"Oh, nothing, it's just your *father*," she says, using

the voice reserved for talking about Dad, a strained, low-pitched sigh.

"Oh," I say, relieved. Dad is always doing something wrong.

"He's being a bit of a pill," she says.

"When is he anything but a pill?" I say, and she laughs.

"He's pretending not to know how to work the washing machine. And, he says that if I don't do more of his laundry I'm forfeiting our marriage vows. I mean, he's now home on Wednesdays, Thursdays, and Fridays, so you think he could do a little housework."

"Ouch," I say. Dad is always sinking to new lows. "Did you tell him that you're going to donate his body to science? That they've never seen a live Neanderthal before?"

Mom laughs again. She must really be angry, because normally she'd feel obligated to say, "Jane, be nice to your father, he works hard."

"And, money's really tight now that your father is only working two days a week," she says.

"Do you need money?" I ask her. Though I don't have any to spare, I'd lend her the $5 I just got for Grandma's Christmas sweater on Ebay.

"No, that's OK," she says. "We'll be fine."

Steph and Missy are suddenly shouting.

"What's that noise, dear?"

"Oh, I've got friends over."

"Don't let me keep you," she says, sounding more cheerful.

I find Missy and Steph screaming and pointing to the television, which is set to CNBC. On the screen Mike is bobbing his head and talking with what seems like conviction. Underneath his giant head, are the words "Mike Orephus, CFO Maximum Office."

Since when did he get a promotion?

"Shhhhhhhhh," I hush them.

I turn up the television's volume.

"So, our profit share is up, and we foresee extended growth in the next quarter . . ." he's saying. I think he's highlighted his hair. He's also gotten his teeth whitened.

"Cocksucker," Steph breathes.

"SHHHHHHHH," I say.

"How about the rumors of a merger? Would you consider merging with the web-based Office Online?"

"Well, it's far too early to talk about any mergers at this point. But I can say that at Maximum Office we are going to keep all our options open."

"Does he have a fake tan?" Missy asks.

"Shut up!" I shout, turning up the TV to absolute maximum volume.

"We're positioned extremely well in the market, and I think we've shown, time and again, that we hit our projections. Our board is not likely to make any hasty decisions."

"Good news for investors," the announcer says. "Thank you, Mike."

"Thank you, John."

"Up next, a look at CEO perks, and the trends toward downsizing them. But first, this message."

I mute the TV and sit down.

Both Steph and Missy are staring at me.

"What?" I say.

"I think it's time we tell her about our plan," Missy says.

"What plan?" I ask, suspicious.

"The plan we *just* made," Steph says, tapping her fingers together in exaggerated glee.

They tell me their plan.

"You are both insane," I say, looking back and forth between the two of them, trying to figure out how long I should play along before calling the police. I suspect this is all some elaborate practical joke, and calling 911 might be exactly what they want me to do so that they can laugh at me later.

"No, listen, it's not that hard."

"You're talking about *robbery*."

"It's not robbery if Fat Ferguson doesn't know his keycard is missing."

I stare at Steph as if she's lost her mind, which I fear she has.

"You're talking about stealing Fat Ferguson's keycard so you can get into Maximum Office. What part of that isn't robbery?"

"Technically, it's not robbery if we don't use a weapon," Missy says. "It's theft."

"Is she for real?" I ask Steph.

"Ferguson is perfect—think about it," Steph says. "He has no friends. He'll be easy to pickpocket, and if something goes wrong with the prank, we'll blame him, because we used his keycard."

"This sounds like a really dumb idea," I say.

At this point, I hear Ron scratching at my fire escape. He's halfway through the window when Steph starts screaming, and Missy, reflexively, beans him in the head with a half-full can of Diet Coke.

"Dude," Ron exclaims, rubbing his head and straightening to almost his full height, because he never straightens completely, always keeping his back in a Shaggy slouch. "What was *that* for?"

"God, Ron," Steph breathes. "You scared us."

"You know him?" Missy says.

"Jane slept with him," Steph answers.

"Hey," I shout, defensive.

"What's up, *chicks*?" Ron says, raising his bushy eyebrows.

"They're plotting to commit a felony," I say.

"Sweet."

"Can he be trusted?" Missy asks me.

"I hardly think so," I say.

Suddenly taken by Missy, Ron says, "Girl, you are seriously hot." He grabs her hand and makes as if to slobber on it. Missy lets him, and it looks as if she's leaning over so he can get a look at her cleavage.

"You're not so bad yourself," she tells him. "Sorry about the head wound."

"Not a problem-o," Ron says, taking a seat next to Missy. "Want some pot?"

"Sure," Missy says, taking one of his joints.

"Don't smoke that in here," I snap. The last thing I want is for my landlord to raid my apartment with off-duty police officers who will arrest me for felony drug possession.

"So," Missy says, lighting up Ron's joint. "All we need is a car."

"I've got a car," Ron says.

U.S. Bobsled and Skeleton Federation
421 Military Rd.
Lake Placid, NY 12946-0828

Jane McGregor
3335 Kenmore Ave.
Chicago, IL 60657

March 13, 2002

Dear Ms. McGregor,

Thank you for your interest in pursuing a career as a U.S. Olympic Bobsledder. We should advise you, however, that bobsledding is a very taxing and grueling sport that requires superior athletic ability and is not, as you mentioned, a sport where gravity does most of the work.

Since you mentioned that you are not, nor have ever been, an athlete of any caliber (and we do not count grade school gymnastics lessons) I am afraid you will probably not be in a position to make the 2006 Olympic team. However, if you would like to learn more about bobsledding, we can offer you professional lessons from any number of our certified bobsledding instructors.

Happy Sledding!
Lee Bryn
Assistant to the Director of Public Relations
U.S. Bobsled and Skeleton Federation

8

Steph and I are in the backseat of Ron's gray Chevy Impala, and I am wondering if I can claim kidnapping should we be stopped and arrested by the state highway patrol. Ron's muffler is attached by a single metal wire, and his back right window is nothing but a garbage bag held in place by duct tape. It flaps in my ear every time we accelerate beyond twenty miles per hour.

"We are not going to do this," I say.

"Look, you said you wanted to come, so I let you come," Missy says, turning around and facing me from the front seat. "So shut it, will you?"

"I only came so I could talk some sense into you," I say.

In the driver's seat, Ron snorts. I kick the back of his seat and he says, "Hey, watch it, man."

His steering wheel, I notice, has a pink leopard-print fur cover. He's only lacking matching dice hanging from his mirror.

"Steph, come on, be sensible," I say, turning to plead with her.

"We're just going to talk to him," Steph says. "We're going to talk to him and pickpocket his key-card."

"You're just going to walk up to him and slip your hand in his pants and walk away with his keycard." I don't even try to contain the sarcasm.

"That's right," Missy says.

Ron's Impala backfires, then shudders and dies in the loading zone of the McCormick Convention Center.

"What are we doing here?" I ask them.

"It's a sci-fi convention," Steph says. "Ferguson is going to be here."

"He's into sci-fi?"

Lord of the Rings," Steph corrects. "How did you miss all those hobbit figurines on his desk?"

I shrug. "I thought they were the new corporate lawn gnome," I say.

"Anyway, he has a booth here or something."

"How do you know this?" I ask Steph.

"He told me in New York," she says.

"Great," I say.

"OK, guys, you better get going. Ron and I will wait in the car," Missy says, sending Ron a flirty look.

"Sweet," Ron says.

"Why do we have to go?" I whine.

"I was kicked out of last year's convention," Missy explains.

I don't think I want to know why.

"Come on, quit whining," Steph says, grabbing my arm.

Apparently, girls who aren't wearing Klingon masks can pretty much slip by the main tables of the convention without paying an admission charge. I haven't seen this many painted faces and bad rubber masks since last Halloween at Navy Pier. Rows and rows of tables and booths line the giant convention room, and banners above our heads announce genres like Star Trek: The Next Generation and "Frodo Fans This Way."

I feel like I might catch nerd by just being here.

"Let's hurry up," I tell Steph, pushing her through the crowd.

After studying the badly laid out map of the convention, we wander through what appear to be hundreds of *Lord of the Rings* booths. There's one of every conceivable character in the books, and enough elves, trolls, and hobbits to fill an insane asylum.

Steph and I seem to be magnets for the weirdos. Already, we've gotten a handful of free figurines and a rolled up calendar poster featuring Sean Austin. While Steph is busy trying to hoard her share of glow-in-the-dark elf necklaces, I nearly collide into a pair of thirty-something men in tights and oversized ears. They look like middle-aged Keebler elves.

"Queen Galadriel!" they cry, looking at me, then drop to their knees. One of them almost splits his tights.

"I don't want any peanut butter fudge sticks, thanks," I say.

"We are here to do your bidding, oh mighty elf queen," the balding one says.

Clearly, they are both virgins.

"I bid you go get a life," I say, tapping each one on the shoulder with my free poster.

"Our life is to serve you, oh our mighty elf queen," the other one says. He has rubber arrows sticking out of a pouch he's wearing on his back.

"You can't be serious," I say.

"What the hell?" Steph cries, turning around and seeing the Keebler guys on their knees. "I turn my back for one second, and you get into trouble."

"They want to do my bidding," I say.

"Why don't you ask them for money?"

"Why didn't I think of that?" I turn to the overweight elves. "You guys got twenty bucks?"

"Bucks—what is this strange currency of which you speak?" says the one wearing the long blond wig that makes him look like the mullet-toting David Spade in *Joe Dirt*.

"That's what I thought," Steph spits. "OK, move it along," she adds, waving them off.

"Here's some free advice, fellas," I say. "You guys might want to try hitting on a woman when you're not wearing tights."

"There's Ferguson," Steph hisses, indicating a man wearing a giant wizard's hat in a booth selling miniature hobbit dolls.

"That's not him," I say, because the man is half the size of Fat Ferguson.

"It is him," Steph declares. "He's just lost weight."

"Wow, he looks totally different," I say.

"For those of us who aren't size zeros, like you, it's not easy to lose weight," Steph tells me. Steph is a size fourteen and resents that I can wear boys' jeans.

"I am not a size zero," I say. Then I add, "At least you have boobs."

"Let's go," Steph says, grabbing my arm.

I squint harder, and see that despite the loss of weight, it is the same semi-balding Ferguson with the '80s square glasses frames, and the cheap, short-sleeved, collared, striped shirt.

"Ed," Steph calls. "Ed, good to see you."

Ferguson turns around and his jaw drops.

"Steph?" he asks, incredulous. "And Jane! What are you doing here?"

Two pencil-thin adolescents behind Ferguson stare. They are clearly not used to seeing grown women in person and not naked on porn Web sites.

"We were in the neighborhood," Steph lies. "Want to get a drink?"

The two boys behind Ferguson snicker. "Dude, score!" one says.

Ferguson ignores them.

"You want to get a drink with me?" he echoes, sounding amazed.

I don't remember Ferguson being so pathetic. It seems like Ferguson probably doesn't get out much, and when he does, it's only to talk to fellow sci-fi geeks about wizards and elves.

Ferguson's face falls.

"Well, I'd love to, but the booth . . ." His voice trails off. "We have one more hour until we shut it down, and then I was hoping to swing by the Next Generation booth. I heard that there's someone dressed up like Deanna Troi."

"She has big knockers, too," one of the adolescents behind Ferguson says.

"Are we seriously going to wait for him?" I ask Steph.

"We don't have much choice," Steph hisses back at me.

I look up and see the Keebler elves haven't given up their quest. They're back and trying to give me a garland of plastic flowers.

Since I'm stuck at Ferguson's booth, I send the elves out to fetch Steph and me snacks and drinks.

"You know they're hoping to get laid," Steph says.

"Well, they can keep hoping," I say. "In the meantime, I'm thirsty."

The elves return with a couple of Diet Cokes and

some popcorn. When one of them tries to braid my hair, I slap at his hands. But the elves aren't easily discouraged. Eventually, I use them like homing pigeons, sending them out to the parking lot with messages for Missy and Ron.

After two and a half hours, Ferguson finally agrees to leave with us.

"Can't we come with you, our queen?" the mullet one asks me.

"No," I say.

"What about getting your number, your highness?" the other one asks.

"Number?" I echo, acting puzzled. "What is this number of which you speak?"

When we get outside, Ron and Missy are waiting at a discreet distance, having been given a heads-up by the Keebler elves. Ferguson offers us a ride in his red Ford Fiesta, and Missy and Ron tail us to the Bennigan's nearby.

Steph only just manages to persuade Ferguson to leave his wizard's hat in the back seat of his hatchback before we go into the bar.

Once inside, Ferguson beams at us.

"It's so good to see you girls," he says, as if we're prostitutes.

"You look great, Ed. Have you lost weight?" Steph asks, once we're sitting at the bar.

"Almost a hundred pounds on the Subway diet," Ferguson says, beaming, patting his markedly reduced belly. "Just like Jared."

I don't say anything, I just squint. Despite his significant weight loss, Ferguson still smells the same. Like rotting oranges and Gorgonzola cheese.

"You know you don't get enough vitamin C on that diet. You could die of scurvy," I say.

"Ha," barks Ferguson, elbowing me in the ribs. "Jane, you always were the jokester."

I can't decide what is more offensive—that he actually touched me or that he used the word "jokester."

"What can I get you girls to drink?" Ferguson says, pushing up his now too-big glasses, a flap of now-loose skin under his chin quivering as he speaks.

"Bombay Sapphire and tonic," I say.

"The hard stuff, eh?" Ferguson says, touching me again with his elbow. I try my best not to shrug it off.

"I'll have what you're having, Ed," Steph says, smiling at him, resting her arm lightly, flirting, on his forearm.

Ferguson hops off his bar stool in his eagerness to get our drinks and stumbles a little. He rounds the bar, waving his hands at the bartender.

"What are you doing?" I hiss at Steph.

"Catching flies," she says, grinning into the face of Ferguson as he returns, cheeks pink with the exertion of getting the bartender's attention.

I am silent for the next thirty minutes, watching Steph drape herself across Ferguson, who seems to actually think he has a chance at a threesome. He seems to have forgotten his many lectures on my bad attitude—in fact, he seems to have forgotten entirely that we were never friends.

"Jane, how many hobbits does it take to screw in a lightbulb?"

I roll my eyes. Steph gives my shin a soft kick under the bar.

"I don't care," I say.

"Come on, Jane. It's a joke. Guess."

"I really don't care."

"Well, think about it—I'm going to take a piss. I'll be right back," Ferguson says, hopping off his stool and weaving his way to the men's room.

"Did you tell him we're prostitutes now?" I ask Steph, watching his considerably slimmer figure disappear into a narrow hall at the end of the bar.

Steph ignores me. She's too busy pouring my drink and hers into Ferguson's glass.

"Hey!" I protest.

"We want him drunk, not us," Steph snaps at me.

Ferguson emerges from the bathroom a few minutes later, his thinning hair coming off his head in small poufs.

"Ed!" shouts Steph suddenly, when he is inches from us. "Bet you can't down that whole drink in one gulp."

Within about two hours, he's completely drunk. His alcohol tolerance is like a little girl's. Another indicator of a seriously dismal social life.

"I'm sorry about how things happened, I am," Ferguson is slurring. He is bleary-eyed and looking as if he might start crying. This is not what I need.

Suddenly, Ferguson reaches for me, and I think he is trying to grab my left boob, except what he's really trying to do is give me a consoling hug, but my reflexes are too fast. I put the palm of my hand straight into his nose, sending him flying backward, the rest of his drink airborne in a fountain above his head. I see him fall in slow motion, the fleshy part of the thin jowls under his chin flapping. He hits the ground with a solid thud, his head bouncing against the rubber mat on the bar floor. The glass tumbler falls down smack in the middle of his forehead, landing with a bone-thumping clunk.

He is out cold.

"Shit—what happened?" the bartender shouts from above my right shoulder. Steph is already on the ground, helping Ferguson sit up, even though he is unconscious, his head lolling.

"Too much to drink," Steph calls to the bartender.

"Is he OK?" the bartender asks, sounding concerned. He is thinking liability. He is imagining a deposition where hostile lawyers ask him about overserving.

"Fine," Steph and I both say at once.

"Maybe I should call an ambulance," the bartender ventures.

"No, we've got him. We'll take him," Steph says. She already has one of Ferguson's arms around her neck. She is motioning me with her head to get on the other side.

I shake my head.

"Jane!" Steph hisses at me. "NOW, Jane."

Something in her voice convinces me that I'd better help. I crouch down and put Ferguson's damp arm over my shoulder. I push up, but my legs are weak from excessive lack of exercise, and Ferguson hasn't lost *that* much weight.

"Are you lifting? I don't think you're lifting," Steph says, hauling up her half higher than mine. Ferguson's head lolls forward and he grunts. Ferguson is coming to a little, his eyes fluttering.

"Come on, Ed, we're going home," Steph says, shaking her side a little. "Can you walk?"

Ferguson murmurs something incoherent, but he's moving his feet, and some of the weight on my side lessens a bit.

"Come on, that's it," Steph says.

"Drive safe," the bartender calls after us.

"What the fuck?" Missy cries from the window of Ron's Impala. She is clearly mad, but not so outraged that she'll actually get out of the car and confront us. She watches as we steer Ferguson to the back door and sink him inside the car, his head clipping the roof on his way down.

"What the fuck happened in there?" shouts Missy, swiveling her neck back around to face us.

"Jane knocked him out cold," Steph says.

"Whoa, dude," exclaims Ron.

"Just drive," Steph spits. "I'll follow you in Ferguson's car."

Ferguson's head lolls back against the seat. He's murmuring something about fried chicken.

We arrive back at my apartment, much against my will—I want to take Ferguson to Ron's, but Missy says we have to make it look like Ferguson came home with us of his own will in case he presses kidnapping charges.

"Kidnapping?" I squeak.

"It probably won't happen." Missy shrugs. This does not make me feel better.

It is difficult getting Ferguson up the stairs, because he's not quite all there, and so we all pitch in to help him up. Once we make it up the stairs, we drag Ferguson's limp, breathing body to the couch. But before I can even catch my breath, Ron has his entire head inside my refrigerator. Apparently, committing a class A felony doesn't make a dent in his appetite. He emerges with a loaf of bread, the last of my coldcuts, and a bottle of mustard. He proceeds to make a sandwich in his mouth by squirting in mustard, then shoving in a whole piece of bread and a slice of ham.

Ferguson, on our coach, groans.

"Well? Are you going to get his keycard?" Steph is looking at me expectantly.

"I'm not touching him," I say, backing away with my hands in the air. The idea of fishing around in Ferguson's pockets makes me queasy.

"Do I have to do everything?" Steph says, stomping forward. She stoops in front of the couch and begins searching Ferguson. She is elbow-deep in brown Sansa-belt pants, but doesn't even flinch in her methodical searching.

She comes up with his wallet, and hands it to Missy.

"I thought you were looking for keys," I accuse, as I watch Missy take a twenty-dollar bill from the fold. She doesn't answer me.

"It isn't here," Missy says, after dumping the contents of Ferguson's wallet on my coffee table. "Keep looking," she instructs Steph.

"Who buys this boy's clothes?" Steph exclaims, wrinkling her nose. "You know he doesn't have a bad body, really, but he needs someone to help him dress."

"You have to be kidding, right?" I ask Steph. She doesn't answer me.

"Here it is," Steph says, pointing to a cord around his neck. He actually wears his keycard and ID badge around his neck when he isn't at work. I don't think I've seen anything so sad.

In one swift motion, Missy rips it from his neck.

"What the . . . ?" Ferguson mumbles, coming around and squinting, trying to make out our faces. He lost his boxy glasses in the bar when he fell.

"He looks a lot better without his glasses," Steph comments.

I give her a look. "What?" she asks, innocently.

"Huh? Where am I?" Ferguson mutters groggily.

"Where do you think you are?" Steph asks him.

"I don't know."

Missy flips on the television, to distract him. *Dude, Where's My Car?* is on.

"You are a wild man, dude," Ron says, suddenly, slapping Ferguson on the shoulder. "Want some?" he says as he lights up a joint.

Ferguson, who is still dazed, takes it and drags deep.

"Sweet," Ron says, nodding at him. Because I've had a long day, I even take one drag of the joint that Ron passes around.

When Missy and Steph push Ferguson out the door around midnight, I am too high to say anything.

After consuming every last Chee•to in our apartment and downing three mustard sandwiches, I finally go to sleep on the couch in my clothes. Steph has passed out on the floor, and Ron, as usual, has snuck out the fire escape. I see he's taken the unfinished sketches of his band's CD cover with him. Typical move, so that he can claim later he doesn't have to pay me the full fee.

To: jane@coolchick.com
From: Hiring@NabiscoWorld.com
Date: March 16, 2002, 10:30 A.M.

Dear Ms. McGregor,

While we appreciate your enthusiasm for Nabisco products, we are afraid that we cannot send you free samples of all our products so that you can further your career as an Official Product Tester.

For your loyal patronage, we are including a coupon for twenty-five cents off a box of our popular Ritz Bits® crackers.

Good luck with your career!
Tom Haas
Product Development

9

I come awake with a sensation of unprecedented dry mouth and a burning in my throat, and the memories of the night before come back in dizzying snippets. I can almost feel the brain cells I've lost, the mismatched synapses firing over dead nerves. There's a dull ringing in my ears, and it takes me several moments to realize that it is actually the phone ringing.

"Sweetheart—I have the best news," Mom says, breathless, into the receiver.

"I hope it's not a blind date," I say, thinking this, too, would be karma.

"Nope—even better," she says. "I've got you an interview at my company."

"When?" I ask. My call waiting beeps. "Mom? Let me call you back."

"Is this Jane I am speaking with?" a woman asks me, sounding perky and entirely too smug. People with jobs generally do sound smug.

"This is Jane," I say.

"Great—is now a good time? Am I interrupting anything?" She laughs after she says this, and I think she is making fun of me.

"I'm Cheryl Ladd and I work with Doris McGregor. She dropped your name and said you were quite talented. We searched our files and saw you sent us your resume a couple of weeks ago."

"Oh?"

"In fact, the boys and I thought it was pretty funny. Your resume is quite interesting." I do not know which one she has—but quite a few of them I've sent are a bit exaggerated.

She begins reading my resume aloud. "Worked as an assistant to Andy Warhol, developed the Pepsi logo . . ."

"Er, right," I say. I must have been particularly bitter and disenchanted when I wrote that one.

"Well, we're a dynamic, creative team, and we need creative people like you—who aren't afraid to take risks."

Cheryl is so peppy on the phone that I am having a hard time listening. I do not do well absorbing erratic inflections in tone.

"I know this is short notice, but are you available this afternoon? I'd love for you to meet the team."

·   ·   ·

Against my better judgment, I leave Missy and Steph alone in my apartment with Ferguson's key. With any luck, they will have decided that this whole breaking-into-Maximum-Office plan is ridiculous.

After I've showered and dressed, putting on my best wool suit and heels, I go to a small office building at the corner of Grand Avenue and Dearborn, feeling like I'm being set up on a blind date. The elevators open to a small, open, bare-floored office with bright blue walls, track lighting, and expensive, full-backed leather chairs. The cubes aren't made of plywood but of Italian maple, and all the accents in the room are a cool stainless steel. All in all, the office space looks like it was designed by Swedish architects on speed. Everywhere there's exposed wood, black, metal, and glass.

I take two steps into the office and am nearly beaned by an orange Nerf football that goes zipping by my head.

"Sorry," says a hunky, dark-haired god who looks like he just walked out of an Abercrombie & Fitch catalog, complete with ruffled hair, coolly frayed khaki shorts and nicely tanned legs. He retrieves the football and then tosses it across the office to his friend, a guy with Buddy Holly glasses like the ones I've left at home and black spiky hair. From where I'm standing I can see into the kitchen and a great glassed-in refrigerator full of soda—brand-name soda. I didn't think these offices existed anymore. I'd thought they'd all gone the way of tech portfolios—in a giant flaming crash. And suddenly I'm nervous, with the feeling you get when you see the date your friends set you up with is far, far better-looking than you are: you want him to love you, but if he doesn't, you want him to have a fatal flaw, like an IQ of fifty.

I see Mom, who is sitting at a nice maple-wood cube in the corner of the room, and I wave. She waves back. I see she's talking to another hunky guy—this one blond, in his thirties, and looking like a J. Crew model.

A perky woman with a sandy-haired bob and a turned-up nose comes up to me and grabs my elbow.

"You *must* be Jane. Oh, I'm so glad you made it." She's even more perky in person than on the phone. People this peppy always have something to hide—usually manic depression or some other kind of serious mental illness. Still, I look past it. Already, I know I want this job. I want to work in a place where Nerf games are condoned and encouraged. I want to sit in a cube with slick, Swedish furniture. "Can I get you a Coke? Chips? A bagel?" She's cocking her head to one side like an airline stewardess.

"Uh, no thanks," I say.

"Well, come on—let's go to the fishbowl," she says, hooking her arm through mine and steering me over to the conference room—a giant glassed-in structure in the middle of the open office space, the one with the track lighting and maple conference table.

Just as we sit down, there's a hard thunk on the glass wall—it's the Nerf football again and Abercrombie sends us an apologetic shrug, while Cheryl *tsks* at him, and gives him an exaggerated "you've been a naughty boy" face.

"Now, *Jane*," Cheryl says, stretching my name out in five syllables in her singsong voice, "can I tell you how much we *love* Doris. I mean we *LOVE* Doris.

"She's like a *mother* figure for us," Cheryl continues. Her nostrils flare out when she speaks, and her eyes bulge when she's trying to be emphatic.

"I can understand that," I say.

Cheryl laughs. "Oh, but *of course*. Now, *Jane*—" again five syllables—"tell me about *you*."

She blinks expectantly. I hate open-ended questions. I shift uncomfortably.

"Well, since the highlight of my day these days is eating peanut butter sandwiches and watching *The View*, I'm afraid I'm not all that interesting. But . . ." I add, trying to turn on the charm, "I've really taken the time to do some introspection. To find out what I really want from a job, and I think I know what it is." I pause, trying to think what it is, exactly. "Swedish furniture," I quip. Better to joke than to say something really dumb, I think.

Cheryl throws her head back and laughs a fake laugh.

"Oh, Doris *said* you were *funny*." Cheryl sighs and wipes under her left eye. "Well, let me tell you about this job. We work hard here at Cook4U.com—it's not all fun and games. Don't let the Nerf ball fool you."

She pauses, as if giving me an opening to laugh, but I don't, so she quickly moves on.

"We can work long hours, but we try to have fun—because after all if you're not having fun, then what is the *point*?"

"Right," I nod my head agreeably. Bobbing it, almost. *Hire me. You want to hire me,* I mentally shout.

"Well *sure.* But what we want here at Cook4U.com is a feeling of *family.* We're coworkers, yes—but we like to think of ourselves as a . . ."

"Family?" I prompt.

"Exactly!"

"Doris is a great maternal figure. And I think you've seen Dave—he's the guy with the Nerf football. He's a great pesky younger brother type. So if you were part of our *family*—what role do you see yourself playing?"

"Graphic designer," I say.

"Right—but what *family* character would you be?"

"I'm not sure I understand what you're asking," I say.

Cheryl hangs her head in mock frustration.

"Come on, *Jane*—" six syllables this time (JA-A-A-N-N-NE)—"you know what I mean."

"The Gay Uncle?" I joke. Cheryl doesn't get that I'm joking. She frowns.

"We're very accepting of all sexual orientations here," she says. "We don't discriminate."

"Sorry, I didn't mean to imply you did," I say. I'm blowing it. Totally blowing it. Time to regroup. "I'd be the artsy younger sister."

"Good—good," Cheryl says, scribbling something on her notepad. She clears her throat and flips her hair off her shoulder. "How much are you 'into' cooking?"

I stare at her blankly.

"Well, we *are* Cook4U.com, and we've survived the

dot-com bust because we believe we have a superior product, and because we really *love* what we do. We take cooking very seriously. I mean, everyone here is *crazy* about *cooking.*"

I don't know what to say, exactly. The only things I can cook come in frozen packages with instructions written on them.

"So how much are you *into* cooking? On a scale of one to ten."

"A ten," I say. "Definitely a ten."

"Jane," she says in a lecturing tone. "*Everyone* at Cook4U is *off the charts* in terms of cooking enthusiasm."

I feel like I've been tricked.

"Oh, I mean, right, off the charts. I'm off the charts," I say. "I'm a fifteen."

Cheryl shakes her head, telling me it's not high enough.

"I mean, twenty, thirty—a hundred," I say, desperate.

"Now you're talking," Cheryl says, nodding.

I know without a doubt that I've blown the interview. Right there. With the scale question.

"Well, we worry about *fit* here at Cook4U.com. Everyone is upbeat—everyone is positive. We all thrive on *positive* energy. Do you thrive on *positive* energy?"

The idea of even trying to pretend to be perky is exhausting me, but I give it my best shot.

"I can be upbeat," I say. "I like positive energy as well as the next person."

"I can tell you're a direct, no-nonsense personality. Clear type Orange. You call things as you see them. Nothing much gets past you. I'm a Blue. I'm a people person." She smiles as she says this, a big, frighteningly fake grin. I stare at her, transfixed.

"OK, *Jane,* I think I've kept you to myself long enough. It's now time to call the team in."

The "team" consists of Abercrombie, his Nerf football partner, and a Russian with a thick accent. They pile into the conference room carrying their free soda like badges of honor and plop lazily into surrounding chairs. I want to work with them so badly it hurts.

"This is the team. Team, this is *Jane.*"

"Hi *Jane,*" they all singsong at once.

"Now, *boys,* be nice." Cheryl giggles as she says this, and sends a flirty look to Abercrombie.

"*Jane.* Tell us. Do you think Vlad is sexy? He thinks you're sexy." Abercrombie is putting Vlad, the Russian, on the spot. He turns red.

"John," admonishes Cheryl.

"Cher, you know I love you babe, come on," Abercrombie says, causing Cheryl to giggle.

"So, what do you like to eat for lunch?" Abercrombie asks me. "That's a very important question around here. What we have for lunch."

I *really* want this job.

"I'm a sandwich person," I say.

"Sandwiches!" the team cries. "Excellent. One more sandwich person."

This is the strangest interview. I don't know whether I'm gaining or losing points. I don't know if they're being jovial or sarcastic. My heart sinks to my stomach. It's like catching your gorgeous blind date scoping out the restaurant for quick exits.

"How about your credentials?" Vlad starts to ask me, but Cheryl interrupts.

"Oh, that's not really that important," Cheryl says. "What is important is how you *feel* about working, and what you *want* from your work."

Now I know how Mom got hired. She can talk about her feelings for hours. This however is one way in which I actually resemble Dad. I don't like talking about feelings. In fact, more often than not, I like to pretend I don't have them.

"Well, I think we've pestered Jane long enough today," Cheryl tells "the team" as if they're a preschool class and I'm a turtle in show-and-tell. Then, she turns to me. "Do you have any questions for us?"

This is the question I hate most in interviews, because the questions you want to ask (i.e., how much do you intend to pay me and how easy is it to get away with two-hour lunches?) don't reflect well on you as a whole. So, you have to make up crappy questions you don't care about so you look interested and committed.

"When will you make a decision?" Damn. This is the best question I can come up with? I'm blowing it, I think. Blowing it.

"In the next couple of weeks," Cheryl says, clearly disappointed with my lack of creativity. "Well, if that's it . . ." Cheryl trails off. "All that's left is the drug test."

Drug test?

"Everyone here takes a drug test," Cheryl says, handing me a slip of paper. "The clinic is right down the street. You can stop by there on your way home."

Before I leave, Mom gives me a hug at the door, which is incredibly embarrassing, then whispers, "Good luck!"

"Thanks for coming by!" Cheryl sings at me as I step into the elevator.

On the way to the drug test, I stop by Starbucks and buy three grande herbal teas, but I doubt they'll do any good. Damn Ron and his weed.

I thought my day couldn't get worse, but when I get home, I discover Missy and Ron making out on the couch like teenagers.

"Oh my God!" I scream, covering my eyes. "I'm going to go blind."

"Don't be so melodramatic," Missy coughs, sitting up and wiping Ron spit from her mouth. Steph, I see, taking a quick peek through my hands, is nowhere to be found. I'm glad she's spared seeing this sight.

"I think I'm going to be sick," I say. Catching Ron making out with Missy is as bad or worse than catching my parents. I feel queasy.

"Dude, you are such a spaz," Ron sniffs.

Almost immediately, they start sucking face again, like there's a tractor beam pulling their lips together.

"Seriously, stop it. You're going to make me throw up," I say. I cover my eyes again, and bounce my shin against the coffee table.

"If you don't like it, why don't you go to your bedroom?" Missy asks me.

"The living room is clearly a *common* area," I say. "Why don't you two go to YOUR bedroom?"

"Fine," Missy declares in a huff. She gets up and drags Ron to what used to be my bedroom and slams and locks the door. Within seconds, there's the telltale sound of squeaking bedsprings.

"Not on my bed!" I shout, but I fear it's already too late.

I go back to the living room and turn up the television as loud as it will go, and then pick up the Working section of the *Tribune* because after my botched interview, clearly I need sound advice.

It tells me I should approach job hunting like a regular job—scheduling in times for "networking" and "resume building" and "classified reading" as if they are business meetings.

If I wrote down my schedule, I think I'd slit my wrists. It would look something like:

8 A.M.–9 A.M.—Lie in bed pretending to sleep.

9 A.M.–10 A.M.—Watch *Oprah*.

10:00 A.M.–10:05 A.M.—Think about exercising. Decide against it.

10:06 A.M.–10:08 A.M.—Eat four slices of peanut butter toast.

10:08 A.M.–10:30 A.M.—Ask Missy to wash dishes, then listen to her twenty minute explanation of life-threatening allergies.

10:30 A.M.–10:45 A.M.—Drink coffee, eat bagel. Watch end of *The View*.

10:45 A.M.–11:45 A.M.—Read through the same job listings that were posted yesterday.

11:45 A.M.–12:00 P.M.—Decide to better self. Attempt to read Important Novel by Important Author that has won Important Prize. Start to get sleepy. Doze. Get woken up by Missy who can't find the remote.

12:00 p.m.–12:05 p.m.—Wake up with a start, positive that new jobs may have been posted online.

12:05 P.M.–12:07 P.M.—Check online. No new jobs have been posted.

12:07 P.M.–12:08 P.M.—Empty already emptied trash.

12:08 P.M.–12:20 P.M.—Watch infomercial on dehydrators. Consider buying one.

12:20 P.M.–12:30 P.M.—Wrestle with Missy for the remote. Lose.

12:30 P.M.—Decide to limit television intake, as it is bad for self-esteem and wallet. Turn off television. Turn on radio.

12:31 P.M.–12:34 P.M.—Sing along to Tom Petty's "Won't Back Down."

12:34 P.M.–12:36 P.M.—Sufficiently inspired to look through job listings again. I won't back down!!

12:36 P.M.–12:38 P.M.—Wind is taken out of sails by unfortunate Jewel song "My Hands."

12:39 P.M.—Turn off radio. Pace apartment. Worry about making rent. Eat spoonful of Jif. Have Missy shout at me to quit pacing because I'm making her dizzy.

12:40 P.M.–12:45 P.M.—Attempt again to read Important Book by Important Author who won Important Prize. Mind wanders. Realize am hungry.

12:46 P.M.–1 P.M.—Eat four slices of bread.

1:00 P.M.–2:15 P.M.—Nap.

2:15 P.M.–2:45 P.M.—Wake up. Attempt more reading of Important Book. Get drowsy. Nap some more.

2:45 P.M.–3:15 P.M.—Contemplate get-rich-quick schemes. Make calls about selling own eggs/blood/organs. Eat another spoonful of Jif.

3:15 P.M.–5 P.M.—Watch reruns of *Gilligan's Island, I Dream of Jeannie,* and *Hogan's Heroes.* Listen to my bed being violated by Missy and Ron.

5 P.M.–6 P.M.—Empty trash. Dream up chores, like refolding clothes in drawers. Reorganize shoes in closet. Clean goo off detergent caps. Eat more bread.

6 P.M.–6:30 P.M.—Contemplate going to bed.

My scheduling exercise is interrupted by my buzzer. I look out the front window and see Kyle.

"Thank God," I say.

"Todd canceled on me tonight. Want to go out?" Kyle says into my intercom.

"Do I ever," I reply, tossing on my coat and heading for the stairs.

"So why do you keep coming around?" I ask Kyle, over a bowl of soup at Noodles down the street from my apartment.

"I don't want you to see you on *Maury Povich,*" he says.

"Nice."

"Seriously, you seem down. You're not like the Jane I know."

"Who's the Jane you know?"

"Jane is somebody who doesn't miss a beat. Ever," Kyle says. "She always has a snappy comeback. She doesn't let anybody push her around."

"I like this Jane you know," I say. "Maybe you should introduce us."

"The Jane I know likes to pretend she doesn't need anybody, but she does," Kyle says.

"I think you're getting too serious on me," I say.

"I'm just saying, if you want to talk, I'm here," he says.

"Thanks," I say.

•   •   •

Several drinks later, we get into a debate about whether or not "Mr. T" or "B.A. Baracus" is a better alias, which naturally leads to the discussion about how a crack team of former military specialists managed never to shoot anyone despite ample rounds of ammo. The sheer volume of bullets should've guaranteed at least one person shot, and not just the dirt in front of their feet.

Kyle tells me he has a talking bobble-head doll of Mr. T, which naturally I have to see, which leads to a trip to his apartment.

Once inside Kyle's apartment, I realize I haven't been here before now, that he always came to my place, or I've met him at Todd's, or he's just shown up at my parents' house. Everything is neutral at Kyle's, tasteful, his CDs hidden away in a cabinet especially for this purpose.

He has all of the CDs I do: Wilco, Radiohead, Coldplay.

"I pegged you as a Celine Dion fan," I say.

"Ouch, that hurts," Kyle replies, coming back to me carrying two glasses of red wine. I'm already a bit tipsy from the wine at dinner.

He puts on Wilco.

"Do you want another glass of wine?" he asks me. I realize I've gulped down my glass in two long drags. I suddenly feel like the fifth-grader again, the one who squished herself in the backseat between Todd and Kyle, hoping Kyle would notice the fact that she was wearing new Jordache jeans.

"Are you trying to get me drunk?" I ask him.

"Maybe I am," he says, then pauses. If I didn't know better, I'd say Kyle might be flirting. He's using The Smile again. And it's beginning to work on me.

"Is that my painting?" I ask, amazed, jumping up from my seat on his couch and crossing the room to the fireplace to put more distance between us.

I squint at it. It is, I realize. It's one of my art projects from my undergraduate days. It looks very different hanging on the wall of a well-furnished apartment. I'm used to seeing my paintings as props for covering cracks in drywall and rips in wallpaper of poorly furnished studios.

"I've got two of your other drawings in frames in the bedroom," Kyle says.

"You've got to be kidding."

There's a funny vibe in the room. My stomach feels like there are small electric charges running through it, making it jump.

"See for yourself."

The framed pictures are drawings of tree branches. Two vague renditions of the ends of branches of the trees in my parents' backyard. I think I sketched them on a whim, one summer when Kyle and Todd were playing tag football in the backyard.

"I've got better work than that," I say, turning around. Kyle is standing close to me.

"Not to me," he says.

Before I quite know what's happening, he's kissing me. On the lips.

For a second, I'm shocked. Literally. It's like an electric surge, like I can feel my hair standing on end. After the initial surprise of it wears off, I'm kissing him back, and all I can think is, wow. I never knew Kyle was such a good kisser.

And before I know it, we're on his bed, and he's on top of me, and his hands are under my shirt. And I'm having trouble remembering exactly why it is that I didn't do this before. Why I had been so quick to give up on my fifth-grader's crush. My shirt is half off, before I finally react to the dull warning sirens in the back of my head, the ones that are screaming: "Alert. Drunken Sex with Brother's Best Friend Is Not a Good Idea No Matter How Good a Kisser He Is."

"Wait," I say, temporarily pulling back from Kyle, my head spinning. Everything's moving so fast.

"I'm sorry," Kyle breathes to me, pulling back, sitting up and running his hands through his hair. "I didn't mean to go so far."

"No, it's OK," I say, seeing the stricken look on his face. "Really."

"Really?" he asks me.

"It was nice. Really," I say.

"In that case," he says, bending down to kiss me again.

"But maybe we should stop for now?" I say, putting a hand on his chest. My body is screaming at my brain to stop being such a killjoy. My body is hoping that Kyle will argue with me.

He doesn't.

"You're right," he says, pulling away. "It's late. I'd better get you home."

Cook4U.com, where everyone is a gourmet™
57 W. Grand Ave.
Second Floor
Chicago, IL 60610

Jane McGregor
3335 Kenmore Ave.
Chicago, IL 60657

March 29, 2002

Dear Jane,

While we felt that you were a strong candidate for the position of web designer and artist, we decided to go with another applicant who better fit our qualifications. We will keep your resume on file for up to one year, and will be happy to consider you for any related future positions.

Best of luck to you,
Cheryl Ladd
Hiring Manager and Director of Content
Cook4U.com

P.S. I feel obligated also to inform you that you did not pass our required drug test. There were detectable amounts of cannabis in your sample. I am sorry to say that this will most likely prevent us from considering you for future positions at Cook4U.com.

10

$\mathcal{I}$ find myself wanting to sing out loud. Kyle *kissed* me, I keep thinking, over and over, like I'm twelve again. I can't sleep. I can't eat. All I can think about is Kyle.

I've been wanting to laugh out loud ever since he kissed me. I wonder if this is what a crush feels like. It's been ages since I've had a legitimate one.

In a couple of days, he calls me to apologize.

"Really, there's no need," I say, practically beaming, because I'm happy to hear the sound of his voice.

"I feel like I took advantage of you," he says.

"I like being taking advantage of now and again," I say.

"In that case, what are you doing tomorrow night?" he asks me.

This makes me laugh.

"Not so fast, Romeo," I say.

"Right, you're right," Kyle says. "We should probably wait the required three days between dates, and pretend we're too busy to actually see one another for another week."

"Oh, definitely," I say. "And then I'll have to put you off for another week, and then *maybe* we can meet for coffee."

"Coffee? Hold the phone, you're moving *way* too fast for me. Next, you'll want to pick out the first names of our children."

I laugh. Kyle is fun to flirt with. I suppose he's had lots of practice. Immediately, I shoo this thought out of my head.

"What are you doing Saturday?" he asks me.

"Wow. You skipped right over the casual weeknights and went right for the Saturday date—that's brave," I say.

"You don't win big unless you risk big," he says.

I smile at this.

"Saturday is Dad's annual Spring Barbeque," I tell Kyle. "Did you forget?"

"D'oh," Kyle curses. "How could I forget enough charred meat to feed a third-world country?"

Dad hosts his annual Spring Week barbeque on the first Saturday in April, which he does every year no matter how cold it is. Dad loves to grill meat, and does so almost every other Saturday from April to October. The first week in April, however, is second only to the Fourth of July in sheer amount of food basted, grilled, and eaten.

"I'll see you there?" I ask him.

"Most definitely," Kyle says. "Can I offer you a ride? I promise to be on my best behavior."

"If by best behavior you mean you're going to try to grope me, then I accept your offer of a ride."

Kyle laughs.

"You're on," he says.

I hang up the phone and sigh. This crush stuff feels pretty good, I decide. I'm not even too bothered by the incessant squeaking coming from my bedsprings in the next room, since Missy and Ron act like they're Serta mattress testers on a marathon mission.

I'm distracted from the merciless grinding of my bedsprings by the unexpected arrival of Steph.

"I've been evicted!" she cries into the intercom.

When she arrives on my landing, she's winded, but manages to tell me her sad story. Her lease is up, and her landlord, being cunning and determined to find a way to get Steph out so she can raise her Wrigleyville rent thirty percent, checks Steph's credit history.

"Well, she found out I'm jobless, and that's it—no lease renewal," Steph says, wiping at her eyes.

I give her a hug. I understand her pain. And, while I know I'll probably regret it, I hear the words come out of my mouth anyway.

"Why don't you stay here?" I ask. "You can sleep in my room, or on the couch for a few days."

Immediately Steph stops crying. "Really?"

"Really," I say.

"I was hoping you'd say that," Steph cries. She disappears down my staircase and comes back again carrying two suitcases. "You're the best!" she says, giving me an air kiss on the cheek.

"You brought over your suitcases?"

"Well, if you didn't invite me to stay, what kind of friend would you be anyway? And I make it a rule not to keep crappy friends."

"I suppose I should take that as a compliment," I say. "I don't suppose you have anything to contribute to the rent?"

"No, but I do have a fabulous shoe collection. You want to borrow any of them, you let me know."

"Steph, I wear a seven. You wear a nine."

"Right, well. Purses then. Borrow away!"

"Thanks," I mutter, but Steph misses the sarcasm.

Not ten minutes later, there's another buzz at my apartment's buzzer.

I look out my front window and see Ferguson standing on the stoop.

"Great," I say. "What am I supposed to tell him?"

"Pretend we're not home," Steph says behind me. Ferguson looks up, catches me in the window, and waves.

"Too late," I say. I buzz him up, and Ferguson wanders into the apartment looking sheepish.

"Hi, girls, I just wondered if maybe I left my keycard here the other night?"

Ron pops out of Missy's bedroom at that moment wearing nothing but a towel.

"Ferg!" he cries, seeing Ferguson. "What's up, dude? Want to smoke a bowl?"

"Well, I don't know." Ferguson hesitates.

"Come on, stay awhile," Ron insists, acting like he owns my place. I'm too busy trying to avoid looking at Ron's pale chest to argue too fiercely.

"OK," Ferguson agrees.

Missy comes out of the bedroom, too, wearing what looks suspiciously like one of my missing Gap shirts.

"Is that my shirt?" I ask her.

"No," she snaps indignantly, as if I'd accused her of hoarding Pop Tarts (which I did a couple of days ago).

"I think that's my shirt," I say.

"You're crazy," she tells me, cuddling up to Ron, who is fashioning a bong out of tin foil and one of my nice Crate & Barrel bud vases.

After an hour of smoking, Ferguson starts telling us how much he loves us.

"Really, I love you guys," he says over and over again.

Missy rolls her eyes. Ron slaps Ferguson hard on the back. "You have to respect a man who isn't afraid of his emotions," he says.

"Maximum Office sucks," Ferguson says suddenly.

Missy, Steph, and I look at him, then each other. By all accounts, Ferguson was a company man. No one ever heard him say a bad thing about Maximum Office, ever.

"What do you mean?" Missy asks, carefully neutral.

"We're having *more* layoffs this month," Ferguson says, his voice dropping to an exaggerated whisper. "And, this time, they're going to throw in a couple of managers so it looks good. Well, let's just say that in three weeks, I'll be looking for a new job."

This news would've made me ecstatic six weeks ago. Now, I'm just numb to it. Nobody deserves a layoff. Well, no one except maybe Mike.

Steph and Missy exchange a glance.

"Why don't we tell him our plan?" Steph asks.

"I don't know," Missy says.

"Come on, he can help us," Steph says.

Missy considers this a moment, then she gets up, walks to her bedroom, and comes back carrying several rolled-up blueprints under her arm.

"You guys aren't seriously going to do this," I say. I thought they'd abandoned the Maximum Office break-in plan.

"You can't be serious," I say.

"As a heartbeat," she says.

"You mean 'heart attack,' " I correct.

"Whatever," she says.

"What's all this?" Ferguson asks, as he takes in the blueprints and our guilty faces.

I expect Ferguson to leap up and call the police, or worse, for an entire SWAT team to descend upon my apartment because he's secretly wearing a wire. I wait one or two beats, but I don't hear urgent footsteps on the stairs or police helicopters overhead. Instead, a giant smile breaks out across Ferguson's face.

"I love you guys. Did I mention how much I love you guys?" He beams, and attempts to hug each one of us. Ron and Steph are the only two who let him.

Days blur together like pregnant pauses in soap opera dialogue, and Ferguson rarely leaves my apartment, except to fetch clothes from home. When I ask him about his job, he snorts. "I'm using up my sick days before they steal them from me."

No one seems to really want to leave my apartment—it's like a Roach Motel. Missy has moved ahead with her plan of breaking into Maximum Office, even though it is becoming increasingly clear that she has no idea how to accomplish her objective. She constantly argues with Ferguson about how to read the blueprint, the pair continually confusing air ducts with hallways.

Steph, who's painted and repainted her toenails, chips in now and again about what she thinks they should do to the executives when they get into the email system. So far, firing them and then sending their wives copies of their expense reports seem to be at the top of the list.

Ferguson, whose pot intake has severely weakened his dieting willpower, consumes all the carbohydrates in my apartment, including an entire loaf of bread.

My apartment, thanks to Ron and Ferguson, now perpetually smells like feet.

Luckily, I have Kyle to think about as a happy distraction. I am trying to soak up this beginning stage—this flirty-talk stage, which has added a whole new dimension to the relationship. A nice one, in my opinion. Steph, who can only be distracted from Maximum Office planning for brief intervals, offers to help me pick out what to wear. Her suggestions pretty much revolve around wearing something with a plunging neckline.

"You forget I don't have cleavage," I tell her.

"Men don't care," she says. "All they want to see is a little bit of boob. They don't care if they're squashed together or not."

"Great," I say.

I don't think this approach will work with Kyle. For one thing, I've known him too long, and he's likely to call me on it by suggesting I look like J. Lo in Versace, or worse, Lil' Kim at practically any awards show.

For another, I don't want a cheap one-night stand with Kyle. I want more than that, because for the first time I realize he's got Potential. He's smart, funny, and sexy. I wonder what it would be like if we started seriously dating, and why I hadn't really allowed myself the luxury of considering him before.

Think of the benefits: for one, he already knows I'm crazy, so there would be no surprises later. Two, he's already met and impressed my parents, and has not been scared off by them. Three, I know, deep down, that he is one of the Good Guys.

"Oh, dear, somebody's got a bad case of smit," Steph observes, as I try on and then discard the fifth outfit I've pulled from my closet. Everything is either too obviously trying (like my power suit) or too horribly frumpy. Since being laid off, my closet seems to have lost any trendy clothes it had.

"I am not smitten," I say.

"Any girl who tries on more than six outfits is smitten," Steph says, as I angrily discard the sixth on my bed.

"If I had money, I'd buy a new outfit," I say.

"That's the second sign of smit," Steph says.

"I am not," I say, but my voice lacks conviction.

"Why don't you wear those dark low-waisted jeans?" Steph points to the back of my closet.

"Serious plumber's butt," I say. When I sit down in them, they might as well be at my knees for the coverage they give.

"Hey, whatever cleavage you got, flaunt it, baby," Steph jokes.

I snort. "I hardly think butt cleavage is the way to win Kyle."

"You'd be surprised what guys go for," Steph advises. "Wear those jeans and these boots," she says, picking up my kitten-heeled boots. "And this," she adds, holding up a black V-neck sweater.

"If I wear these, it means I can't sit down in view of anyone," I say.

"Sitting down is overrated," Steph says.

Kyle calls while I am still in the shower, and Missy takes a message. Apparently, something came up and he can't give me a ride to my parents' house.

"Did he say why?" I ask Missy, feeling a tiny stab of disappointment.

"What do I look like—your social secretary?" she spits.

"What did he sound like?" Steph prods, attempting to help.

"He sounded like a guy who was calling to say he can't pick you up," Missy says.

"That is totally unhelpful," I say.

"I was aiming for rude, but I'll take unhelpful," Missy says.

"Don't jump to conclusions," Steph orders me, when she sees my mind working. "You've known this guy forever, right? He's probably just gotten a flat tire or something."

Or something, I think.

With some trepidation, I take the train wearing my super low-riding jeans and manage to arrive at my parents' house early. This is a first.

I barely make it through the front door before Dad is handing me a giant platter of raw meat, because he is barbequing enough sausage for a third-world country. I scan the living room, but there's no sign of Kyle. Just Todd and Deena, who are cuddled up together on Mom's couch. No matter how early I am, I can never beat Todd.

Seeing Deena is a shock. Usually, between my birthday dinner and Dad's spring barbeque, Todd's changed girlfriends three or four times.

"Nice jeans!" coos Deena. Since she is wearing what looks suspiciously like sprayed-on black spandex pants, I am not sure whether or not to take this as a compliment.

"Have you heard from Kyle?" I ask Todd, trying to be nonchalant, but failing. I still can't shake the feeling that something is wrong.

"He had something he had to do." Todd shrugs. "He may be here later."

"*What* was he doing?" I ask.

Todd gives me a funny look. "Why do you care? And why are you all dressed up all of a sudden?"

"I am not dressed up," I say.

"Jane, I'd say these days if you shower that's dressing up," Todd teases. "Actually coordinating an outfit that hasn't been sitting on the floor of your closet for days constitutes formal wear."

"Very funny," I say.

Mom interrupts before I can say more.

"Jane? Can you help me in the kitchen?" Mom asks, raising her eyebrows in the secret signal that she has news to tell me.

"It's your Dad," Mom says, surprising me in the kitchen. "He's officially been laid off."

I say nothing for several seconds.

"Well, you know they were cutting back his hours,"

Mom tells me. "And, well, they finally just cut them back to zero."

"When?"

"Last week."

"Last week!" I cry, sounding outraged like Todd. "How come nobody told me?"

"Well, I tried to call," Mom starts. "But no one seems to be answering your phone."

"How is he taking it?"

"Not well, so be extra nice to him, OK?"

Being extra nice to Dad is difficult, because he has had a few beers and is ranting about the fact that he wouldn't be out of work except for the bad foreign policy decisions of Bill Clinton.

"We should never have gone into Somalia," Dad says, while flipping burgers. He is wearing a NRA T-shirt that says "From My Cold Dead Hand."

"That's when our economy went south."

"Dad, there's no way you can blame your unemployment on Bill Clinton," I say.

"Oh, you just watch me," he says.

I sigh, and glance out to the front yard, hoping to catch a glimpse of Kyle's car.

"What you need to do, Dad, is get your resume on Monster and Hotjobs," Todd advises. Leave it to Todd to start in with the suggestions before Dad gets his first unemployment check.

"That's a waste of time," Dad tells Todd. "Most jobs aren't advertised. It's all who you know."

This should be interesting—watching my brother going head-to-head with my dad in a career advice-giving contest. Neither one would ever admit to not knowing everything there is to know about everything.

"But I'm thinking maybe I'll let your mom earn the bread around here for a little while," Dad says, suddenly. "I could get used to this women's lib stuff."

Dad is the only person I know under the age of seventy who uses "women's lib" seriously in conversation.

"Or maybe your mom and I can move into that grand apartment of yours," Dad tells me. "Lord knows you have enough space in there."

Dad is surprisingly upbeat about his situation, and I think it's because he hasn't yet made a trip to the unemployment office.

"Everybody have a seat," Mom declares, when Dad finishes grilling. I keep nervously checking the front door, thinking maybe our doorbell is broken.

"Jane, why aren't you sitting?" Mom asks me, as I stand in the corner of the kitchen eating off my plate.

"I just prefer to stand," I say.

"Come on, sit," Dad commands.

Reluctantly, I take a seat at the far end of the table, with my back to the wall. I try to pull my sweater down over the back of my jeans, but it's short by about two inches. I can feel a breeze.

"So, Jane, have you heard from Cook4U? I can't get a straight answer on what they're doing with that graphic design position," Mom says.

"Er," I say. "Well, they probably just decided not to hire anyone and didn't say anything."

"It's weird. Cheryl won't even talk to me about it," Mom says.

I am saved by the sound of Kyle's car in our driveway. I only just manage not to bolt to the door like I'm ten again. I beat Mom to the door by a half second.

Kyle has on his scarf, and he doesn't make a move to come inside. Behind him, his car is still running.

"I wanted to come by and say hello, but I can't stay," he says in a rush.

He looks like he'd rather be anywhere than on my mom's stoop, and I am struck by the awful thought that he wants to avoid me. He won't even look in my direction, instead staring over my shoulder to my mom, standing behind me.

"Oh, nonsense. Come in and get something to eat," Mom says.

"No, really, I've got someone in the car," he says.

I am trying to see who it is sitting in Kyle's passenger seat, but the glare from the windshield makes that impossible.

"Bring your friend in, too," Mom says congenially. "Come on, one minute won't kill you." Mom, ever the good hostess, gives the car a welcome wave.

Just then, as we watch, the passenger door of Kyle's car opens, and out comes a long, slinky leg. Shiny brown shoulder-length hair follows, then the perfect 36C boobs, an impossibly small waist, and perfectly rounded hips complete the picture. Nobody looks that much like Catherine Zeta Jones except Caroline. As in Caroline, Kyle's girlfriend for three years who ran off to Australia one summer with only a phone call as explanation. Caroline, as in the same woman Kyle thought he might marry. Caroline, his ex who's supposed to be halfway around the world, but isn't because she's standing in my parents' driveway.

"It's just silly for me to wait in the car," she's saying to Kyle, as she comes up the drive. "Mrs. M, it's been far too long!" she cries, coming up the drive and opening her arms up wide to give my mother a hug. Caroline's parents used to live on our street before they moved downtown. Still, it's no reason for her to practically step on me to get to Mom, who takes the hug with a surprised look on her face.

"Caroline, I thought you were . . ."

"In Australia? Well, I'm back," she says, turning to throw a look over her shoulder to Kyle. "And this time, it may be for good."

I have never had my appetite so fully and utterly quashed as it is in the seconds that follow the arrival of Caroline. The one chicken wing I've eaten, in fact, feels in danger of launching itself into my mother's living room.

Caroline.

Her shiny, perfect hair and her spotless white cable-knit sweater, brown corduroy miniskirt, and suede camel boots. Her easy, throaty laugh. The way she simply captivates a room with a charming half smile and flip of her hair. How am I supposed to compete with that?

I look over at Kyle, who seems to be at Caroline's mercy, who doesn't flinch when she gives Kyle's arm a possessive pat.

Todd looks nearly as stunned as I am. Apparently, Kyle did not let him in on this little secret either. Deena, unnerved by the presence of another busty woman in the room, frowns slightly as she takes in Caroline's appearance. Dad, who's the only one in the room incapable of picking up on the obvious social tension, barrels into the room and gives Caroline a bear hug.

"How long have you been in town?" Dad asks. "I hope you're here to stay."

"Just a couple of days," Caroline says. "You could say I'm feeling out my options."

I feel light-headed. I sit down.

"Jeez, Jane," Todd cries, laughing, drawing the attention of everyone. "Quit flashing us all."

I realize I've sat down on Mom's ottoman and exposed my plumber's butt to half the room.

"Excuse me," I say, springing to my feet with such speed that I nearly drop my paper plate full of bratwurst on Mom's living-room rug as I head to the bathroom.

M&M's/MARS
800 High Street
Hackettstown, NJ 07840

Jane McGregor
3335 Kenmore Ave.
Chicago, IL 60657

April 5, 2002

Dear Ms. McGregor,

While we are sure you are an excellent graphic designer, we do not have a job available for the hand-coloring of our M&M's chocolate candies. That is done by an automated process in our factory.

Also, we are not considering the addition of any new colors to our candies at this time. However, we will keep your suggestions of Magenta and Burnt Sienna on file.

Sincerely,
Ray Lopez
Human Resources Professional

11

I wonder how long I can stay in the bathroom before I'll be missed. Five minutes? Ten? Twenty? I stare at myself in the mirror, my hair up in a I'm-not-trying-too-hard ponytail, and my this-is-almost-natural-but-better makeup, and wonder how I misread the signals so badly. Hadn't Kyle been flirting with me—and actually kissed me? Hadn't we been dancing around the idea of *dating*?

Was I so far gone after the Mike fiasco that I couldn't even read basic dating signals anymore?

I let my head fall against the mirror. Someone should take me out of the dating game before I hurt someone—namely, myself.

I take a few more breaths. Calmly, I analyze the situation. Kyle kissed me. Kyle *definitely* flirted with me on the phone. Kyle calls an hour before he's supposed to pick me up and cancels. Kyle arrives at my parents' house with his once-serious ex-girlfriend who is acting like they're back together.

I'm not the crazy one here.

Fueled by something very close to hostility simmering just below the surface, I re-emerge from the bathroom and spend the rest of Dad's barbeque standing in the corner with my arms crossed, not eating.

Kyle doesn't look at me the whole time, not even once, not even an uneasy glance in my direction. I don't know how he can stand not looking at me. I am practically glaring at him. Caroline, who is flipping back her shiny dark hair like she's starring in her own Pantene commercial, sends me a look, every now and again, that in my paranoid state, I take as gloating.

Caroline steals the conversation spotlight, as usual, telling us all how she decided "on a whim" to visit home, and how Kyle was nice enough to pick her up from the airport today, and how she hasn't even been home to see her parents yet.

This is good news, I suppose. This means they probably haven't had sex yet, unless they did it while they drove down the Kennedy. This is also why Kyle must have canceled picking me up. Why? So he could go get *Caroline* from the *airport*.

Predictably, I feel my anger toward Kyle slip ever so slightly and find a better, juicier target: Caroline.

Caroline, who is self-absorbed and totally uninterested in other people's feelings, who essentially left him without a word a year ago and now drops back into his life and expects him to pick up where she left off? She is wrong for him in so many ways. For one thing, she's totally unstable. Who just leaves the country and the continent "on a whim"? You could never trust her to stay. Not to mention, why is he rewarding that kind of behavior? For another, she's bossy. She tells him what to do and how to do it at almost every turn. Like now, she's asking him to fetch her a drink of water, but not just any water—filtered, and in a glass with ice. But not too much ice, she says. Just a couple of cubes.

I try to imagine her in bed, giving him directions like the workers guiding in planes on the jetway. Left. Back. Back. Left, I said! Back. Right. Back! Stop!

As a worse twist of fate, Kyle has never looked better. He makes jeans and a sweater look like they belong in a catalog. The curve of his shoulder, the strong line of his chin. I look at his lips and remember how warm they were on mine. I can't forget the feel of his chest, hard and firm, under my fingers. You don't just step over a friendship boundary, discover a spark, and then pull it all back in again. I feel like I've just ordered a seven-course meal and the waiter, after the appetizer, comes out to tell me the kitchen's closed.

Kyle's elbow brushes my forearm as he walks past me, and I wonder if I'm the only one who feels the charge of the touch.

"Sorry," he says, giving me a quick glance, a shy one.

And for a moment, I think he may be apologizing for more than just the bump.

I don't say anything. I just watch as he fetches Caroline her glass of water with ice.

When I come back to my apartment, I discover that Ferguson has fallen asleep on my couch and is snoring. Steph is drawing permanent marker mustaches on the models in my J. Crew catalog and Missy and Ron are making loud sucking sounds on each other's faces. This is the last thing I need.

"Guys, seriously, do you have to do that in the living room?" I ask them.

After a few more seconds, Ron is the one to disengage.

"You're such a buzzkill," Missy tells me.

"Whatever," I say, rolling my eyes.

"How did it go?" Steph asks me.

"One word: Caroline," I say.

"But when? How?" Steph stutters. Shocked, she listens as I recount the events of the afternoon.

"If he's got an ex in the picture, you don't want him," Missy tells me.

"Thanks for stating the obvious," I say.

"What was he doing inviting you on a date if he was going to get back with her?" Steph asks me.

"I wish I knew," I say.

"Well, chicks, this little foray into *As the World Turns* has been fascinating, but I've got to motor," Ron says, standing up and stretching, as he brushes lint off his giant, oversized pants.

"Where you going?" Steph asks, too eagerly.

"Home, then a gig," Ron says.

Steph looks at me, and I know we'll end up going. I'm in that frame of mind where I doubt things can get worse, so a night out with Ron doesn't seem so bad.

"What about Ferguson?" Ferguson has a line of drool that's threatening to travel from his mouth to one of my Pier 1 throw pillows. Quickly, I snatch the pillow away. The motion abruptly wakes Ferguson, who sits up, blinking.

"Hey, where are you guys going?" He rubs his eyes, not waiting for us to answer. "Can I come?"

We travel in Ron's Impala to his two-flat in Bucktown, where he is living, along with his three bandmates. As far as I can tell, only a couple of them actually work, holding down odd jobs here and there, and the rest of them survive on the lead singer's trust fund. It pays to have rich friends with expensive hobbies. The two-flat is even nicer than my spacious, overpriced apartment, although instead of furniture, they have mostly giant floor pillows. A trio of wilted hippie chick wannabes are lounging on the giant Oriental rug at the center of the room and passing around a huge bong. The air is thick with pot smoke. The Poser Hippie Chicks are wearing tattered rags that look like they came from a reject bin at the Salvation Army, but probably cost them $500 apiece. They're large women, and they're wearing skimpy tank tops that only barely hold in their ample chests. Each has a roll of fat hanging over her gypsy skirt.

Ferguson puts his hand out and introduces himself as if he's at a networking convention.

"Groupies?" I ask Ron, who shrugs.

"That's Heather, Ganesha, and Vishnu," he says, not bothering to differentiate between the three. Missy looks at them appraisingly, as if trying to size up her competition. Not picking up on any threat, she decides to ignore them.

"We're muses," one of them says.

"They *kick ass* with creative energy," Ron says. He doesn't explain further, just plops down next to one and takes a hit from the bong she offers. Missy also takes a drag, and then she and Ron start licking one another's face. I look away quickly before I'm overcome with motion sickness.

"Don't you find them gross?" I ask Steph.

Steph shrugs. "Mildly," she says.

When Missy lets Ron come up for air, he points to me and tells the muses who I am.

"She did the CD cover," Ron says by way of introduction.

"Nice work," the three muses say.

"And that's her friend," Ron adds. "They're both having career crises."

The three muses snicker.

"If you're too busy having a career," says one, who's

falling out of her red-and-white striped halter, "then you won't ever have a life."

"I get that you're very in tune with the spiritual," another muse says with a yawn. "I think you should be a psychic. Channel that energy."

"How much does that pay?" I ask.

"Money isn't important," another one says.

"You're wasting your time," says the third. "She's closed to new possibilities."

"She is, a little," Ferguson agrees.

"I am not," I say, defensive.

"She's got cynic written all over her. She's barred to happiness."

"Vish, I think you're being harsh," says the other. "She's just trying to find herself."

A knock sounds at the door, and Ron pulls himself away from sucking on Missy's tongue to go answer it. Standing on the landing are a couple of college kids, wearing striped rugby shirts and baseball caps. Ron hands them a couple of Ziploc bags and takes a wad of bills from them. The college kids leave, and Ron returns to his position in the circle of pot smoke.

"You're a dealer!" I exclaim, though I am not entirely surprised.

One of the Poser Hippie Chicks cackles. "I told you she was closed," she says, smug.

"I'm leaving," I declare.

"Don't freak out, Jane, shit," Ron says, putting a hand on my arm. "It's only a side business."

One of the Poser Hippie Chicks snorts.

"Come on, don't be tight," Ron pleads, his eyes droopy from pot. "Why don't you have some hot tea and settle down?"

"I'm going to make popcorn," Vishnu says.

I wonder what would happen to me if I simply stayed, for days, weeks, or months here, in Ron's apartment.

I see myself six months from now, sitting on the couch next to Vishnu, my eyes bloodshot and bleary, unable to remember what day it is, completely and utterly wrapped up in the life of Ron. My most ambitious thought of the day will be to minimize my movements as much as possible, not even bothering to change channels on the television set, instead fixating on the shopping network for hours. I'd have a steady diet of Doritos and hot tea, and pretty soon, I'd start to wear hippie rags and call myself an Eastern Mystic Muse.

Then I think of Caroline rubbing up against Kyle, and I think, there are worse things than being one of Ron's muses. I could be stuck watching Kyle and Caroline cuddle and coo at each other at countless family gatherings from here on in.

One tub of popcorn and two cups of strong tea later, and I am beginning to feel a bit more magnanimous. I'm not sure if it's the fact that I have food in my stomach or that I'm getting a contact buzz from the pot smoke in the room. Ferguson and Missy both turn down the tea, but eat more than their share of popcorn, and Steph, who is definitely buzzed, starts laughing uncontrollably at something Ferguson says.

"I need to pee," I announce. One of the Poser Hippie Chicks points to the back of the apartment.

The bathroom has rose wallpaper that inexplicably causes me to laugh hysterically. The thought of Ron with a powder pink bathroom is hilarious. I look up again at the wallpaper and notice that it seems to be moving. Like some holographic image. The rose petals are dancing.

Maybe I'm more buzzed than I thought.

Only it's not the spins, where everything moves at the same pace. The images are moving at different intervals, each at its own speed. I blink a few times and shake my head. I put my nose right against the wall, to see if it's a trick of the light, but just as I do, one of the rose petals jumps straight out of the wall and onto my nose.

"Ack," I say, stumbling backward out of the bathroom and nearly into the arms of Vishnu or Ganesha, I'm not sure which.

"Don't worry," she tells me, smiling. "It was the tea. Shroom tea."

I am too busy watching her eyebrows dance to be angry.

"We thought you could use a break from reality," she says, smiling at me. I think her teeth are made of gold. Or diamonds. In either case, they're shiny and hypnotic.

"Shroom tea?" I ask. "Does Lipton make that?"

The muse does not laugh at my joke.

"Just don't fight it, OK?" she says.

• • •

I have never taken a hallucinogen before. I must say it is a bit disappointing. I mean, where are the pink elephants? The parade of talking monkeys?

The Poser Hippie Chicks, Missy, Ron, Ferguson, and Steph—who is studying her hand intently—and the rest of the band, gather together to leave for the gig, which starts in a half hour. I hear a voice that sounds like gravel, and realize my Doc Martens are speaking.

"You could stand to lose a few pounds," the right one says.

"Stop slouching. It's bad for my arch," the left one adds.

We end up at Gunther Murphy's, where the band is putting on a show of the four songs they know. Russ, the guitarist, knows the general manager, which is how they got the gig. Russ plays with his eyes closed, and Ron is rocking his shaggy head back and forth completely out of sync with the music. The lead singer is mumbling as usual, and has both hands wrapped tightly around the microphone. They like to bill themselves as a jazz infusion band with Grateful Dead influences, but that's only because impromptu "jamming" is the only thing they do well since they are too lazy to learn new songs. It sounds less like jazz and more like a bunch of guys who taught themselves how to play.

Missy takes up a position front and center and starts

elbowing any remotely respectable looking women who attempt to stand within ten feet of Ron. Steph and Ferguson are doing some odd version of the Jitterbug, while Vishnu, Ganesha, and Heather throw themselves into some kind of gypsy dance, twirling in circles in the middle of the bar room, their ragged skirts trailing along the floor. Vishnu, I see, is barefoot. My Doc Martens disapprove.

"Girl of loose morals," the right one says.

"Can't you ever find any nice friends?" the left one asks me.

"It's clear why Kyle chose Caroline over you," the right one says. "Just *look* at the people you hang out with."

Ron looks remarkably good on stage. The red stage lights beaming down on Ron even out his skin tone, just like for strippers. My eyes wander off through the crowd, which is surprisingly dense and filled with women who look just like the trio of Poser Hippie Chicks. In the middle of the crowd, I see someone who looks like Kyle. Now I know I am hallucinating, because when I look back again, he's gone.

"Boys only want one thing," my right Doc Marten chides.

"But you already give it away," the left one adds.

The two shoes laugh.

I am feeling light-headed, and so I stumble over to the bathroom, locking myself in the far stall and sitting on the closed toilet lid. I prop my Doc Martens up on the door, so we can have a proper conversation.

"You should've taken finance courses in college," the right one tells me.

"Or at the very least marketing classes," the left one adds.

"You believed Mike was going to marry you," my right Doc Marten tells me.

"And that Kyle was going to actually *fall* for you," the left says.

They have a good laugh at my expense.

Ganesha finds me in the bathroom stall, and hands me a large plastic cup filled with ice water.

"You should drink this," she says. "It will make the comedown easier."

"Maybe I don't want to come down," I say.

"Everyone does eventually," she says, smiling at me sweetly, one curled red dreadlock falling forward across her face. "Life is a roller coaster, baby. Up and down, round and round."

I sit for a moment longer in the bathroom, and Steph comes in, laughing.

"I am the master of the universe," she tells me. "And Ferguson—who knew he was such a good dancer?"

"Now I know you're high," I say. "By the way, my Doc Martens can talk."

She ignores that completely. "Did you know that your skin is totally transparent?" she asks me. "I can see your bones. You really ought to eat more calcium."

"Slut," my left Doc Marten says.

"Office slut," my right one corrects.

"Shut up," I say.

"Hey," Steph protests.

"Not you," I say, sighing.

"You don't look so good," Steph tells me as we both stumble out of the bathroom. She has a huge pink streak of lipstick down the front of her chin, where she's attempted to apply her MAC gloss vertically instead of horizontally.

"I don't feel so hot, either," I say, as the room takes a spin.

"Hey, is that who I think it is?" she asks me, looking over in the direction of the bar. I look where she's looking and see him.

Mike.

To: jane@coolchick.com
From: Mary Kay Cosmetics
Date: April 8, 2002, 10:35 A.M.

Dear Jane,

   We'd love for you to become part of the Mary Kay family. However, we insist that all Mary Kay sales representatives use our products. We feel that our products are a superior beauty line, and our representatives must believe this, as well, to make them good sales representatives.

   You mentioned in your email that you are allergic to the color pink. This should not be a problem, because while some of our packaging is pink, none of our facial products, excluding some shades of eye shadow and lipstick, are actually pink.

Best,
Elizabeth Van Etten
Mary Kay Representative

12

$\mathcal{B}$efore I can think about pretending I never saw him and running for the nearest exit, he catches my eye. And even worse, he picks up his drink from the bar and makes his way through the crowd in my direction.

"I don't feel so good," Steph says. "I think I'm going to throw up." Before I can stop her, Steph runs back into the bathroom. That leaves me, alone, to face Mike.

"Hey," he says.

I am too whacked out to be suspicious of his motives, and too high to deliver the speech I'd planned time and again in the shower, the one that tells him that we're both adults, and that I knew it was a fling, and that he really doesn't have to worry about me, because I'm fine. I'm a big girl. I can take care of myself.

Besides, he looks even better than usual. Put together,

as always, and in control. And even as I tell myself I'm going to resist his charm, I know that part of me needs the attention and wants his interest, especially now that I've lost Kyle's.

"Where's the fiancée?" I say.

"Smooth," my right Doc Marten tells me.

"Real smooth," my left says.

"Ouch," Mike says. He doesn't even *look* sorry. He's unflappable. Completely. "She's in New York, actually. We're fighting."

He leaves this vague tidbit of information hanging in the air, as if I'm supposed to gain some sort of hope from it. Instinctively, I compare him to Kyle. Kyle has a better smile, better eyes. Better almost everything. Objectively, Kyle is more handsome, but Kyle isn't here right now is he? He's not the one flirting with me, grazing my forearm with his hand.

"Nice. And I suppose you want me to feel sorry for you, then?"

My right Doc Marten groans.

"No, I should have told you," Mike says. "I screwed up. I really didn't think we would be more than a fling."

"You were right about that," I say.

"Oh, come on, Jane. I really care about you, I do," Mike says.

"Save it for someone who gives a damn," says my left Doc Marten. Mike, however, doesn't seem to hear it.

"I'm not going to fall for this again," I say.

"Yes, you are," my right shoe sighs.

"I can't tell you how broken up I've been about how things worked out," he says, as if he had nothing to do with the course of events. As if his breaking up with me and his firing me were events out of his control, like natural disasters.

"Yeah, me, too," I say, trying to keep guarded. I should be angry. Instead, I'm relieved. He's apologizing, like I hoped he would.

"Here she goes," my left shoe chirps.

He smells so good, it's not fair. How am I supposed to resist him when he smells like clean laundry and soap, and the hint of something just a little bit spicy? Mike is like deep-fried food. You know it's bad for you. You know you're going to regret it, but you know it's going to taste so good.

"How are you? How have you been? Do you need anything? Really, let me know if you need anything."

I want to ask him for rent money, but I refrain.

"Letting you go was the hardest thing I ever did," he tells me, leaning close to my ear so that only I hear him.

"Do you mean breaking up with me or firing me?" I quip, but the tough girl act is all for show. Inside, I feel my will melting. The pit of my stomach is buzzing. My neck, where I can feel his breath, tingles. And still I tell myself, futilely, one last time, I should walk away. Now. Before I can't resist.

"You've never looked so damn sexy," he whispers, and I know it won't take much more before I'm trapped.

• • •

Ron is still on stage playing, with Missy dancing in front of him. Steph, who looks a bit woozy, but intact, emerges from the bathroom with help from Ferguson, who seems to be holding her up. She looks up and sees me talking with Mike.

She waves, but it's no use. My shoes are right. I am easy, and I'm not going anywhere. For a second, I think maybe I should just walk away.

And then I start thinking of Kyle with Caroline, and how they're probably, right at this moment, a tangle of naked limbs in Kyle's bed. Fine, I think. Two can play that game.

I do what I swore I'd never do again, I lean over and tell Mike what I'd like to do to him, Monica Lewinsky style. That's when he puts his hand to the small of my back and we stumble outside and into a cab.

I am giggling because I can't seem to fit the key into my door lock, and Mike has his hands up my skirt and is yanking on the edges of my underwear. I'm glad I wore the lacy ones and not the grungy gray-white ones with the hole at the waistband. I like to be prepared. As soon as Mike's confident groping is about to turn X-rated, I turn the key in the lock and we tumble into my apartment.

The floor is spinning and Mike has his hands up my shirt. This is a cause for concern because my breasts are not my best feature. They are relatively flat and grope-less, and I am wearing a bra with some push-up power (i.e., padding) and Mike is finding that out as we speak. But I let him, and we kiss—a sloppy, wet kiss, and all I can think of is, Kyle is one hundred times the kisser Mike is. Kyle's kisses aren't rough and off-center like Mike's are. Kyle is deliberate, gentle, and knows just what he's doing. Mike is careless, rushed, and even now he's unzipping his pants, offering himself up like some kind of delicacy.

I don't bite.

"What?" Mike asks me. "What's wrong?"

"Maybe this isn't a good idea," I say.

"Come on, baby," he says, nuzzling my neck, planting a trail of kisses down to my collarbone.

"What are you trying to prove?" my left shoe screams.

"And will it be worth the therapy you're going to need? That's what I want to know," the right adds.

"You're still going to marry her, aren't you?" I ask Mike.

"What?" he mumbles into my neck.

"Your fiancée?"

"What does this have to do with her?" he asks me, pulling away for the first time.

"Are you going to marry her or not?" I demand. My desire for Mike is dying with each extra second he takes to answer this question.

"It's not important," he says.

"It is important to me."

"Fine," he sighs, exasperated. "You want me to lie to you? You want me to tell you some fairytale about how

I'm going to leave her and be with you forever? Real life just doesn't work that way."

"So you are going to marry her."

"Yes," he says. "I am."

I knew this, deep down, all along. The small part of me that clung to the hope that I could change his mind dies. Not that I wanted to be with him, I tell myself. Who would want to be with someone like Mike? Life as his wife would be a life sentence of suspicion—every night, rifling through his pockets for receipts, snooping through his email, obsessed with finding proof of what you know must be the affair happening right under your nose.

"Does she know about me?"

"No," he says, not looking at me.

"Are you going to tell her?"

His eyes narrow, and his voice drops. "No, and you aren't going to either." His voice is cold and emotionless. I don't know if it's the shrooms, or if his face is as ugly as I see it—drawn, hard, threatening. The look scares me, and if I had any doubt as to where I fit in his life, I know now. I'm the girl who's supposed to play nice and keep quiet.

And this hurts—surprisingly, because I didn't think I could let him hurt me again. And right then, I decide, I'm over him. Done. Finished. This doesn't make me feel strong or empowered. Instead, I feel brittle, like cracked glass, as if anything he might say now could shatter me into a thousand pieces.

"I think you should go now," I say to him.

. . .

After I hear the front door close, I sit dry-eyed on my bed, knowing that this is probably the moment I should congratulate myself on finally getting over Mike. But I don't feel like a winner. All I feel is alone. So alone, that part of me feels like calling Mike back, if only for the twenty or so minutes of intimacy, even if it is fake.

"Sometimes the right thing to do is the hardest thing to do," my left shoe says.

I fall asleep, and wake up to what sounds like a hive of bees.

I then realize it's not bees at all, but snoring.

My living room is a disaster. There's a body curled up on nearly every piece of my furniture—the couch and my two chairs. Ron is snoring on his back, with his head on the floor and his feet propped on top of my glass coffee table. Missy is curled up next to him. Steph is lying on her side on the couch, and Ferguson is fast asleep on the floor at her feet.

No flat surface in my apartment is without trash, clothes, or a body. On the bright side, my shoes are no longer speaking to me. And I am too hungover to feel anything but an overwhelming desire for coffee. After five minutes of intensive searching in my refrigerator, I find the coffee—hidden behind an old *TV Guide* and what looks like one of Ferguson's shoes. Measuring out the coffee grounds feels like doing calculus. My brain hurts.

I find myself staring at my coffee machine in complete amazement. I feel like I have never seen anything so incredible as water being transformed into coffee drop by precious drop.

"I'm going to pretend I didn't see you leaving with Mike last night," Steph says, stumbling into the kitchen, yawning. "Do I even want to know what happened?"

"I didn't sleep with him if that's what you mean," I say.

"Thank God," Steph says, fanning her face like she might faint. "So, it's really over then?"

"Beyond over," I say.

We both stare at the coffee machine.

"Did we *both* ingest hallucinogenic drugs last night?" Steph asks.

"Yep," I say.

"Just checking," Steph says.

There's another beat of silence.

"And so I didn't *really* invent Skittles candies, even though I was sure I did and that I'm secretly worth a fortune?" Steph asks me.

I nod. "That's right. You didn't invent Skittles."

"Dammit," Steph curses. "And Ferguson isn't really secretly Luke Wilson in disguise?"

"No." I laugh, but the motion causes a sharp pain to jolt through my brain.

"The shrooms have made me feel really dumb," she says.

"Me, too," I say.

"No, I mean it. I think I've lost IQ points," she says.

"Me, too," I say.

"Like, what's that flashing light for?" She points to the red light on my the answering machine.

"Phone messages," I say. I realize that it's been forever since I've actually checked my answering machine. I got into such a routine of expecting no one to call, that I stopped even looking.

"Oh, right, you're supposed to press this button." Steph hits "play."

Beep.

"Jane, it's Kyle. We need to talk. Call me."

Beep.

"Kyle again. Look, I think we should talk about this, OK?"

Beep.

"It's Kyle. Call me, OK?"

Beep.

I am rubbing my temples trying to figure out why it makes me happy that Kyle has been stalking me. My brain is working two speeds slower than usual. Still, I think I should be mad. There is something I definitely should be mad at him about, but my memory feels like a connect-the-dots picture, only half the dots are missing.

Beep. "Jane. This is Gail Mindy from the law firm and we've got some temporary work that I think you'd be qualified for . . ."

I don't quite hear the rest. I don't remember sending

my resume, but then I've sent it almost everywhere, so I'm not surprised that I applied for a clerical job.

"You'd better call her," Steph says. "We're almost out of food."

Dialing numbers proves too complicated for me in my current post-shroom state, and Missy, the only one of us besides Ferguson who didn't drink shroom tea, ends up calling Gail Mindy and pretending to be me. She agrees with almost everything she says and adds, spontaneously, that I have good Excel spreadsheet skills. I am not sure I can even open an Excel spreadsheet, much less use one. I can, however, type, because in college I got out of a math requirement by taking Numerical Typing.

"You're supposed to be there in twenty minutes," Missy tells me when she gets off the phone.

Under different circumstances, I would be filled with glee that I finally have a job, even a temp one, except that this emotion is tempered by the fact that I don't think I have enough presence of mind in my hungover state to operate the shower knobs very effectively, much less a telephone, computer, or fax machine. Somehow, I manage to shower and get dressed, despite the fact that I spend ten minutes transfixed by the pull string on my interior closet light. My post-shroom comedown has clearly reverted my brain to its primate ways and fixations on all things shiny.

Outside, Missy puts me into a cab, telling me to make sure they pay me up front, as if she is my pimp.

• • •

The cab drops me off in front of the Goldhagen, Haynes, and Keinan law firm, where they need someone to answer phones.

I go through the revolving door once without stopping, and then nearly miss the entrance again as I'm distracted by sunlight glinting on the interior glass. The security guard at the front desk is staring at me strangely.

The office manager, Gail Mindy, is a wide-set woman with bright red hair and pale, almost translucent skin. She shakes my hand with a viselike grip and proceeds to run through instructions at such a rapid clip that it's unclear to me whether she's actually speaking English. She tosses out a few words I understand: "Coffee, Fax, Phones," pointing to various corners of the office, before sitting me down at the front desk and giving me a headset.

It takes me four tries before I've put the thing on correctly, and by then there are already four lights blinking on the oversized phone. I press one and nothing happens.

Another several minutes pass before I realize that my headset is not plugged in. I attach it, and press the button again.

"Law firm," I say, because holding in my head the names of the firm partners makes my head want to explode.

"Barbara, please," a man says on the other end of the line.

I am at a loss. I look through the massive bible that is
the firm's directory hoping that Barbara's last name starts
with an *a*.

I can't find it.

"What is Barbara's last name?" I ask.

The man sighs loudly.

"KEINAN," he says slowly and with exaggerated care
as if I might be deaf. "As in one of the partners in the
firm?"

I find Barbara Keinan's extension, and shortly there-
after realize that I have no idea how to transfer calls. Hit
transfer, then the extension, then transfer? Or is it hit
hold, then the extension, then transfer? Or is it hold-
transfer-extension? Or is it hold-transfer-extension-
transfer? Or extension-hold-transfer-transfer?

My head hurts. The lights on the phone are transfix-
ing.

I go with transfer-extension-transfer and the light
disappears, as do the other three blinking lights.

Gail the Office Manager materializes at the front
desk, eyeing me suspiciously. She has a way of doing
that, as if she can magically transport herself from place
to place in a cloud of Jean Naté perfume.

"Everything OK, here?" she trills at me.

"Fine," I say, nodding, and when she turns the corner, I put my head down on my desk because it suddenly
feels too heavy to keep up a moment longer.

The phone lights up again, and when I answer, it's
the same man looking for Barbara.

"I got disconnected," he tells me, sounding accusatory, as if I did it on purpose.

"Please hold," I say, hitting hold-extension-transfer, and hanging up.

The phone lights up almost immediately. It's the same man again, this time not bothering to be polite.

"Just give me her extension," he shouts at me.

I want to tell him that I do have a bachelor's degree, but I'm not sure that will really help my cause at this point.

Sometime midmorning, a blond paralegal walks by my desk and this reminds me of Caroline. Right. Caroline. Evil Caroline. It's all coming back to me now.

When Jean Naté goes to lunch, I sneak a call to Todd. I need to know the status of their relationship.

"I got a job," I say, right off.

"Congratulations."

"Yeah, it's temp work, but at least it's work."

"See? I knew you could do it. Persistence pays off!" Todd sounds legitimately proud of me. Temporarily, I feel warm and fuzzy inside.

"So?" I say.

"So?"

"So what's up with Kyle and Caroline?" I sigh, frustrated.

Todd gives a long sigh. Todd and Caroline don't get along that well. This probably stems from the fact that when Caroline and Kyle were seriously dating, Kyle never had time for Todd, always claiming to be busy doing things for Caroline (like remodeling her kitchen).

"I don't know, but whatever it is, I hope it's temporary," Todd says.

"Do you think it is?" I ask, for the first time hopeful.

"God, I hope so. At this point, I'd be happy to buy her a plane ticket to Australia if it would help things," Todd says.

Todd hates picking up a bar tab, much less a two thousand dollar plane ticket. This shows how serious he is.

Jean Naté comes back early from lunch and finds me on the phone. "No personal calls," she barks at me.

When I get home after a long day of hold-number-transfer, my apartment smells like a circus, and there are three more people here than when I left in the morning: Ron's three muses.

The muses are sitting in a circle, flipping through my old *InStyle* magazines. Ferguson is willingly rubbing Ganesha's feet. Ron is squeezing Missy's butt while she makes ham sandwiches, and Steph is sleeping in the spare bedroom, wearing a pink, silk eye mask.

"You're out of Diet Coke," one of the muses informs me.

"Oh, and peanut butter," Heather says.

"Oh, and your landlord came by looking for his

rent," Vishnu says. "What's his name? Bob? I couldn't quite understand what he was saying, but he said he's going to charge you late fees."

"Why the hell are they here?" I ask Ron.

"The police raided my apartment," Ron says, matter-of-factly. "The muses and I are homeless."

"Oh, no," I say, shaking my head. "Absolutely not. No way. You cannot live here."

"It'll only be for a couple of days," Ron says.

I think my face is turning purple.

"Maybe one day—just one? And Russ and Joe may come by later."

"Besides, we can help you with that Maximum Office thing," Ganesha says.

I stop and stare at her, and then at Missy.

"You TOLD them?" I ask Missy, who's sticking a knife dripping with mustard into my mayonnaise jar.

Missy shrugs.

"She had some good ideas about how to word the emails we're going to send out," she says.

I almost hear the veins in my temples popping.

Pop. Pop. POP.

I am tired of pretending that everything's OK.

Everything is not OK.

Everything is not even remotely OK.

I am losing my shit.

I'm facing financial ruin, and my once pristine apart-

ment has turned into a halfway house for every lazy degenerate within a scope of three miles. Even if a new job
came through tomorrow, and they doubled my previous
salary, there's no way I can even cover my minimum
credit card payments, not to mention the thousands in
back rent I owe Bob the Landlord. Short of winning the
lottery or marrying Ted Turner, I see no way of avoiding
declaring bankruptcy. My best romantic prospect in
years, Kyle, has hooked up with his old girlfriend, and I
am losing it.

Oh, sure, I'm not living on the street. I'm not homeless. I'm not in the middle of a campaign of genocide.
I'm not a ten-year-old boy going blind weaving rugs in
Pakistan. I know there are worse things in the world. I
know that in my head. That only makes it worse. Because this is the worst thing that's happened to me so far
in my short life, and I'm not handling it well. I'm not really handling it at all. So what happens when someone
dies? When something really bad happens? I'm not the
strong, independent person I want to believe I am.

In fact, nothing in my life is what it seems.

Nothing is in my control—not my job, not my love
life, not even my own apartment.

"I'm going to my bedroom and then counting to ten," I
say, in a voice that's shaking as I try to keep it steady.
"And when I come out, I want everyone out of my apartment."

I slam the door, so they all know I'm serious.

• • •

"One."

I can't believe I've let this go so far.

"Two."

Is it possible for my life to get worse?

"Three."

What on earth did I do in another lifetime to deserve seven squatters in my own apartment?

There's a knock at my door.

"I hope whoever that is, you're coming to tell me goodbye," I say.

"Jane," says Steph. "Jane, let me in."

"Four. I'm not going to, Steph, I'm sorry."

"Jane, we're not the people you should be angry with," Steph adds. "You know who's to blame in all this, and it's not Ron, and it's not Ferguson, and it's not me."

"FIVE," I practically shout.

"It's Mike, and you know it. Don't you want to get him back? Don't you want to imagine the look on his face when he finds out he's fired?"

"Six," I say, but softer this time.

"Come on. It'll be cathartic. You can do this one thing and move on with your life. Don't you want to move on, Jane?"

I pause. "Seven," I say.

"Come on. You need closure. You had a bad breakup. You lost your job. You need closure."

"I'm fine. I don't need closure. I just need everyone

out of my apartment." I pause. "Eight AND NINE," I add.

"Come on. You've been moping around for months. You've been pretending that you were unfairly singled out, when we all were handed bad deals."

I shake my head.

"You're not the only one suffering here," she says. "We've all suffered."

I nod.

"So, are you going to help us or are you going to sit and feel sorry for yourself for the rest of your life?"

I consider this a moment. Either my brain is still muddled by shrooms, or Steph is starting to make sense.

I have been stuck. I do need to move on. It's more than time for me to be over this.

"You think if we do this one thing, then I'll have closure, and I'll be able to move on?"

"Definitely," Steph says.

I think about this for a second.

I open the door.

Missy has some duct tape in her hand and a baseball bat.

"What are you doing?" I ask her.

"Well, if Steph didn't convince you, I'm afraid we were going to have to tie you up," Missy says.

"That's not funny."

"I'm not joking," she says.

I stare at her, but she doesn't blink.

"We're breaking into Maximum Office tonight," she adds, after a moment. "Are you in?"

I look at Steph and then back to Missy. Steph's right. I need to get Maximum Office out of my system.

"I'm in," I say.

To: jane@coolchick.com
From: Headhunters Central
Date: April 9, 2002, 10:35 A.M.

Dear Jane,

In response to your email, we do not systematically discard resumes of people with art degrees.

We understand that answering phones in a temp job is "destroying your will to live" but we're afraid we can't place you in jobs that we don't have.

Please stop emailing us.

Sincerely,
Lucas Cohen
Headhunters Central

13

I tell myself that breaking into Maximum Office is a harmless prank. Missy will send out emails to the top management and maybe take down Maximum Office's Web site. We'll throw a little toilet paper around, and then we'll be out of there. In and out. Nobody gets hurt. No felonies take place. And the most they can do to us if they catch us, according to Missy, is charge us with trespassing, since Ferguson is still an active employee (for the time being) and we are technically his guests. Missy, who has gone over our severance agreements with a magnifying glass, says that there's no clause specifically barring us from the premises of Maximum Office.

The parking lot at Maximum Office is brightly lit by high-wattage fluorescent lights beaming out over the wide expanse of asphalt. There is a security guard circling the parking lot in a mini pickup truck, which looks like a cross between a golf cart and a Jeep. It has a yellow light on top that's flashing.

Missy and Ron are in the front seat of Ron's Impala, and Ferguson, Steph, and I are crammed into the backseat. The muses decide to stay home, since they claim to be only good for the planning stages of a project and not the execution.

Missy is cursing.

"You didn't count on security?" I ask her.

"Shut UP," she hisses at me, clearly peeved. She spent so long trying to memorize the building floor plan that she didn't count on how we would actually get in undetected.

"Why can't we just walk in?" Steph asks, annoyed. "Just pretend to be with Ferguson."

"That's a last-resort excuse," Missy says. "We don't want to be seen if we don't have to. Besides, that guy's got to leave the parking lot sometime."

We sit in silence, safely hidden behind a large shrub with our engine and lights off, watching the security guard doing donuts in his golf cart in the parking lot.

"He looks like he's having a lot of fun," I say.

"Shut up, I mean it," Missy says.

I'm quiet. I'm beginning to think that perhaps I was a bit hasty in agreeing to this little escapade. I've never been one for acts of stupendous courage. I'm more like Kenneth Lay—hiding from Congress for weeks, and then finally showing up only to plead the Fifth.

I look over at Ferguson, who is taking our stealth mission far too seriously. He has painted his face commando-style and is wearing black combat boots and a utility belt, complete with tape measure, knife, flashlight, walkie-talkie, and keys.

"Don't you think you're overdoing it a tad?" I ask Ferguson. "I mean, what's with the commando makeup?"

Ferguson refuses to speak to me unless I speak into a walkie-talkie, even though I'm sitting right next to him in the backseat.

"You're a dork," I say into the radio.

"You're supposed to say, 'over,' over," Ferguson whispers.

"You're a dork, *over*," I say.

As we watch, the guard finally stops doing wheelies and pulls around to the other side of the building.

"Now's our chance," Missy says, opening her car door.

It takes Ferguson a few minutes to extract himself from the back of the Impala. His flashlight gets tangled in the seatbelt, and he spends a second disengaging it.

"Hurry up," Missy is hissing at Ferguson. Once free, he clambers over to us and we begin our twenty-yard walk to the door. Ferguson, who has been crouched low and giving us all hand gestures like a Navy SEAL, stops midway there, winded. He bends over and puts his hands on his knees to catch his breath.

"You've got to be kidding me," Missy hisses.

Once at the front doors, Missy uses Ferguson's key card to slip inside. Ferguson does an elaborate spin move, as if he's a SWAT commander trying to avoid laser light triggers. I walk normally over the threshold, giving him a look. He gives me the "OK" then "thumbs-up" signs.

"Strike Team is in place, *over*," Ferguson says into his walkie-talkie.

"We're all on the same team," I hiss at him. "There's only *one* team."

"You're supposed to say, 'over,' *over*," he whispers back.

"Come on," Steph says, dragging him away.

We take the stairs up to the second floor, and almost immediately come upon Steph's old cube. It's now covered in framed pictures of someone's Scottish terrier, along with a terrier calendar, and an oversized postcard that says "Dogs Are People, Too!"

I have to wrap both arms around Steph to prevent her from actually dismantling the cube.

"Let me break just one framed picture, just one!" she pleads with me as I wrestle her back into the hall.

"That wouldn't be very obvious, now would it?" I ask her, trying to settle her down.

"Well, let's go visit your cube, and see how you like it," Steph whispers.

My cube is two sections over from Steph's. It faces a window, so I know someone's bound to have moved into it the very afternoon I left.

What I am not prepared for is to see that the entire IT department has moved into my old space. Part of me was hoping for the poetry of the lone empty cube, a standing memorial to the significant loss of my leaving.

Instead, my old desk is nearly unrecognizable. It has been converted into a *South Park* mecca, every available surface covered in pictures of Cartman and cows.

It's like I never existed at all.

Steph shrugs. "Well, on the bright side, at least it's not decorated entirely in Scottish terrier," she says.

Missy takes two wrong turns before we're in the server room, which is really nothing more than an oversized janitor's closet, with lots of dusty shelves containing stacked electronic equipment like some sort of storage room for Star Trek props. Wires hang out everywhere.

Ferguson knocks over the trash can in the corner with a clang, causing us to stare at him.

"Sorry, *over*," he cackles into the walkie-talkie.

"Is someone going to take that from him, or do I have to do it?" I ask the group.

Missy sits down in front of the only computer screen in the room and begins typing.

"Commander, permission to secure kitchen area, *over*," Ferguson demands of Missy.

"Permission denied," Missy says.

"But I'm hungry, *over*," Ferguson whines.

"Why didn't you eat before we left?" Missy hisses.

"I did eat before we left." Ferguson is holding his stomach and making a pinched face. *"Over."*

"We'll eat later," Missy says.

With chilling precision, Missy takes a crowbar out of the bag she's carrying and jimmies the lock on the file drawer in front of her. She picks up a notebook inside, containing, she says, all the system's passwords. With ease, she gets into the email system, and times the email, which will fire all the executives, to go out the next day. Then she starts on payroll.

"One month or two?" Missy asks me. "Should we suspend their pay for one month or two?"

"Two," Steph says.

"Where's Ferguson?" Missy asks me.

Steph and I find Ferguson crouched in the corner of the office kitchen, trying to eat someone's Dinty Moore stew.

"Kitchen secure," he says, jumping up and wiping his mouth. *"Over."*

"Give me that walkie-talkie," I hiss, jumping at him. We get into a tug of war before Steph pulls us apart.

"Stay focused, people," she commands.

"Copy that, *over*," Ferguson says into his radio.

On our way back from the kitchen, we pass by Human Resources. The door is open, and a couple of desk lights are on.

"Let's do it," Steph says.

"Do what?"

"See what other people make," she says.

The personnel files are locked, and so it takes us a little while to get them open using nothing more than a ruler and the leverage of my Doc Martens. Unlike Missy, we are not seasoned in the techniques of larceny.

"Look at this," Steph says, pulling out the file on Mike.

He has three documented counts of sexual harassment against him, and one pending lawsuit. Looks like he tried the old let's-have-an-expensive-dinner-and-sex trick with a few other people in the office. But not all of them had been as willing as I was to accept it. I am strangely peeved. I thought I'd been special.

"The company settled two cases against him already," Steph says, flipping through a few other pages in his file.

"How much?"

"Doesn't say."

"Give me that," I say. I'm copying it. I don't know what I'm going to do with it, but I'm taking it with me.

"Come on, we're done," Missy says, clamping a hand on my shoulder.

"Where's Ferguson?" I ask Missy.

"Who cares?" she replies.

"We can't leave him," I say.

"I'm going. If you want to stay that's your business," Missy says.

Steph looks from me to Missy and back again.

"I'll help you look for him," Steph says.

Steph goes one way, and I go another, and we each whisper Ferguson's name. Before we even cover half the floor, a blaring alarm sounds. Missy's tripped up a fire alarm, either on purpose or by accident. Knowing Missy, she probably deliberately set it off to make us her patsies.

I run toward the kitchen, where I nearly collide with Ferguson, who is trying to eat someone's week-old left-overs. I grab him by the hand and start running, and see across the row of cubes that Steph has the same idea. We're both headed for the stairwell. We push open the door, fly down the stairs, and are suddenly out the door and into the underground parking lot—the executive parking lot. Ferguson's shoes are making clacking sounds against the concrete enclosed garage.

Suddenly, there are bright white headlights in front of us. Steph grabs us and shoves us behind a car.

The headlights have to be the guard, or the police. We're dead.

I heard once about a plane that lost part of its roof mid-flight, the force of lost air pressure sucking out several rows of seats.

I often wondered what you would do in a freefall. You have seven minutes or more before you hit the ground. You'd grow tired of screaming. You'd have to take several breaths to scream. And then, nothing to do but wait. You have an eternity to watch the ground come up to meet you. You see it coming the whole way. Faster and faster. A tiny road map growing bigger and bigger. Circles becoming trees, lines, roads—the Monet turning into a photograph, sharp and clear. Until you smash into a hundred blades of grass, and beneath, hard earth.

What Color Is Your Parachute? does not have a chapter on worst-case survival advice for plummeting 1,000 feet at terminal velocity.

I am bargaining with God.

Never again will I ever do anything illegal, I vow silently, as I watch the bright headlights stop in front of us as we crouch by the bumper of the Lincoln. I swear, from now on, if I am not caught, I will say hello to Mrs. Slatter every day—that is, if she ever gets back from Las Vegas. I will bring her cookies. I will ask if she has enough heat in her apartment. I will be nice to my brother Todd. I will make an effort to be nice to my dad. I will be more supportive of my mom. I will stop feeling sorry for myself. I will stop blaming other people for my problems. I will get out of debt.

I will happily answer phones at any law office that will have me. I will return Kyle's calls. I will be nicer to Ron. I will pay all the rent I owe Landlord Bob, even if he is a gambling addict and double-dealer. I will not press charges against Missy. I will be nicer to animals. I will be nicer to the homeless. I will do charity work. I will volunteer.

I will go to church. I will pray regularly. I will confess my sins. I will consider joining the Peace Corps.

.   .   .

The engine stops, and I hear the sound of a car door opening.

I will never again say anything bad about anyone with a "Jesus Saves" bumper sticker. I will faithfully pass along any chain email letters I get professing to be sent from angels. I will always let people over into my lane when they are trying to get on the expressway. I will never again shun people giving out fliers on the street. I will even be nice to Scientologists.

"Dudes, what are you doing?" I hear Ron's voice. I open my eyes and see Ron standing in front of the headlights of his Impala. I have never been so glad to see him, ever.

Ron, however, doesn't want to leave without Missy, and so we circle the parking lot until it's obvious she's already gone. He won't even go when the fire truck arrives, and we wait, lights off, at the far end of the parking lot, while we watch the firefighters pile out of their truck and investigate the false alarm.

"Missy was just after my bod, I guess," Ron says, sadly, as he starts up the Impala and takes us home.

Kinsella and Wood
Attorneys at Law
635 N. St. Clair Street
Chicago, IL 60611

Jane McGregor
3335 Kenmore Ave., #2-E
Chicago, IL 60657

April 10, 2002   Certified Letter

Dear Ms. McGregor,

   We represent Robert Mercier, the owner of the property located at 3335 Kenmore Avenue, where you currently reside. According to our records, you owe Mr. Mercier two months' rent ($3,300) along with additional late fees and penalties ($650), and the security deposit ($1,650), which Mr. Mercier says he has no records of you paying him.

   We urge you or your representative to contact us immediately to work out a payment of this outstanding debt or face legal eviction. If we do not hear from you within three business days, we will petition the court to have you physically removed from the premises.

Sincerely,
David Wood
Attorney at Law
Kinsella and Wood

14

At my apartment, we find the muses painting one another's toenails and watching reality TV. None of us says anything about the break-in. We are all too stunned to speak.

Missy doesn't come home, which is good news as far as I'm concerned. In fact, it seems she's already somehow planned her exit, by removing most of her stuff from my apartment. I wonder if she planned this escape from the beginning.

The muses use up the last of Steph's Biolage shampoo, and so by the end of the weekend, she's had enough and moves out to stay with her sister. Ferguson, after fending off a nasty bout of food poisoning from the bad leftovers he stole from Maximum Office, decides that he ought to go back to his own apartment. When he leaves, he gives me a tight hug and says that he owes me his life.

"I didn't do anything," I say.

"You saved me, and I won't forget it," he says. "You could've left me behind and you didn't."

"Really, it's nothing."

He gives me a mock salute and hugs me again.

Ron, who is taking Missy's sudden departure hard, won't even smoke pot when offered, and instead stares out the back window like a Lab waiting for his owner to get home. I put the copy of Mike's file underneath my bed. I still don't know what I'm going to do with it. I am tempted to mail it to his fiancée, but I don't want to make any hasty decisions.

The muses stay, after offering to do some housework, and besides the fact that Vishnu likes to do yoga poses naked in my living room, things are almost normal.

Monday comes and, miraculously, I discover that I have not been fired from my temp job working for Jean Naté as the front office receptionist. It figures that the one job I want to be fired from I may keep forever.

After a long day of answering phones, I get a letter from Landlord Bob, threatening eviction. Immediately, I march up the stairs and start pounding on his door.

I know he's there, because I can hear the television on inside, but he's not answering his door.

After I start banging the tune of "Oops! . . . I Did It Again" on the door, he finally shouts at me.

"TALK TO MY LAWYERS, YES?" he shouts through the door.

"Bob, it's not my fault that you have a gambling problem," I say. "You can't do this to me. It's extortion."

"TALK TO MY LAWYERS!"

"Admit it Bob, I only owe you one month's rent."

"ZOO LATE ON RENTS, NOT MY PROBLEM," Landlord Bob shouts through his door.

"One month, Bob. One."

"LAWYERS!" Landlord Bob shouts.

Talking to Landlord Bob is like trying to get a Parisian to admit to speaking English; it's a futile exercise.

At my temp job at the law firm the next day, I find myself so preoccupied with my current state, and with thinking about Mike's folder, that I nervously tangle up the phone cords so that my headset is only a foot from the console. I am trying to untangle a pretty serious knot when the elevator doors in front of me open and in walks Kyle Burton.

His eyes widen a bit in surprise, but he recovers quickly. I must look as shocked as I feel because Kyle says, "You look like you've seen a ghost."

Hastily, I jump up from my seat—I don't know why, but the force of my movement unplugs my headset, sending the endpoint of the cord straight into my eye. This is not the Ice Queen act that I so desperately wanted to play out the next time I saw him.

"Ow," I say. I feel like I'm ten again and have a crush on Kyle, and he's just caught me kissing his yearbook picture.

Kyle hides a smile.

"Same old Jane. How long have you been working here?"

My brain can't seem to function. "A week," I finally say. I want to shout at him, but I doubt that would win me points in the office.

"I tried to call you," he says. "I left you messages."

"I got them," I say, curt. Here we go, I think. That's the tone I'm looking for.

"Never mind," Kyle says, waving a hand. My heart sinks. Never mind? Never mind what? Never mind he's back with Caroline for good and I can shove off, never mind?

"How's Caroline?" I ask, almost before I can help myself.

"Fine, as far as I know," he says.

They're together then, I think.

"But I haven't seen her lately," he says.

Lately? What does this mean? He's being infuriatingly vague.

"What have you been up to?" he asks me.

I think about the Maximum Office break-in, and me and Mike. "The usual, too. Except for the temp job."

"That's good," Kyle says. He stares for a minute at his shoes. I'm so rattled, I can't think of another thing to say. Is he with Caroline or isn't he?

"I'm here to see Barbara Keinan," he says before I can speak. "We have a ten o'clock."

"Er, right. Well, I'll call her for you." I can't seem to

get my fingers to work properly. They keep wanting to punch all the wrong numbers. Since when does Kyle have this effect on me? I'm so nervous, I can feel my heart pumping hard in my rib cage.

"Ms. Keinan, Kyle, er, Mr. Burton is here to see you," I say, before I realize that my headset is still unplugged. Hastily, I plug it back in, only to hear Barbara Keinan shouting "Hello? Hello?"

"Ms. Keinan, Mr. Burton is here," I say again.

"Show him into the conference room."

"Right this way," I say to Kyle. I go in front of him, acutely aware that he has a full view of my back as I walk, my slightly wrinkled gray wool pencil skirt and my not-so-small run in my pantyhose that's creeping up the back of my knee as we speak. My heels, new ones, Mary Janes with nearly three inches of stiletto (I couldn't let the Manolos I bought for Mike go to waste), teeter slightly on the thick office carpet.

I give Kyle a quick backward glance, but his expression gives nothing away. We meet Barbara Keinan halfway to the boardroom.

"Kyle," she says, shaking his hand like they've known each other forever. "Good to see you. Can Jane get you some coffee? Tea?"

"Coffee would be great," Kyle says.

I squint at Kyle. The last thing I want to do is get him coffee.

I'm so angry, I fill the mug too full and manage to splash some on my skirt and on the toe of my right shoe.

"Ow," I say. The coffee is scalding hot—as usual. Jean Naté insists on it being practically boiling at all times.

Inside the boardroom door, I try to steady myself, walking carefully into the conference room, too-full coffee mug in hand. Just as I'm almost to Kyle, I hear Barbara ask, "I haven't seen Caroline in ages. Not since our reunion. How is she?"

Almost at this exact moment, my heel catches on a snag in the carpet, and I feel myself teeter off balance. In my haste to right myself, I overcompensate and the jerking motion sends coffee out of the mug and over my hand, which causes me to yelp and drop the mug. I watch in horror as it shoots straight down like a missile onto Kyle's knee, toppling over, and spraying scalding droplets of dark coffee over his gray wool pants, onto the top of his leather shoes, and sploshing the entire left leg of Barbara Keinan, who is wearing (until then) spotless Donna Karan cream-colored pants. The shocked look of anger upon Barbara's face tells me that I probably won't be serving coffee to anyone else anytime soon.

"I am so sorry," I squeak, too late. The thunderous look Barbara sends me says it all.

I am positive I'm fired, but Jean Naté tells me otherwise later that afternoon. "You're very lucky to still have this job," Jean Naté tells me later when she finds me in the bathroom with my blistered hand under the tap. "You're lucky that gentleman was so agreeable. Barbara was ready to fire you on the spot, but he convinced her that wasn't a good idea."

I'm beginning to wonder what it will take to get me fired around here.

"But, we had to put that incident in your employee file," Jean Naté says. "One more screwup, and I'm afraid you're gone."

When I get home, I'm not sure who I should be mad at, exactly, but I'm mad. Even walking through my front door and seeing Vishnu clothed is not enough to brighten my mood, nor is seeing the huge bouquet of pink and yellow roses on display in my kitchen.

"They're for you," Ganesha tells me. "From some guy."

The card says, "I hope my misplaced knee didn't get you fired. Sorry. Kyle."

He's *sorry?*

He thinks one flower arrangement (even if it is an expensive and tasteful one) is going to make up for his behavior? Oh no. Not by a long shot.

While I'm considering whether or not I should dump out the flowers, my phone rings. I let the machine get it. It's Kyle.

"Look, Jane, I am so sorry about today. I hope you didn't get in trouble, and well, I just wanted to tell you that. OK? I'm sorry. Really. And I think we should talk, because there are some things we need to sort out. Please call me, OK?"

The sound of his voice, contrite, so perfectly *nice,* sends me off. Why should he sound so nice? Why? He's not nice. Nice guys don't make out with you one night and get together with their ex-girlfriends the next.

"You should really talk to him," Ganesha advises me.

For once, I decide she's right.

It's pouring down rain outside, but I run out wearing only my work clothes and a raincoat, forgetting my umbrella and deciding I don't want to go back for it. My hair is soaked almost instantly, but I don't care.

I am going to tell Kyle how I really feel, Caroline be damned. I'm going to tell him that he can't just go playing with a girl's feelings this way. He can't go kissing a girl, then getting back with his ex-girlfriend, then sending her a giant arrangement of roses. He is the king of mixed messages, and I plan to tell him so.

Outside Kyle's apartment building, I lay on his buzzer hard.

"Jane!" he says, surprised to see me. I must look like a drowned rat, dripping water on his welcome mat.

"Surprised?" I ask him.

"Well, I was expecting the pizza guy," he says.

"Is she here?" I ask him, pushing my way past him, and into his apartment, leaving wet footprints on his hardwood floors.

"Who?"

"You know who," I say. "Caroline."

"Right, about Caroline . . . uh, I think we should talk," Kyle says. "I'm really glad you're here."

"I bet you are," I snap. After doing a sweep of his apartment, I discover he's in it alone.

"You have every right to be upset," Kyle says. "I'd just like to explain."

"I bet you would, but first, I have a few things I want to say to you."

"OK," he says. "Do you want a towel first?"

"No, I want you to shut up and listen," I say. I push back my wet hair from my eyes and poke him once in the chest. "Sit down," I command. He sits.

"First of all, you can't just send a girl roses and think *everything's* going to be fine. I know your mother and I think she raised you better than to go around toying with one girl's feelings while you plan to get back with an old girlfriend," I say.

Kyle makes a movement to speak, but I shush him with a hand.

"I'm going to finish this, whether you like it or not," I say.

"Two, you could have just *told* me you and Caroline were getting back together instead of bringing her over like some sort of sick surprise to my parents' house," I say. "Are you *that* insensitive or just *that* dumb?"

Kyle flushes red. "Right, you're . . ."

"Nope, not finished," I say.

Kyle turns a shade redder.

"And *finally*, I want to tell you that getting back with

Caroline is a mistake, a big one, because she doesn't appreciate you and takes advantage of you, and she's self-absorbed, and, frankly, you can do a million times better. Despite the fact that you're an insensitive jerk sometimes, I think you're a good guy and you deserve better than a woman like Caroline."

Kyle is looking at me with a half-smile on his face.

"What's so funny?" I ask him. "Nothing about this should be funny."

Kyle's smile grows bigger. I'm perplexed, my anger fading away into puzzlement. "You better not think of laughing at me," I say.

"Are you finished?" he asks me.

"Yes, I guess so," I say.

"Good, because I have some things I want to tell you," Kyle says, getting up and affectionately pushing a clump of wet hair off my forehead.

"One, I acted like a royal jerk, and I am very sorry," he says. "Two, I didn't mean to bring Caroline to your parents' house.

"And, three, Caroline and I are *not* back together."

Gap Customer Relations
100 Gap Online Drive
Grove City, Ohio 43123-8605

Jane McGregor
3335 Kenmore Ave.
Chicago, IL 60657

April 11, 2002

Dear Ms. McGregor,

While we are sorry that you have not been successful in your job application at our Gap stores, we can assure you that Gap does not discriminate against people who hold college degrees. Many of our employees have college degrees or are currently earning their college degrees, and we in no way discriminate against potential employees based on education level, race, age, religion, or creed.

In regards to any other job application questions, I refer you to the individual store manager.

Sincerely,
Kelly Joy
Gap Customer Service Representative

P.S. I am afraid we do not offer special discounts to the unemployed.

15

*W*hat?" is all I can manage to say, because I think I have forgotten how to breathe. "What do you mean you and Caroline aren't back together?"

Kyle puts his hands on my arms and draws me closer to him.

"*She* wanted to get back together," Kyle says. "I didn't."

"But she was draped all over you at the barbeque," I say.

"Well, that was before I told her we definitely weren't getting back together," he explains.

"But why?" I can't imagine Kyle not wanting to get back together with Caroline. She has a perfect body— everything about her, except her personality, is perfect.

"Because she is self-absorbed and because she does take advantage of me, and because she only came back to me because she's broke," Kyle says. "I didn't even know she was coming home. She called me from the airport because she didn't have enough money for a cab and her parents weren't home."

"But, I thought . . ."

"And, most importantly, I didn't get back together with her, because I'm crazy about you." He pauses. "In fact, I think I'm in love with you."

My ears start ringing.

"Love me?" I echo. "Love me as in love-me-like-a-sister love me, or love me as in I-want-to-see-you-naked love me?"

"I definitely want to see you naked," Kyle says.

"So that speech I just gave . . ." I say.

"Was totally pointless except that it told me you were crazy about me, too."

"Oh," I say, feeling sheepish.

"Jane, you're the most dynamic and complicated and most contradictory woman I know," he says. "And, if you weren't so busy trying to build a wall around yourself so no one can hurt you, you'd realize I've had a crush on you for years."

I am stunned.

"It's your turn to say something," Kyle says.

"How about we stop talking?" I offer, pulling him closer for a kiss.

· · ·

About fifteen years of repressed attraction is unleashed in a wild, sweaty groping that amounts to us knocking down two pictures from his wall as we tumble into his bedroom.

I pull away first. I am out of breath, my heart pounding wildly in my rib cage.

"Are you sure you're not just looking for an easy lay?" I joke.

"You're anything but easy," he tells me.

He presses me against the wall, kissing me as he undoes my shirt buttons, one by one. He runs his hands up my back, and down again, and I can think of nothing but what his hands feel like: strong, assured. I feel like eating him alive, and wonder why it is I've never been willing to admit how attractive he is, how perfect. He's holding me now, holding me up, and I wrap my legs around his waist. We're moving toward the bed as he whips away my shirt and tosses it on the ground behind us.

It is much different than with Mike. Sex with Mike was awkward because I was always preoccupied with putting on a performance. It was what sex looks like under garish fluorescent lights. Sex with Kyle is shimmering and liquid, like the reflection of a swimming pool. I realize I've been afraid to go here because it means something different. It is not squalid sex with Ron. It is not scrapbook sex with Mike. It is something with higher stakes.

I'm on my back and he's kissing me, licking me, from

my neck to my belly button, causing little shivers down my stomach. I have my hands on the zipper to his pants, and for a split second, I wonder what Todd is going to make of all this, and then I decide that I don't care. All I care about is what's going to happen next, because nothing in my mind is working except the most primal parts, and I don't even have time to think about sucking in my stomach, or pushing out my chest, or worrying about my A cup demi-bra.

Kyle reaches over to the nightstand for a condom, and I try not to think about all the other times he's done that. I take it from his hand and put it on him myself with my mouth—a parlor trick I picked up in college. I only do this when I really want to impress somebody. It took months practicing on a zucchini to get it right.

Kyle lets out a small laugh.

"I can't believe you just did that," he says.

"I bet you won't believe a lot of things about me," I say.

"Tell me what you like," he whispers in my ear, the first time a guy has been on the ball enough to actually ask.

"Do you like this?" he asks, kissing me hard on the lips, flipping me over on my back. I murmur a yes.

"And this?" Kyle's fingers find me, and it seems like he's got a few tricks of his own. He's got me so worked up that I beg him not to stop, and he doesn't, not until I'm so close I want to scream. That's when he pushes inside, and it feels like it's never felt. I can't think of anything but how good it is. It's the first time I don't have to put on a show. Kyle is whispering in my ear about the things he wants to do to me. He only gets to the second before I've gone tumbling over the edge, a surprising rush so strong I can't help but make noise. It's the first time I've never had to fake it on the first go 'round.

Afterward, Kyle cradles me in his arms, holds me close in a protective spoon and runs his hands over my body like he's trying to store up information, his hands memorizing the curves.

"I've had a crush on you since eighth grade."

"You did not," I say.

"I did. I thought you'd laugh at me if I told you."

"I would have," I say.

"I know," he says. "I had to wait until your defenses were down. You are so rarely vulnerable."

"I had a crush on you when I was ten," I admit.

"You did?" Kyle sounds genuinely surprised.

"And if you liked me for so long, why didn't you say something?"

"Well, you *always* had a boyfriend. I swear, you were always surrounded by boys."

"I hardly think so. You were the one who always had a girlfriend," I say.

"The point being, there was a serious lack of opportunity."

"So your plan of seduction was flaunting your old

girlfriend and then almost getting me fired from my temp job?"

"I wouldn't call it a plan, exactly," he tells me, kissing my nose.

"You're lucky I'm easily impressed," I say.

I fall asleep in Kyle's giant king-size bed, and he cradles me and strokes my hair, and I feel funny and weird, and it's been so long it takes me awhile to remember contentment.

I come awake to the feeling of Kyle squeezing me close, and for the first time in months, I don't seem to care about my joblessness. I don't come awake seized with that familiar sense of doom. I feel, for once, optimistic. Maybe it's the fact that Kyle's kissing me, courageously unconcerned about morning breath. Or maybe it's the fact that I'm kissing him back, and I know where this is headed, and it isn't to awkward goodbyes and the avoidance of eye contact.

Kyle sits up and stretches.

"I'm going to make us coffee," he says. I watch him as he pulls up his boxers and pads softly to the front of his apartment. Yawning, I get up, taking most of the sheet with me.

Kyle insists on driving me to work, where I arrive wearing pretty much the same clothes (with a different shirt—one of Kyle's) that I wore yesterday. And for once,

I'm not worried that Kyle won't call, or that someone at the office will talk about me.

But the tranquil, lazy feeling of satisfaction doesn't last.

Waiting in my email inbox, like a land mine, is an email from Steph. Attached is an article from the *Chicago Tribune*.

"Prank Gone Bad?" it reads. "Officials Investigating Break-In at Major Office Supplier."

I skim the article in a kind of panic.

I see the words "vandalism," "break-in," and "police" and I nearly stop breathing. It says:

Prank Gone Bad?

Police believe two or more disgruntled employees of Maximum Office broke in, ransacked the employee files, and broke into the company's email system.

Several vice-presidents and other high-ranking managers of the company received email notices that claimed they had been fired. At least two weeks of high-ranking managerial pay, totaling somewhere in the neighborhood of $55,000, has been diverted from payroll and is currently missing.

I can't seem to breathe properly.

Did Missy steal the payroll money?

Of course she did.

This whole prank was probably just an excuse for her to get into the system and then blame it on one of us.

I keep reading.

The break-in comes several months after a significant round of layoffs of nearly 1,000 employees, none of whom were in high-level managerial positions.

Police say they have no suspects at this time, but are currently reviewing the roster of recently laid-off employees who may have had access to the company's buildings.

So far, officials say they don't think the break-in will affect the planned merger with the number-two giant office supplier, Office Online, Inc.

The police are probably at this moment figuring out that of all the disgruntled employees, I am the most disgruntled. I imagine they have already sent out a herd of black-suited federal agents, who at this very moment are probably interviewing Bob the Landlord, who will be telling them how he always suspected I was into something illegal, given my inability to pay the rent on time. I imagine Steph being interviewed, spewing expletives, and being carted off to jail in the backseat of an unmarked police car.

I call Steph.

"WHERE have you been?" she breathes at me.

"Booking a one-way ticket to Mexico City," I say.

"Don't even joke about that," Steph says.

"What are we going to do?"

"Just stick to the alibi Missy said to use."

"What's that?"

"You know, we were at home. We watched *Office Space*."

"I haven't seen *Office Space*," I say.

"Who hasn't seen *Office Space*?" she asks me.

I ignore that. "Well, can you at least tell me what it's about?"

"Well, these guys get laid off and then they decide to steal from the company," Steph says.

I am silent for a beat or two. "You don't see the irony there?"

"What?" she asks.

"Never mind," I say. "What if that doesn't work?"

"I'd say we both need a good attorney, then," she says.

I call my own apartment, figuring that while Missy is probably still gone, I can at least tell Ron that there may be police coming to my apartment. That might entice him to leave and take his muses with him.

Vishnu answers.

"Is Ron there?" I ask her.

There's a clatter and the sound of grunting (she's probably doing Downward Dog naked), and then Ron comes on the phone.

"Yo," he says.

"Ron, it's Jane. Listen to me very closely."

"Jane—DUDE, you won't believe what's happened."

"Are the police there?" I cry, panicking.

"Police? No, no, no. Sink Gunk, DUDE. We've got our own single out. Like, we're on the RADIO."

"Great, Ron. That's just great. But I have something important to tell you."

"We're going to be on the *Crash and Burn* soundtrack or something. It's going to be wild."

"Ron. I have something important to tell you, OK? Let me talk for a second."

I finish explaining about the news article, and Ron doesn't say anything for several long seconds. Then, he says, "Hey, on your way home can you pick up some nitrate-free lunch meat? We are like totally out of sandwich filler, dude."

"Ron. Did you hear a word I said?"

"Ganesha wants turkey, but I'll take ham or roast beef."

There's no use trying to talk seriously to Ron about anything.

When the police aren't waiting for me when I get home, I manage to relax a little. Maybe they *won't* find me. Maybe I'm so far down the list of the hundreds of disgruntled Maximum Office employees that they'll give up interviewing people before they even reach me. Besides, Missy said it is a misdemeanor. I think about Mike's file under my bed, but I still don't know what I want to do with it, if anything.

Because rationalization always has been one of my talents, I decide that maybe, for once, God will not punish me for wrongdoings.

• • •

There's a commotion on the stairwell, and I realize it's Mrs. Slatter, because I can hear her lapdog yipping. I open up my door and peer down the stairwell in time to see Mrs. Slatter, wearing a nylon jogging suit made entirely of silver sequins.

"How'd you do in Vegas?" I shout down at her. She looks up at me and squints through giant plastic sunglasses.

She shrugs. "You win some, you lose some," is all she says. I notice, however, that her dog is wearing a rhinestone collar, and mini star-shaped doggie sunglasses.

Kyle calls around six, proving that he's after more than a one-night stand.

"I thought guys like you were supposed to wait three days before calling," I say.

"That's far too predictable. I like to keep my women guessing."

"The sign of a true player," I say.

"Are you free tonight? Can I buy you dinner?"

"Only if it's incredibly expensive and you expect sex afterward."

"Naturally," Kyle says, and I can tell he's smiling.

Citibank Financial Offices
Customer Service
Wilmington, Delaware 19801

Jane McGregor
3335 Kenmore Ave.
Chicago, IL 60657

May 6, 2002

Dear Ms. McGregor,

We are writing to inform you that you have exceeded your MasterCard credit limit by $338.09. Per the written agreement you signed with us, we will charge you $50 for exceeding your balance and another $50 in late fees.

Please call our customer service line immediately to address your outstanding balance and late minimum payment. Failure to do so will require us to turn over your account to a collection agency.

Sincerely,
Jen Keith
Citibank Customer Services Manager

P.S. Per your inquiry, we are unable to accept the following in payment: human organs, sexual services, or indentured servitude.

16

*W*hat I feared would be a one-night stand with Kyle has turned into a month-long relationship. I have kept my temp job, miraculously, and a boyfriend for longer than four weeks. For the first time, I feel like my luck is changing. Either that, or I'm in the eye of the bad luck storm. It's the latter, I discover, during a night when we're eating pizza at Kyle's and watching CNN, and a story about the Maximum Office break-in airs. Since when did misdemeanor trespassing merit national news coverage?

"Oh yeah, I heard about that break-in," Kyle says. "You know anything about that, Jane?"

"Are you saying I did it? Because, I didn't do it."

"I didn't imply that you did." Kyle looks at me strangely.

"I mean, I wouldn't do something like that," I say.

"What's your problem?"

"Nothing," I say, too quickly.

"Calm down," Steph commands after I call her the next morning. "First, nobody has even come looking for us, so I really doubt that they have any clue about who did this."

"We should all get our stories straight, just to be sure," I say.

The next afternoon, Ferguson, Steph, and I meet covertly away from any of our neighborhoods, in the Ennui coffee shop in Rogers Park. I take elaborate measures to make sure I'm not followed, including circling around the block twice because of a car parked out front that looks like a federal agent's. I shouldn't have bothered, because when I walk in, I see that Steph and Ferguson are sitting in a front-window seat.

"Don't you guys want to sit somewhere a little less obvious?" I ask.

"Calm down," Steph says. "Who's going to see us?"

When I protest more, Steph sighs dramatically and agrees to move.

Of the three of us, I am most worried about Ferguson caving under police interrogation because he tends to bow easily to peer pressure.

Ferguson is looking less nerdy than usual. He's got on a regular Gap shirt and jeans and is looking slim, like he's almost back to his pre-pot-smoking weight. And instead of his boxy glasses, he's wearing contacts. If I didn't know any better, I'd suspect he has a girlfriend.

"Ferguson, you're the only one they can tie into this mess because we used your keycard," I say.

"I told them I lost my keycard," Ferguson tells us.

"They interviewed you?" I nearly choke on my coffee. "Why didn't you call us?"

"I called Steph," Ferguson says, then blushes a deep red.

Steph, who is trying to look anywhere but at me, stares intently at the discarded coffee stirrers piled in the middle of the table. I look at Steph, then back at Ferguson.

"You guys hooked up," I accuse.

"Well, you know what they say about adrenaline-causing situations and sex," Steph says.

I really don't want to hear any more of this.

"Then it grew into something more," Ferguson says, clasping Steph's hand on the table. "I'm so lucky. Don't you think she's the most beautiful woman you've ever seen?"

"Isn't he soooo sweet?" Steph says, interlacing her fingers in his. I decide that maybe I should start charging admission to my apartment. It has more successful love stories than Match.com.

It is hard to make a plan sitting across the table from Ferguson and Steph, who—now that they're outed—

can't seem to keep their hands off one another. I'm the victim when their game of footsy goes awry and Ferguson accidentally kicks me in the shin.

"Guys, we need to focus here," I say.

"It was just a prank," Steph says. "Who cares about a stupid little prank? Fergie says that they're not even sure the payroll money has been stolen."

"Did you just call Ferguson, 'Fergie'?" I ask.

Ferguson sends Steph a flirty look, and I fear he might kiss her in my presence. He's looking at her as if she's a foot-long Subway club sandwich.

"Never mind," I say. "I think it's obvious that Missy stole the money. She's probably in Tijuana by now. And when they find out the money is really gone, then it's not going to be a dumb little prank anymore."

"It'll take them a while to sort out all the details," Ferguson says.

"And even if they do, there's nothing linking us to the scene," Steph says. "Jane, just relax, OK? Don't panic and everything will be fine."

Not panicking has never been my strong suit. Everyone knows I can't keep a secret, and that I crumble under even the hint of pressure.

In fact, I only last a few hours, until I have to tell Kyle.

We're on his couch, watching a rental tape, or, not really watching it so much as making out in front of it, and I ask him what he thinks of attorney-client privilege.

"I mean, what would you say if I told you that I committed a crime? Would you have to report me to the authorities?"

Kyle, who is kissing my neck, mumbles something I can't hear.

"Kyle, I'm serious. What if I told you I shoplifted something. Would you have to turn me in?"

"Technically—no," Kyle says. "And I think the statute of limitations on shoplifting is like three years. So unless you've shoplifted at Saks Fifth Avenue recently, I'd say you're probably fine."

"So, if I told you something, you couldn't repeat it because of attorney-client privilege."

"Technically, I'm not your attorney, so that doesn't apply," Kyle says, burying his face in my neck.

"What if I gave you a dollar and hired you?" I ask him.

"What's this all about?" Kyle asks me, sitting up.

"Here's a dollar," I say, pulling one from my pocket.

"That buys you about twenty seconds of consultation."

"Even at a discounted rate?" I cry.

"Jane. What's the problem?"

"I broke into Maximum Office."

Kyle is completely silent for a moment.

"Say that again," he says.

"I broke into Maximum Office. We suspended paychecks for upper management and messed with the email system. We sent out emails that told vice presidents they were fired. And that's all we were going to do, except I think Missy stole some payroll money, maybe $55,000. I saw it on the news. It's been in the newspaper and on TV."

Kyle straightens and withdraws his arms from me. He sits on the couch and runs his hands through his hair.

"You committed a felony," he says.

"Missy said it was a misdemeanor."

"It's a felony," Kyle corrects. He lets out a long breath. "Do you have any idea—ANY idea—how completely and totally dumb that was?"

"I'm beginning to get an idea," I say.

"Jane, you have to go to the police and tell them what happened."

That's not what I want to hear.

"I can't do that. Then I'll go to jail, and it was all Missy's idea."

"Listen to me very carefully, Jane," Kyle says. "We need to get you an attorney—a criminal defense attorney—and then you need to go turn yourself in."

"I'm not turning myself in," I say.

"Jane." Kyle's face twists into an even more stern and disapproving look. "Jane, listen to me. Legally, you will be in much better shape if you give yourself up. And, morally speaking, it's the right thing to do. I think you know that."

"It was just a stupid prank," I say.

"I think you're old enough to have outgrown stupid pranks. You've got to start acting like a grown-up sometime. You can't just think the things you do don't have consequences. At some point, you've got to take some responsibility for who you are."

I have nothing intelligent to say to that, so I snap, "I don't have to sit here and listen to this."

I stand.

"I'm just saying, Jane, that this is not like you," he says. "You're smarter than this. You're not someone who's easily taken in."

I used to think I wasn't a person so easily taken in. Then came Mike.

I feel like I might start crying, so I head for the door.

Kyle doesn't make a move to stop me. I feel his disapproval and disappointment.

"I think I'm going to go home," I say, but I want him to ask me to stay.

He doesn't.

"Maybe that's for the best," he says instead.

The View
320 West 66th Street
New York, NY 10020

Jane McGregor
3335 Kenmore Ave.
Chicago, IL 60657

May 7, 2002

Dear Job Applicant,

We regret to inform you that we are not hiring at this time.

Thanks for thinking of *The View!* For more information about this funny and lively daytime show, please visit our web site at abc.com/theview.

Sincerely,
Stacey Seiler

P.S. Star Jones is one of our most popular co-hosts, and to my knowledge does not plan to leave the show in the near future.

17

The muses are feng shui-ing my apartment when I return. They tell me that part of my problem is that I have my kitchen trash can in my money sector, and a dead plant in my spiritual sector.

"What's in my love corner?" I ask them.

"A pile of unpaid bills," Ganesha says.

The next morning at work, I keep transferring people to the wrong extensions. I can't think of anything except what Kyle said. He's clearly right. He's the most grown-up person in my life, next to my parents, and I don't think they count, exactly. The fact that he thinks I've made a mess of things means something. I think about going to the police, but the minor detail that I am a coward gets in the way of me actually picking up the phone to call them.

And then there's the file under my bed, which I still don't know what I want to do with. Mail it to his fiancée? Mail it to CNBC? Mail it to him and demand money? Shred it? I haven't decided.

At lunch, I meet Dad at the unemployment office, because Mom makes me promise to help him navigate the unemployment lines.

Dad, who doesn't even get a driver's license without complaining loudly and at length about the bloated nature of liberal government, gives a running narration of his experience of the unemployment office that would make John Stossel proud.

"Is this what my tax dollars are paying for?" Dad declares at a volume intended for everyone in a two-mile radius to hear. "We are CUSTOMERS. We are paying their salaries, and they're sitting there doing their NAILS."

Technically, the two women at the front desk are bickering because one claims the other intentionally left a paper clip askew, which caused her to break her nail. I try to tell Dad that hostility will only make them conveniently "lose" his unemployment check, but he doesn't seem to care.

Dad bristles at filling out forms and demands to speak to the manager when the woman behind the glass partition tells him to step out of line.

"I'm paying your salary," he says, and is surprised when she doesn't immediately begin apologizing and asking him if he'd like a refreshing beverage while he waits.

"Unbelievable," he says when they call security and tell us we have to come back at a later date. "And this is what Bill Clinton had us pay all those taxes for."

"Dad, Bill Clinton isn't president anymore," I say. "It's time to move on."

"If you forget the past, you're just going to repeat it," Dad says.

I decide to ask Dad, in a veiled way, what he thinks about breaking and entering.

"Dad, if you did something illegal, and you were going to get away with it, but the right thing to do was turn yourself in, would you?"

Dad stares at me a moment.

"Is this about your rent money? Because I told you, you can't afford that apartment."

I sigh. Why does everything come back to my apartment?

"It isn't about me. I'm just asking you a theoretical question."

"You and your mother. Always with these theoretical questions. They're a waste of time. Women want to know in theory and men want to know in fact. That's why men and women don't get along."

"Never mind," I say.

When I get home, Vishnu is doing naked yoga in my living room, contorted in a pose that really ought not to be attempted in the nude. I avert my eyes and go to the fridge only to find that even the ketchup has been consumed. There is nothing there but what looks like Ganesha's bra and a Nerf football.

I don't even want to know.

My buzzer rings and I go to answer it, hoping against hope it's a lost pizza delivery guy.

Two fraternity boys with SAE caps are standing at my door.

"Is Ron here?" one of them asks.

"We've got the green," the other says, waving a few $50 bills in front of my face.

"I'll take that," says Vishnu, who has wrapped herself in one of my Pottery Barn afghans. She hands the boys a paper sack filled with God knows what.

"Were those drugs?" I demand of Vishnu as she closes the door.

"I hope so," she says.

"I really don't want you or Ron dealing drugs from my apartment," I say.

"Don't be such a buzzkill," she tells me.

My buzzer rings again.

I don't answer it.

"Don't," I tell Vishnu, who's headed to the door. She ignores me, and buzzes up the guests. Then, she quickly goes back to her yoga poses.

"Just give them one of the bags," she says, pointing to a neat row of brown baggies sitting on my foyer table.

I swing open the door, ready to tell the fraternity boys to go somewhere else, when I see two men in sport coats and Dockers. I have a bad feeling almost immediately about them. For one thing, neither one of them smiles. For another, they don't look like they're in the market for E.

"Jane McGregor? I'm Detective Mason," says the beefy one in the blue tie, "and this"—he indicates his partner—"is Detective Johns. Can we speak to you a minute?"

My mouth goes completely dry. I can't speak. I can't even move. I think my heart has stopped. I don't actually feel it beating at all, and I think I am starting to feel lightheaded. I slip out of my apartment and try to keep the door mostly closed behind me, although Detective Johns is trying to see inside. I try to close the door further so he can't see the rows of brown baggies.

"We're investigating a break-in at your former place of business," says Detective Mason. He makes it sound like Maximum Office is a brothel or a drug den.

"Yes," I squeak, and then swallow. "I mean, yes, I heard about that on the news."

The detectives look at each other and one of them scribbles something in his notepad.

Suddenly, I think of Mike's personnel folder sitting under my bed. With great force of will, I don't turn my head to see if I can see it poking out from my bedroom door.

"I see," Detective Mason says. "Well, we're interviewing people who worked for Ed Ferguson, to see if they might be able to tell us if he was behaving suspiciously in any way the week leading up to the break-in."

The folder is like Poe's *Tell-Tale Heart*. It seems to be thumping in my ears, and I keep thinking I hear papers rustling in my apartment.

"Ferguson?" I say, trying to collect my thoughts and focus. "I worked for him once, but I was laid off more than three months ago," I say.

"Oh," Detective Mason sounds surprised as he looks down at his notepad.

I can't believe Maximum Office gave him outdated information. It seems the human resources department is as inefficient as ever. I wish payroll would be as lazy in terms of updating their records.

"Have you spoken to Mr. Ferguson in the last couple of weeks?" Detective Johns asks.

The folder. They are definitely going to see the folder. Maybe Ganesha found it and put it on our coffee table. With great force of will, I do not turn around and look to see if she has.

Detective Johns doesn't notice me pause before I answer because he seems to be transfixed by the sight of Vishnu contorting over my left shoulder. I suspect she is doing a handstand behind me.

"I think I did run into him maybe once," I say, trying to be as vague as possible.

"Do you remember when?"

"Maybe a couple of weeks ago," I say.

"Where?"

"Uh . . . on the sidewalk, actually." This isn't a lie. During Ferguson's extended stay in my apartment I did see him once or twice on the sidewalk in front of my building.

Detective Mason scribbles something else in his notepad.

Why did I take the folder? I think. It's the only real piece of evidence linking me to the crime.

"Did he seem strange?" he asks.

"No," I say. "No more than usual."

Neither detective laughs. I forget policemen aren't supposed to have senses of humor.

"I was kidding," I add for clarification.

"Oh—right," Detective Johns says, without so much as upturning one side of his mouth.

Both detectives are now looking over my shoulder. I hate to think what they're seeing.

"Is there something else?" I ask.

Both men have their mouths slightly agape.

"No, I don't think so," Detective Johns says, looking behind me.

"Thanks for coming by," I say, as if they are party guests.

Once they're gone, I run to my bedroom, nearly knocking over the naked Vishnu, and grab the folder from under my bed. It's there, intact, without pages missing. I still don't know what to do with it. I consider trashing it, but something stops me. Instead, I shove it between my mattress and box spring.

"Don't panic," Steph instructs me on the phone later that night. "They don't have anything on us. They're just trying to shake us down."

"So says you," I say. "You're not the one who had police hanging out at your apartment today."

"Besides, Vishnu probably distracted them," Steph says. "Did you give them our *Office Space* alibi?"

"No," I say. "I didn't think you were serious. I thought you were kidding."

"Never mind," Steph says quickly. "That probably doesn't hurt us too badly."

"You were *serious* about the *Office Space* alibi?" I ask, incredulous.

"Calm down," Steph commands. "Do you watch *Law and Order*?"

"No," I say.

"What sort of unemployed person are you if you don't at least watch one of the bazillion *Law and Order* reruns?" Steph doesn't wait for me to answer. *"Anyway,* if you watched the show, you'd know that they always trick one person into informing on another. That's how they win their cases."

"How does that help us?"

"If you don't crack, and I don't crack, and Ferguson doesn't crack, then we're all set," she says, matter-of-factly.

"You do realize how ridiculous you sound, don't you?" I ask her. "You're basing our defense on a TV show."

"Just don't panic, OK?"

I do panic, and I decide I need serious legal advice. It's time to grovel and beg for Kyle's forgiveness. Clearly, I am in the wrong.

A woman answers Kyle's phone.

Surprised, I hang up.

Must have misdialed. I am careful this time with the numbers, punching them all deliberately.

She answers again.

"Who is this?" she demands, annoyed. Territorial. She sounds like a girlfriend, not a first date, or a one-night stand. She sounds comfortable answering Kyle's phone. Possessive, even. She sounds like Caroline.

"Who is THIS?" she asks again, more insistent. Jealous, maybe? Suspicious?

I hang up without saying anything.

Two minutes later, I am in a cab going to Kyle's apartment. I am going to get to the bottom of this. I'm not going to be a fool twice.

I buzz Kyle's apartment, and the same female voice crackles over the intercom.

"*WHO'S* there?" she barks, annoyed.

A Thai food delivery guy arrives at that moment, and hands me some menus. He buzzes the apartment below

Kyle's. When he slips into the building, I follow.

I bang on Kyle's door, not thinking about anything except getting a hard look at who is on the other side. A woman answers, wearing cut-off sweats, with her hair up in a messy bun, youthful face completely without make-up. She looks like she lives there. She's wearing a Northwestern University sweatshirt, and eating ice cream from a pint carton.

"You could've just left this on the door," she says, grabbing a Thai restaurant menu from my hand and shutting the door in my face.

NASA

Johnson Space Center

Houston, TX 77058

Jane McGregor

3335 Kenmore Ave.

Chicago, IL 60657

May 10, 2002

Dear Ms. McGregor,

We're afraid you do not qualify for employment as an astronaut with the NASA space program. While you may have earned a Quantum Physics degree from Harvard, we have other very strict requirements for astronauts, including:

- At least 1,000 hours pilot-in-command time in jet aircraft; flight test experience is highly desirable.
- Ability to pass a NASA Class I space physical, which is similar to a military or civilian Class I flight physical, and includes the following specific standards: for vision-distance visual acuity—20/70 or better uncorrected, correctable to 20/20, each eye. For blood pressure—140/90 measured in a sitting position.
- Height between 64 and 76 inches.

Competition for the astronaut program is fierce. We encourage you to try again after completing some of these requirements.

Best of luck,

Matt Toddson

NASA Hiring Official

18

$\mathcal{I}$ have no idea what I'm supposed to do next. Call Kyle? Confront him? Discover that he isn't one of the Good Guys after all, that he's just one of the Mikes?

I can't believe this is happening to me—again. I feel like my life is an endless loop—layoffs, cheating boyfriends, followed by more layoffs and more cheating boyfriends. Just what do I have to do to get a karmic break, anyway? I would've thought committing a felony in between might've broken that cycle.

Kyle saves me from having to make the decision by calling me first.

"Look, I want to apologize for my behavior the other night," he starts. He's talking about our Maximum Office fight.

"I don't care," I say. "I want to know why you lied to me."

"Lied? What are you talking about?"

"I know you have a girl at your place. I saw her there," I say.

"What are you doing? Spying on me?" Kyle asks, flabbergasted.

"Don't change the subject. Who is she? Your other girlfriend? Your fiancée?" I feel the rising of the Ghost of Mike hovering above me in the room. The bitterness is coming through, and before I can stop it, it's bubbling up, overflowing. I am turning into a one-woman Spanish Inquisition.

"Jane, calm down," Kyle says, sternly. "If you're talking about Laura, she's my eighteen-year-old cousin. She's staying with me for the weekend to scout out colleges."

"She's your cousin," I scoff.

"You remember Laura. I think when you last saw her she had braces and her hair short."

The anger fades away as I remember that he does have a cousin named Laura. A blond cousin I haven't seen in years.

"Your cousin," I spit, still not sure if I believe him.

"What? You've known me how long, and you think I'd be sleeping with another woman right under your nose? You think I'd start a new relationship with you— my best friend's sister, when I wanted to play around with a *teenager*? Is that the kind of guy you take me for?"

I suddenly feel really stupid. I suddenly wish, more

than anything, that I had a time machine and could jump back in time about ten minutes.

"I thought you knew me, Jane," Kyle says, sounding sad. "But I don't think you know me at all."

The next thing I hear is a dial tone.

I'm beginning to feel like I am the opposite of King Midas. Everything I touch turns to shit.

I don't need the confirmation, but Todd gives it to me anyway. It *is* Laura, Kyle's cousin, who is staying at his place. A fact I would've known in advance if we hadn't had the fight about Maximum Office, and if I'd just asked him rationally instead of ambushing him like some sort of crazed jealous woman.

Clearly, I need help.

Friday, I end up on the CTA headed to Evanston, where Mom insists I come for a family meal because I sound "down" on the phone. This is not an act. I am down. Between the police and Kyle and my lack of job prospects and the fact that I am flat broke, I am pretty down.

When I arrive home, the house is filled with smoke and Dad is thwacking the smoke alarm with a broom handle, using curse words he usually saves for December when he's hanging up the colored lights on the roof.

"Dad? What the hell is going on? Where's Mom?" I say, because the sight of my dad swinging a broom handle is a bit disconcerting.

"Your mother is working late," Dad says, enunciating

each syllable with exaggerated clarity. "She told me to put in the roast. Can you believe that?"

Dad says this as if Mom asked him to give up a kidney or sell his body on the street.

I wander into the kitchen, where smoke is billowing out of the oven. Mom's roast is sitting on the oven rails, sans pan, which Dad thoughtfully left sitting on the counter. The bottom of the roast is blackened. The top is raw, and the drippings have coated the bottom of the oven in a black, chalky mess.

"Dad, you're supposed to cook the roast in the pan," I shout from the kitchen. He doesn't respond. I hear the plastic of the smoke detector crack, and the sound of the plastic cover hitting the hallway floor.

I walk back into the hallway, but Dad has abandoned the broken smoke detector, leaving the broom handle lying against the wall and the smoke detector on the floor. He returns to his leather recliner and resumes watching *The O'Reilly Factor*.

"Dad? What are we going to do about dinner?" I ask him, even as he's fixated on the television.

"Here," he says, digging around in his pocket and retrieving a crumpled ten dollar bill. "Go order a pizza."

Dad has no idea how much things cost. He thinks a family of eight can eat happily on $5 a day.

Mom arrives home an hour later. She's carrying two huge accordion files full of paper and a laptop bag, looking like the breadwinner she now is.

"Is something burning?" Mom asks me, nose in the air.

"Not exactly," I say.

"Where's your father?" she demands, after she sees the mess of the roast. Mom has that clipped tone she saves for serious arguments. Now, I suppose, would not be the best time to ask if I can move back into my old room.

The three of us eat pizza in relative silence. Mom is angry at Dad. I can tell because she is pretending he is not sitting at the other end of the table. She looks at me, but never at the other end to Dad. Dad has his head down as usual, hunched far over his dinner plate—the best angle at which to shove pizza in his mouth at light speed.

"The foundation is leaning again," Mom says, to a spot somewhere over Dad's head.

"Well, I can't see how we can afford to fix it now," Dad grumbles, between forkfuls.

"I think we should take out another home equity loan," she says.

Dad just grunts.

"How's your new roommate working out?" Mom asks me, ever the good hostess.

"That apartment," Dad barks, immediately. "How many times do I have to tell you, you can't afford that place?"

"Would you quit pestering the poor girl about her apartment?" Mom shouts, suddenly, from the far end of the table. Mom, who rarely raises her voice indoors, much less at the dinner table, causes us to jump. "She's gotten a roommate. That shows fiscal responsibility."

"Doris, she's still living beyond her means, and if it had been up to me, we'd have taught our *children* the real *value* of money."

Mom turns beet red.

"Since *when* did you care about *parenting*?" Mom's voice is thunderous. "You couldn't be bothered with even doing the *smallest* of things. I don't see why *now* you're taking such an interest. I was the one who raised our children. *Not* you."

"Doris, I don't think this is proper dinner conversation," Dad says quietly. This is usually Mom's cue to back down, recover her composure, and apologize for her outburst.

"That's IT," yells Mom, tossing down her linen napkin onto her piece of pizza. "I want a divorce."

"Doris," Dad says, unfazed. "I think you'd better calm down."

"I'm tired of being calm," Mom declares.

"Be reasonable, Doris," Dad cautions.

"For once, I am, Dennis. I'm leaving."

With that, Mom stomps up the stairs to the bedroom. I can hear her furiously opening and closing dresser drawers.

"Dad?" I question.

"Don't worry," Dad says, going back to eating. "She says she wants a divorce all the time now."

"Don't you think you should listen to her?"

"She'll calm down."

As Dad chews, Mom comes down the stairs dragging a large, wheeled suitcase behind her.

"I'm sorry you had to witness this, Jane," she tells me before she makes her way out the back door.

Dad and I sit at the table, listening to her start up the engine of her Volvo station wagon. We hear her back out of the garage, and watch her lights go down the street.

"Does she always pack a bag, too?" I ask him.

"No," he says, shaking his head. "That's new."

Bewildered and not sure what to do, I spend the night on the couch, waiting, I think, for Mom to return. She doesn't.

Dad, who put on such a nonchalant front, becomes a bit more rattled in the morning, when it's evident Mom stayed out for the night.

"She'll come back," he says, but with a little less confidence than the night before.

"Maybe you should try calling her sister's," I suggest.

"I will," says Dad, who is clearly still in denial. "If she doesn't call me in an hour or two, I will."

I sigh and shake my head.

I call in sick to my temp job and wait most of the afternoon and into the night, but there's still no sign of Mom. Not sure what else to do, I take the train back to my apartment, leaving Dad sitting by the phone in his recliner.

When I get to my apartment, it's wall-to-wall people and there's serious techno bass thudding from my old stereo, and someone has moved the furniture against the walls, and people are dancing in the middle of my living room. In my kitchen, there's a beer keg, and the air is thick with pot smoke.

"RON!" I shout, enraged, pushing my way through the crowd of barely clad groupies that are gyrating to the sound of some awful dance music. I bump into Ganesha, who's doing some sort of swirling circle of a dance on my ottoman.

"What are all these people doing here?" I shout at her. She shrugs.

"Record launch party," she shouts back to me, "for Sink Gunk."

I find Ron smoking a joint on my fire escape, talking to his bandmates, Russ and Joe.

"You have to get these people out of here," I shout at Ron.

"Chill, Jane, geez," he says. "It's just a little party."

"Ron, this is MY apartment. You have NO right to invite people over."

Just then, I hear a crashing sound coming from my living room. It sounds suspiciously like someone broke my vintage porcelain cat clock.

"I think you all should leave," I say.

"Hey, dude, calm down," Ron says.

"HEY!" comes a loud voice from above our heads. It's Landlord Bob.

"WHAT ZOO DOING DOWN THERE?" he shouts.

"Celebrating, dude," Ron yells back. "Want a cold one?" Ron attempts to offer Landlord Bob a beer across two stories.

Landlord Bob considers this a moment.

"BE RIGHT DOWNZ," he says, tightening the belt of his pink terrycloth robe.

Great. Perfect. Just what I need.

"See, Jane? All you have to do is be NICE to people and they really respond," Ron says. "No need for all the hostility all the time."

"I AM NOT HOSTILE," I shout.

"Dude, you SO need to get wasted," Joe tells me.

"I'm going to call the cops," I threaten, but even I don't believe me.

"Jane, maybe you should go lie down," Ron says, putting his arm around my shoulder. I bat it away.

"Ron's the one with the broken heart, here," Russ says. "Maybe you should show him a little sympathy."

"Yeah, this is a record launch slash who-needs-that-bitch-anyway party," Joe clarifies.

"Hey, don't talk about Missy like that," Ron says.

"I don't care what kind of party it is, you can't have it," I say, resolute.

"Didn't I tell you she still had the hots for me?" Ron asks Russ and Joe. They nod knowingly.

"I do NOT," I say.

"Jane, it's so obvious how jealous you were of Missy, and now that she's gone you think you're going to make the moves on me. But, look, it's OVER, OK? I just am not attracted to you," Ron says, patting my shoulder sympathetically. "It's time you move on."

"I have moved on," I say, helplessly. "You're the one who keeps coming around here. You're the one who moved in."

"I moved in for Missy," he says.

"I am not still attracted to you," I protest.

"Whatever you say, babe. *Whatever* you say."

Disgusted, I go back inside.

Landlord Bob, who knows better than to come down his own rickety fire escape, has entered through my front door, which is wide open. He's got a beer in one hand already.

"Count that toward back rent," I tell him.

"OH, ZIS REMINDS ME," he says, digging around in the front pocket of his bathrobe. He pulls out a crumpled piece of paper and hands it to me.

"What's this?" I ask, taking it by the thumb and forefinger. Anything that has touched Landlord Bob's bathrobe is contaminated.

"EVICTION NOTICE, YES?" he says. "ZOO OUT OF ZHERE."

"What did you lose on this time? The Bulls?" I ask.

Landlord Bob shrugs. "DOG RACING," he says.

"Great. Just great," I say.

"HEY, MY DOGGIE, HE ALMOST WON."

"This is not fair," I say.

"JANEZ, MY COUSIN, HE PAY TWO MONTHS' RENT IN ADVANCE FOR YOUR NICE APART-

MENT. IN A WEEK, I CHANGE LOCKS, YES? UN-
LESS YOU CAN OFFER ME MORE, EH?"

"Bob, I'm not going to get in a bidding war with your
cousin," I spit. I can tell it's going to be pointless arguing
with him. He holds up his beer as if toasting my eviction
and takes a deep gulp.

Somehow, above the din of the music, I hear the
phone ringing. I manage to unearth the receiver under
piles of used cocktail napkins and answer it.

It's Mom.

"I just wanted to see if you were OK," Mom says.

"Mom, of course I'm all right, but where are you?" I
squeeze myself into a hall closet to get some quiet to hear.

"Never mind that now. I'm fine."

"Mom, Dad's really worried about you and he really
feels badly about what happened," I say, even though he
never actually voiced either of these sentiments.

"Jane, your father and I haven't been right for awhile,"
Mom tells me.

"Mom . . ." I start.

"And I just need some time to think about things,"
she says.

"Mom, I think maybe you should talk to Dad."

"I will, soon, I promise," Mom says.

Someone crashes into the closet door, and I can't
quite hear what Mom says next.

"What's that?" I shout into the receiver, but all I hear
is the dial tone.

· · ·

A bit dazed, I open the closet door.

Can more go wrong?

I look up and see that Ganesha is wearing one of my scarves around her head. A quick glance around the throng of dancers and I see more articles of my clothing dotted throughout the crowd. I go into my room, where there's a half-clad couple exchanging bodily fluids on my unmade bed.

"You!" I shout. "You both, out!"

They don't even stop their tongue-kissing to look at me.

My room is a disaster area. My closet's been pilfered, and my clothes are on the floor, tossed haphazardly over the closet door, spread out under the couple humping on my bed.

I am trying to get my favorite pair of jeans out from under them when I hear a pounding on the door that's loud enough to be heard above the din of techno bass. I push through the crowd to my front door and there's a uniformed officer on my porch.

I nearly faint.

I expect him to whip out a warrant for my arrest on felony burglary charges.

Instead he says, "We've had a noise complaint, ma'am," resting his hands on his utility belt, inches from a very large gun. I am sure it is Mrs. Slatter who complained. Now that she's back from Vegas, I'm sure she's been calling the police every hour on the hour, given the number of people in my apartment.

A quick look behind me and I take in the scene as he sees it: loud, thumping music that is shaking the walls. An apartment jammed full of drunk, disorderly groupies smoking pot. Bob in his pink bathrobe. Vishnu, who looks like she's in the process of removing her shirt.

"Can I speak to a Jane McGregor? The person who lives here?" he asks me.

"Er," I pause. Now would be a good time to lie. "I don't know her."

"Jane!" shouts Ron from the back of the room. "Jane McGregor! I've got something that will cheer you up."

I ignore him.

The officer looks at me.

"Jane!" he cries again. "JAAAAAAAAAAAAAAAA-AAANE."

He's staring right at me. So is the officer.

"You don't know her?" the officer asks me skeptically.

"Er," I say.

Ron, who is coming closer, is doing a few wild, gyrating spin-moves to the dance music.

"Right, well, I'll turn it down, officer," I say.

"Turn it down now," he says.

"I will," I say, watching Ron making progress toward me.

"Now," he says.

"OK."

" 'Now' means I'm not leaving until the music is turned down," he says.

Ron is almost to me. He does one last spin-move,

during which his curled-up flip-flops get trapped in the giant cuffs of his oversized pants. Flailing, he wildly flaps his arms, looking like some scrawny, plucked bird trying to take flight. I see him coming in slow motion, his long, wirelike body a tangle of limbs headed for me. He collides into me, sending me into the officer, and the impact of the collisions shoots a small baggie of white pills into the air, which I see explode over our heads as we tumble into the hallway.

We land in a heap on the floor, and a small shower of white E pills rains down upon our heads.

The officer sighs loudly, before struggling to his feet.

"I really wish you hadn't done that," he says, dusting off small white pills from the front of his uniform. He grabs me by the arm and lifts me to my feet. Ron, who is notorious for getting out of tight spots, points to me.

"Those aren't mine, officer. They're hers," he says, beating me to the punch by about half a second. I would be quicker, except the fall knocks the wind out of me.

"Would you believe they're aspirin?" I cough, lamely.

The officer is examining one of the pills.

"Aspirin, right," he says, taking me by the arm. "Let's go."

"Go? Where?"

"I'm going to have to take you both in," the officer tells me. "Don't try anything funny, all right?"

I can't think of a single, solitary joke, anyway.

IN THE CIRCUIT COURT OF COOK COUNTY, ILLINOIS
MUNICIPAL DEPARTMENT

Robert Mercier *Plaintiff*	No. 08071999
	Rent amount claimed <u>$7,025</u>
Jane McGregor *Defendant*	Trial date: 5/30/02 Time 9:30 A.M.

SUMMONS FOR TRIAL

The plaintiff(s) named above has filed a complaint in this court to have you evicted. A true and complete copy of this complaint is attached.

THEREFORE, you, the defendant(s) is/are hereby summoned to appear in person before this Court on <u>May 30, 2002 at 9:30 A.M.</u>, at which time and place a trial will occur.

Signed:

DOROTHY BROWN
CLERK OF THE CIRCUIT COURT,
COOK COUNTY, ILLINOIS

<u>IMPORTANT INFORMATION FOR DEFENDANTS:</u>

ON THE DATE AND AT THE TIME SHOWN ABOVE, THE COURT WILL DECIDE WHETHER YOU WILL HAVE TO MOVE OR WHETHER YOU CAN CONTINUE TO STAY. YOU MUST BE ON TIME FOR COURT. HAVING TO GO TO WORK, BEING ILL, OR DOING SOMETHING ELSE DOES NOT MEAN YOU CAN MISS YOUR COURT DATE. IF YOU DO NOT COME TO COURT, THE COURT MAY ORDER YOU TO MOVE WITHIN A PERIOD OF NO MORE THAN TEN BUSINESS DAYS.

19

$\mathcal{R}$on and I don't speak as we sit side by side in the back of the squad car.

Ron attempts a conversation with a "Dude, this sucks," but I ignore him. I am so angry at him, I could spit.

At the county jail, which looks less like a jail and more like a really old college dorm, I am booked, fingerprinted, and photographed. Of all the people at Ron's party, I can't believe that we're the only ones who get dragged away in handcuffs. Ron and I are separated after the booking, when Ron shouts to me, "Don't tell them anything until you get an attorney," which causes all the cops in the place to give me a suspicious look.

"I don't have anything to tell, you moron," I shout back at Ron.

. . .

I am put in an open cell-like room with a few metal cots cemented to the walls. It looks more like a really poorly funded camp than a jail, and I almost expect to find the guards wearing red T-shirts with Camp Woebegone on them. In the corner, there's a pay phone, with a line of three by it. I take my place in line and try not to make eye contact.

One woman, who smells strongly of gin, is passed out in the corner, and next to her are two very pregnant women sitting and talking.

I have never had much upper body strength. I suspect if any one of the women wanted to take me—even one of the pregnant ones—she could. But they seem less interested in fighting and more interested in talking about whether or not J. Lo has had a butt implant.

"You know that's just not natural," one of them is saying.

"It is," another answers.

"It doesn't *move* like a natural butt."

"What does that even mean?" the other one says.

And on and on.

I feel like I'm in a salon, not a jail.

"What are you in for?" says a woman to my right. She's wearing a bandanna across her forehead like the Karate Kid.

"My ex-boyfriend threw Ecstasy pills into an officer's face," I say, and then immediately wish I'd said murder.

Bandanna woman laughs. "I boosted my ex-boyfriend's car," she informs me.

The woman on the phone starts to yell.

"You just tell Marla she better stay away from my man," the woman says. "I mean it. I don't want to find *one* of that skank's Lee Press-Ons in my bedroom, or I swear, I'll kill that bitch."

It figures that women let men drive them to jail. What sort of power do they have over us anyway? It just doesn't seem fair.

I finally get the phone after waiting an hour, and I call my dad collect. For health reasons, I hold out the phone about a foot from my ear, which makes hearing and speaking difficult.

Dad answers, sounding bleary, like he's been sleeping.

"Charges? What charges?" Dad is shouting at the operator who is trying to get him to accept the collect call.

"Dad, it's Jane. I'm in jail," I say. "Accept the charges!"

The operator asks Dad again.

"Who?"

"Jane. Your daughter, Jane," I say, but the operator is blocking me out.

"We don't need any vinyl siding," Dad shouts, and hangs up the phone.

I sigh.

I call Todd next. Surprisingly, he does accept the collect call charges. It seems he's been expecting me to call from jail.

"Why didn't you tell me about Mom?" Todd cries,

first thing. He doesn't even seem interested in the fact that I'm in jail.

"Todd, I was going to call, but everything happened so fast."

"Well, you *should* have called me. Mom called me herself and told me about everything."

"Did she tell you where she was?"

"No, but she said she's talked to a lawyer."

"Really?" My heart sinks. As much as I think my dad has been a terrible pill the last few months (and really, almost their entire marriage), the thought of my parents separating makes me feel sad and more than a little guilty. It's clearly partly my fault for bad-mouthing Dad constantly and for living in an apartment I can't afford.

"Who's going to take care of Dad?" Todd asks, as if Dad is an invalid. "What will he eat?"

"It's about time he learned to cook for himself, I think," I say.

"Excuse me, but I *really* need to use that phone," says the woman standing behind me. I can only imagine she is a prostitute, since she's wearing silver platform boots and a flamingo-pink micro-miniskirt.

"Enough parent-talk, Todd. Can you get me out of jail?"

"Everything is *always* about you, isn't it?" Todd sighs.

"I'm in jail. Forgive me if I can't afford to be sensitive at the moment," I say.

"What have you done this time?" Todd asks me, as if I am a repeat felon.

"It's a long story," I say. "It's not my fault."

"It never is," Todd says.

I give the short version of events. Todd is laughing so hard on the other end of the phone he can barely talk.

"That's not helping me," I say.

"Only you, Jane," he manages after taking a few deep breaths. "Only you would end up in jail because of an ex-boyfriend drug-dealer. Wait until Kyle hears about this."

I panic. "You CAN'T tell him," I shout.

I can't imagine anything worse than Kyle knowing.

"I am so going to tell him," Todd says, reverting to a kind of Valley girl lisp.

"You can't. I'll kill you. I swear."

"I am going to call him right now."

"TODD," I scream, desperate. "Please don't. PLEASE. He'll never let me hear the end of it. Todd, I'm begging you. Don't."

"Maybe I will. Maybe I won't."

"TODD! If you tell him, I'll tell Mom and Dad who REALLY broke grandmother's antique vase."

"I doubt they'll care about that now," Todd says, but he sounds uncertain.

"Mom cried about that for a week," I say.

"Well," Todd hesitates. "Breaking a vase doesn't compare to jail."

Everything is always a contest to Todd.

"Just don't tell Kyle. I will KILL you."

"Maybe," he says.

"Now, will you get me out of here?"

"OK, I'll make some calls," Todd says, switching into problem-solver mode. "Oh, and Jane. Don't drop the soap."

"That's only in men's prison," I snap.

I suppose it is official. I am now not only an unemployed degenerate, but also a jailbird. I think this is about as far as I can fall.

I've never wished so hard to be back at my parents' house, even if it may be a broken home. There are many worse things, I decide, than having to go live at home again. Jail is definitely worse.

I spend the night awake, fearing that one of the pregnant women might stab me with a shiv while I sleep (I've seen *Oz,* I know how it is), and blinking back the garish fluorescent lights overhead that never go off. It's almost like being trapped in a cubicle, except for the gray metal bars and the fact that instead of plastic potted plants as decoration, there's a small pool of vomit in the corner, next to the seatless aluminum toilet.

The next morning, as most of the other women get out, I sit and wait.

And wait.

And wait some more.

My clothes are beginning to smell. I wish that during my layoff period I'd taken some Zen meditation classes. They would have come in handy now.

I decide that perhaps I let things go too far. That perhaps my whole problem is that I don't set up boundaries with people. That despite the fact that I can be hostile and generally unfriendly, no one seems to take me seriously. I must look like the sort of person people can walk all over. I must look like a wimp.

How else to explain the fact that my apartment is now a halfway house for the city's worst degenerates? Or that I'm in jail because I'm friends with the city's worst degenerates? When I get out of jail, I decide, I am going to work on setting up boundaries. I'm going to work on telling people "no." Maybe that's my whole problem. Maybe it's not that men like Mike take advantage of me, but that I let them do it.

The guard calls my name around ten, when I'm starved, and I think I might eat my own shirt. Todd is waiting for me in the adjoining room. The minute I walk through, he snaps my picture with the digital camera.

"Blackmail material," he says.

"Great," I say.

"You smell," he tells me when I get close enough to punch him in the arm.

"Thanks," I say.

"You know I had to take a sick day for this," he says. Todd never calls into work sick, and he hardly ever takes his vacation time. He hoards it as if, like precious metals, it will gain value over time.

"I appreciate it," I say.

"Do you have any idea how much it cost to bail you out?" he asks me. He doesn't wait for me to finish. "Let's just say you really owe me."

"OK, I get it," I say.

"I'm thinking indentured servitude," he says.

"Fine," I say.

"You're lucky Mom isn't around at the moment to see you like this," he says.

"Great," I say.

"Between jail and losing your jobs, you sure make it easy to be the good kid in the family," Todd says.

Todd drives me home in relative silence. He asks only what jail was like, taking an unusual interest in small details like the group toilet.

"Todd, are you gloating?" I ask him.

"Maybe," he says.

At my apartment, I discover that Landlord Bob has made good on his promise to change my locks. My key no longer works. I ask Todd to wait for me.

"What's wrong *now*?" Todd whines.

I am buzzing Landlord Bob's apartment, but he refuses to answer. I know he is in there, I can hear his raspy breathing, but he refuses to open the door.

Finally, after ten minutes of pounding and tapping out messages in Morse code, he shouts, "GOEZ AWAYZ. NO TALK."

"Bob—open up and come talk to me like a man!"

I don't know why I felt the need to add "like a man" because Bob in his pink fuzzy robe is not much of a man to begin with. Still, I have the court notice in my hand and it says I have a place to sleep for another twenty-four hours.

"At least unlock it for me and let me get my clothes," I say.

Bob considers this a moment. "NO!" he shouts.

I kick his door hard in frustration, then I remember my bedroom window, and in a few minutes I am snaking up my fire escape like Ron and attempting to sneak into my own apartment. The window slides open, and I sneak inside. There's no sign of the muses or any party-goers. I try not to assess the damage to my apartment, although I can see plenty of empty beer cans and there's the distinct smell of a fraternity house. Instead, I run to my bedroom and throw clothes in a bag, along with Mike's folder from under my mattress.

"You've been evicted?" Todd cries, when I come down carrying my duffel bag. "Unbelievable."

"Can I stay with you?" I ask, hopeful.

Todd scoffs. "Well, you can if you'd like, but my girl-friend's moved in."

"Deena? You let Deena move in with you?"

"We've gotten to *that* stage," he says.

"Todd," I say, flabbergasted. "You *never* get to that stage."

"Well, what can I say? Even I'm not immune to love."

"Now that's a serious personal milestone for you, Todd. I'm really proud."

"Oh, stop it," Todd sighs, but he's smiling. "At any rate, it's probably better if you go back and stay with Dad."

"Great. But I need you to take me someplace first," I say.

Todd pulls up in front of the Kinko's near Dad's house and puts the car in park. Todd has assumed I am making photocopies of my resume.

"I'm surprised you want to do this now," he says. "Surprised but impressed."

"I'll be fifteen minutes," I say.

Dusk falls and the wind picks up as I duck into Kinko's. Instantly, I smell Wite Out and photocopier toner. There are college kids on the computers in the corner, dark circles under their eyes, hunched over their grande lattes. I'm going to finally make Mike pay, I think. I'm going to make two copies of his personnel file and send one to his fiancée and one to CNBC.

I pick a machine, put the card in, and start making copies. One piece of paper comes out before the machine jams.

I glance over my shoulder at the Kinko's worker behind the counter who is trying to pick up a stick of a woman wearing red-striped jogging pants. She's trying to get pricing on spiral-bound notebooks, and he's trying to look down her shirt.

I move over to the next empty copier, and start copying.

The second machine spits out a piece of paper that's black. Entirely black. I touch it and my hands come back covered in toner—the powdery substance flaking off my fingers and spilling onto the toe of one of my shoes.

I look up, but the Kinko's guy is still occupied. There are no other empty machines.

I wonder if this is a sign.

At the front service counter, I wait in line behind the woman in the red-striped jogging pants. She can't seem to decide whether she wants a blue binding or a red binding for her term paper. The Kinko's employee can't seem to decide whether he wants to concentrate on her left or right boob.

I look at the folder in my hands. Mike deserves it and much more. He deserves to lose his job, and his fiancée, and his new shiny silver Porsche. If there were justice in the world, these files would be printed on a double-spread in the *Chicago Tribune* and the *Chicago Sun-Times,* and there'd be a billboard on Waveland, outside Wrigley Field, detailing his many misdeeds.

He deserves this and more. He deserves to suffer.

But this won't get me my job back. It won't erase the outstanding debt on my credit cards, or get me my back rent to save my apartment, which at this point, is probably a lost cause. It won't undo the gap on my resume, or the fact that I spent the night in jail.

Nope. It won't do any of those things.

I get out of line and head toward the door. On my way out, I drop Mike's folder into the trash and turn my back on it. I don't know if that makes me feel better or not, but I'm pretty sure it's the right thing to do.

"That was quick," Todd says when I get back in the car.

"Line was too long," I say. "I'll do it later."

My parents' house—my mother's pristine house—looks like I do the morning after a drinking binge. Disheveled and unkempt. Old newspapers are tossed everywhere. Trash cans are overflowing. There are two empty cardboard pizza boxes lying facedown on the kitchen floor. Dishes are piled in the sink; magazines are tossed haphazardly throughout the living room. I have not seen the house looking so out of sorts since I lived here my senior year of high school.

Three days without Mom and Dad has let everything go.

When I walk into the house, I expect Dad to start yelling, but instead, he sits up from his recliner and rubs his eyes. He's unshaven, and his hair is sticking straight up. He looks like he hasn't left his chair in days.

"You OK?" he asks me. There are no accusations of drug abuse, or lectures about how I've disappointed the family. Dad looks tired and for once, unsure of what he should be doing.

Dad has no reaction when I tell him I'm moving home. He just nods at me and tells me to try to keep the noise down so he can hear the phone if Mom calls. I can't believe my parents are breaking up. It feels surreal, like I'm watching an after-school special, except I know there's not going to be a happy ending.

My mom has kept my room exactly how I left it at age eighteen. There are The Cure posters on the wall, along with Siouxsie and the Banshees and Sting. It is like the world froze in the year 1988. I half expect to look under my bed and see black nail polish bottles, goth lace stockings, or clunky military boots. I was a morose teenager, so it's no wonder I grew into a morose adult. There is not a single color in my room. Even my comforter is black.

I wonder who will own this room now. Mom? Dad? Will they sell the house? I try not to think much more about it.

I crawl under my comforter and try to sleep.

But I can't sleep.

Because my mom has gone missing on her own accord, and may or may not be back, and my parents' thirty-five-year union is disintegrating before my very eyes. And I realize, this is probably my fault for failing so miserably at the basic responsibilities of adulthood: finding your own food and shelter and avoiding jail. I was the straw that broke the back of their marriage, and this makes me feel two inches tall.

I need advice on what to do next, on how to fix things, and I find myself wanting to talk to Kyle. But then, that's impossible, because I've made a mess of that relationship, too.

I think it must be the fact that I am again in my old room, that all of the world's greatest problems boil down to boy troubles. It must be that I am regressing to my junior high school days of torturing myself with unrequited love of boys about as sensitive as lava rocks. I'd be thinking about the universal truth of Robert Smith's lyrics, while they would be trying to get to third base so they could tell their friends what it smelled like.

I sigh, roll over, and wonder for the first time if I might be clinically depressed. Clearly, something is wrong with me.

I call Jean Naté and discover that she's found someone to hire permanently, who isn't me. Apparently, even from the least appealing jobs, going to jail and missing work will get you fired.

"We just didn't feel you had the right qualifications for the job," she tells me.

"I understand," I say.

"If you'd had more filing experience," she says.

"Really, it's no problem," I say.

For once, I am not upset about being let go from a job.

There is no word from Mom, and Dad and I sink into our own silent, separate depressions as we sit together watching daytime television.

"Why are they bothering with those damn DNA tests?" Dad shouts.

I laugh.

"I *know,* that's *exactly* what I said," I say.

We look at each other and share a smile.

"I really screwed things up with your Mom, didn't I?" he asks me.

Dad looks so shrunken, so completely defeated, I feel like crying.

"Well . . ." I say.

"Go ahead, tell me the truth, I can take it," he says.

"Dad, she's had a hard time of it. Working and all. You haven't exactly been supportive."

"I *thought* I was being supportive—in my own way," Dad says.

"By supportive, I mean cooking your own meals and doing your own laundry."

"I did do one load of laundry," Dad insists.

"But one load, Dad, come on, that sounds pathetic," I say.

"You're right. I know you're right," he says.

"Maybe you should try finding out where she is," I suggest.

"I have," Dad sighs, exasperated. "She's not at her sister's."

"Have you tried calling her at work? Sending flowers?"

Dad's face lights up.

"I will," he says, getting up out of his recliner. Then, he pauses. "Where is it that she works again?"

Citibank Financial Offices
Customer Service
Wilmington, Delaware 19801

Jane McGregor
3335 Kenmore Ave.
Chicago, IL 60657

May 13, 2002

Dear Ms. McGregor,

Thank you for writing us and apologizing for not making your minimum credit card payments this last month, and for your desire to successfully complete the twelve steps of Spending Addiction.

While we appreciate your contrite manner, we're afraid this is not going to make your financial obligations to us disappear.

Please contact our representative so we can work out a payment plan for your MasterCard.

Sincerely,
Todd Matthew
Citibank Customer Service Manager

20

Dad is not exactly successful with Mom. But he's not totally unsuccessful, either.

Mom does not take him back, but she agrees to a trial separation, instead of an immediate divorce (which is what she'd been planning).

In the meantime, I am still living in my old room. One day blends into the next, and Dad's time is spent reading self-help books and watching his newly acquired library of Dr. John Gray relationship tapes. He's attacking the salvaging of his relationship with Mom like he would yard work, with both sleeves rolled up. I haven't seen him this energized in years.

Mom returns a week later to gather up more clothes. She has rented an apartment downtown, closer to her work, and she says she needs a period of separation from Dad to decide what her next move will be.

Mom is more understanding than I thought when I tell her about my night in jail.

"We all make mistakes," is what she says.

"I want you to know your dad and me . . . it isn't your fault," Mom adds.

"I know," I say, even though I can't help but think that if I'd given up the apartment sooner, maybe I wouldn't have started the argument that ended in my mom storming out of her own house with a packed bag.

"And your apartment has nothing to do with this either," she says.

Saturday morning, I wake up to the sound of pounding on my door. Dad is shouting at me to "get a move on" like he did when I was in high school.

I glance over at my clock. It says 8:00 A.M. I squeeze my eyes shut again.

"Your brother's making breakfast," he shouts through my door. "And you're going to damn well enjoy it while it's hot."

Dad is often shouting at me to enjoy things. "I hope you enjoyed yourself" is one of Dad's favorite phrases. He sounds almost back to his old self. Almost.

After I don't answer him, he adds, "I sense hostility from you, Jane. You know hostility is not good for our relationship."

This is the *new* Dad. The Dad concerned with relationships and self-help books.

"As a woman, I understand you need time in your well, but now is not the time," Dad is saying.

"I'm coming," I say, rubbing my eyes and yawning. I'd rather do anything than listen to Dad's self-help mumbo-jumbo.

I stumble out of my bedroom, tugging on my old flannel pajamas, the ones with the Dalmatians and fire hydrants on them, and half slide, half slouch down the stairs. I can smell strawberry waffles.

"There she is, Sleeping Beauty," Todd quips, flipping over some sausage on the grill.

In the dining room, I skid to a stop, nearly falling on my face, at the sight of Kyle sitting at the breakfast table, sipping a cup of coffee and reading the newspaper. I blink, but he's still there.

"Why are you always so surprised to see me?" Kyle asks me, because I guess I look shocked.

"Uh," I say. I can't seem to speak.

"I heard about what happened, and I'm sorry," he says.

I still don't know what to say. I'm having trouble not rubbing my eyes and doing a double-take. I tug on the corner of my flannel pajama top. I am all too acutely aware that he thinks I am a nutcase, someone who flies into jealous rages for no reason and who commits felonies.

Kyle has on a long-sleeved T-shirt and jeans. His

hair is covered neatly under a baseball cap. He has never looked so utterly delicious. Just looking at him hurts.

I am painfully aware that the ratty old flannel pajamas I am wearing have a hole in the left leg, midthigh. Also, I haven't showered in a couple of days. I must smell like a barnyard. I sit and fight with the urge to stare at Kyle and demand to know what he's doing here and, of course, if he still thinks I'm a psycho.

"What are you doing here?" I ask, unable to contain myself a moment longer.

"He came over because we asked him to help get you out of this fix," Dad barks.

I turn bright red. My dad, unlike myself, has never been shy about demanding help from people he knows.

"I know a few good lawyers," Kyle says.

"You really don't have to do this," I mumble into my plate, not daring to look Kyle in the eye.

"I don't mind," he says.

I fight the urge to bolt up the stairs and cover myself with a robe. I'm pretty sure the baggy flannel does nothing for my figure.

"There's someone we want you to talk to, Jane," Todd begins.

"He's a defense attorney," Kyle says. "A good one."

At this moment, I would rather be anywhere but here. I take the name and number that Kyle has written on a piece of paper.

I still can't look him in the eye.

"Well, I'd better be going then," Kyle says, abruptly standing and straightening his baseball cap.

I feel a sharp pang. He's leaving. Already. The worn doggie flannel pajamas are men repellant.

Dad is up on his feet and vigorously shaking Kyle's hand. "You sure you don't want to stay for breakfast?" Dad asks him.

"No, I really ought to be going," Kyle says casually, before disappearing out of the kitchen and through the front door.

He hates me.

Clearly.

He still hates me. He still thinks I'm a crazy woman. And why wouldn't he? I've given him no reason to think otherwise. First, there was the burst of insane jealousy, and then I get arrested. Not exactly the calling cards of a sane person.

"None of this would've happened if you had just listened to me about that apartment," Dad starts. "I knew you couldn't afford it, and now look at what's happened."

Something inside me cracks.

"Would you STOP, Dad? I know I'm a complete disappointment, you don't have to remind me what a complete and utter failure I am."

My voice is starting to waver. I can feel the hot tears pressing at the backs of my eyes.

"I KNOW I can't do anything right," I say, voice

wobbly and bottom lip quivering. "I know you hate me. I know you wish I was more like Todd."

With that, I flee the table, run up the stairs, and bury myself under my covers.

A few minutes later I hear a soft knock at my door.

"Go away," I say.

"Janie," says Dad, using the name he hasn't called me since I was in grade school. "Janie, let me in."

Reluctantly, I get up and move the chair I've haphazardly thrown in front of the door as a makeshift barricade.

My dad, who has never been good at comforting, being the opposite of the dad in *Sixteen Candles,* awkwardly places his hand on my shoulder.

"Your mother and I don't hate you," he says. "You know we love you very much."

"I don't see how you can," I say. "I've made a big mess of everything."

"Everybody makes a mess of things once in a while," Dad says. "Look at me. I've lost my job, and your mother is moving out."

"Are you guys going to get a divorce?" I ask, sounding like a bad child actress in an after-school special.

"I don't know," Dad says, and I realize he's as lost as I am, that he doesn't have any more answers than I do.

"I've made a lot of mistakes," he continues. "I'm just not sure."

"Maybe if you tried harder," I say.

"I am going to try," Dad says. "But sometimes there's nothing you can do to make a person love you."

I wonder if he's not just speaking about Mom. I wonder if he's referring to Kyle.

Dad sits down on the bed next to me and gives me a hard squeeze. Dad's hugs are like bear hugs, rough and jolting.

"Do you remember the time when you got stuck on the roof?"

"Yes." I was seven. Todd and some of his friends took sport in launching some of my Barbie dolls on top of the roof. So I climbed a nearby tree to try and rescue some of them. But when I tried to climb down again, I lost my nerve.

"You were always the kid who jumped in with both feet without looking first," Dad says.

"I guess I haven't matured all that much," I say.

"My point is," Dad says, "that being fearless means that you don't always think about the consequences."

"I don't feel fearless," I say.

"You are. You always have been. You were always the one who wanted to go on the roller coasters. Todd was always the one who would cry even on the kiddie rides."

I laugh. He did used to cry on all the kiddie rides, even the slow-moving ones.

"I don't want you to be Todd," he says. "I love him, but one Todd is enough."

Dad clears his throat.

"And, if it seems like I'm nagging, it's just because I

care about you. And the only reason I keep bringing up your apartment is that I never wanted you to leave in the first place," Dad says, squeezing me harder.

"So, it's OK if I move back in with you permanently?" I ask, hopeful.

"Well, let's see what Kyle's lawyer friend says first."

The Executive Touch
Executive Headhunters
59 West Grand Ave.
Chicago, IL 60610

Jane McGregor
3335 Kenmore Ave.
Chicago, IL 60657

May 15, 2002

Dear Ms. McGregor,

It was a pleasure to receive your resume, and we would like to commend you on a stellar career in top management at many blue chip companies. It's not every day we receive a resume of this caliber, or are lucky enough to meet the youngest female CEO of Hershey.

After verifying your resume, we'd like to meet with you in person. We have a good many executive positions we are hoping to fill.

I look forward to meeting you in person.

Sincerely,
Jordan Carroll
Executive Placement Officer
The Executive Touch

21

I call up Kyle's attorney friend Dan Schmidt, and he agrees to meet me in person.

His office is of a decent size, and he has a giant leather chair with arms. It nearly swallows him up, because Dan Schmidt is no taller than my shoulder.

When he stands, I can see almost the entire top of his head. He is shorter than me by four inches. Maybe even five. I could pick him up, roll him into a ball, and slip him in my tote bag. He's that tiny.

"Jane, Dan," he says, approaching me first and shaking my hand vigorously with three hard pumps. "I understand you've gotten yourself into a little trouble?"

I nod and give him the short version of events: Ron, the Ecstasy pills, the officer, my night in jail, and my eviction.

Dan Schmidt lets out a low-pitched whistle.

"Well, first things first," he says, shuffling the papers around his desk like a three-card-monte street dealer. "I'm pretty confident that the drug charges we can probably get dismissed, especially if you can find your friend Ron to testify, or some other party-goers who may have witnessed the events. Second, even if we can't get them dismissed, you have no criminal record, so we can probably get the assistant D.A. to plead down the charges to a misdemeanor."

My eyes must light up, because he's quick to add, "Not that I'm promising anything here, mind you."

"Right," I say quickly. I look up at the law degree hanging on the wall behind his head. It reads, "Daniel E. Schmidt."

"What's the E stand for?" I say.

"Let's not get personal, OK?" he says.

I look down at the floor and notice his feet are about two sizes smaller than mine.

Dan continues. "About the apartment, I'm no expert in tenant law, but if your landlord has changed your locks before your hearing, then that's illegal. I'll write his lawyers a sternly worded letter and see if we can't get them talking about an out-of-court settlement."

At the word "settlement," I feel a hint of hope, like when I buy a scratch-off lotto ticket.

"I can't promise you everything will work out, but I think that we can probably have you out of your lease and free of any liens without actually going to court. Let me see what I can do, OK? OK."

I nod, trying not to look disappointed. This is clearly not the sort of settlement that makes the *Ricki Lake* show, or the kind that involves me getting money.

"I don't think I need to tell you that you've landed yourself in serious trouble and that you should avoid any further confrontations with the law," he says.

"Does that include not paying my credit cards?"

Dan Schmidt smacks his forehead.

"As your attorney, I suggest you sort out your credit," he says.

"I have another problem . . ." I say, thinking about Ferguson, the Maximum Office break-in, and Kyle's advice that I turn myself in.

Dan Schmidt, who is mentally billing me by the hour, nods for me to continue.

I give him the Cliffs Notes version of Maximum Office—including my relationship with Mike and his double life, the prank break-in gone awry, Missy's disappearance, and the missing payroll money.

"I have to say, Jane, that you're one of the more interesting clients I've had lately," he says when I finish.

"Is that a compliment?" I ask him.

"No. It definitely isn't." He sighs.

"Let's take care of the charges that are actually filed against you at the moment," he says. "I'll tap some of my sources in the D.A.'s office and see what I can find out about the case. In the meantime, stay out of trouble, all right?"

"What's this going to cost me?" I ask him.

"No charge," he says, waving his hand. "Kyle Burton and I go way back." I wait for him to elaborate but he doesn't. Instead he stands, showing our meeting is over.

I am thinking about why Kyle would ask one of his friends to represent me for free, when I look up and see a billboard advertising an agency to help people get out of debt. "Getting evicted? Over your credit limits? Maxed out? We can help!"

For the first time, I realize this ad is speaking directly to me. I am its target audience.

I decide this is the first step on the path to financial solvency, and while I'm doing responsible things (like consulting with a defense attorney), I might as well start tackling my debt, too.

Credit Counselors U.S.A. is located in a strip mall, crowded in between an adult bookstore and a Weight Watchers. I can see the business logic: put all the things you'd be embarrassed to be seen going into in one place, a one-stop trench-coat/sunglasses sort of place. That way, if you lost your nerve, you'd have nowhere to easily hide. No Subway. No 7-Eleven. Each hiding alternative is worse than the storefront you're supposed to go to in the first place.

Inside Credit Counselors, there are cubes jammed into what I can only guess used to be a Domino's Pizza, since there's still red and blue paint along the walls and an ordering counter up front where you're supposed to sign in.

"Been here before?" asks the woman behind the counter. She's wearing frosted pink eyeshadow and bright white lipliner. Over her head is a large poster that shouts "Be Debt Free!" It has a bald eagle soaring on it.

"No," I say.

"Fill out these," Frosted Pink Eyeshadow tells me, handing me a hot pink clipboard and pointing to a suspicious-looking brown and tan plaid couch that serves as the waiting area.

Reluctantly, I sit. I wish there were an equivalent of paper toilet seat covers you could put on communal couches and chairs in waiting areas, especially waiting areas in government buildings and credit counseling offices. I can only guess, in terms of clientele, that I'm the upper echelon.

I turn my attention to the forms, speeding through the name and address stuff, not bothering to use an alias. I assume this won't help me in court if I claim to be more than one person.

I pause at the line that reads, "Total Credit Card Debt: _____."

Being an art major, I have never been good at math. I have only been good at getting out of math credit requirements.

Let's see. I have four credit cards, all currently at their limits, which, given the additional credit lines opened, probably puts my current debt at somewhere near . . . well, five figures certainly. I round down to be safe. $15,000 sounds like a good number. I'll go with that.

Next line says "Other Debt." Hmmm. Including back rent? I skip that one.

"Any late payments?" I check "yes" and put in parenthesis "all."

Current monthly income? I write, "Varies."

Hmmmm. Even with my poor math skills I know that can't be good.

"Jane McGregor?" calls a woman with rather severe bangs chopped straight across her forehead. "I'm Sheila. Nice to meet you."

Sheila doesn't shake my hand. She keeps her hands firmly in her pockets. I try not to take this personally. I'm sure after a while, you might begin to think that credit card debt is contagious. Or maybe she knows something I don't about that brown couch in the waiting room.

"Please, take a seat."

We're sitting in her tiny cube. It's the tiniest cube I have ever seen. There is not even room for a full desk, only a half desk, and my chair juts out into the main part of the room.

"I'll take those forms," she says. I hand over the clipboard. She reads it, remaining expressionless.

"How many late payments do you have?" she asks me.

"All of them," I say.

"What does that mean?"

"It means all the bills I ever receive are late," I say.

"Give me a number," she says.

"Twelve," I guess.

She looks at me a moment then types in the number without saying anything. I feel like I am in the student health clinic on a college campus and the nurse suspects I have a venereal disease.

She's clicking away on her computer. She has many sets of brochures on her desk. They scream out titles like "Create a Budget!" and "Nine Rules to Money Management" and "Bankruptcy IS NOT the Easy Way Out."

I haven't given much thought to bankruptcy before. That might be the answer—if big corporations can do it, why can't I?

"OK, I have your credit report here," she says, after a moment.

"That was quick," I say. I figured there would be much more on it. That it would take years to pull up. It would have my mug shot on it like a rap sheet, along with all the times I pretended that I lost my Nordstrom's bill.

"Hmmm," she says, looking it over. She's jotting down notes. "All right," she says, ripping off the top of her Post-it note pad and handing it to me. "This is what your debt actually is, according to these records."

I look at the number and blink.

"Is that a two or a one?" I ask, hopefully.

"A two," she says.

She's written down: $28,527.80

"Are you sure?"

"Positive," she says.

That's almost a year's salary.

"That's more than I thought it was," I say.

"It usually is," she says briskly, taking back her Post-it note, and sticking it to the top of my file. My heart is beating a little faster, and my palms are beginning to sweat.

"Right, well, first, we'll consolidate your loans and come out with a figure, roughly . . ." Her nails are clacking against her calculator buttons. She's so quick I can't tell what she's entering. "Four hundred and fifty dollars a month," she says.

I cough.

"I think that's a little out of my price range at the moment," I say.

"Well, if you raise the interest rate and extend the loan, I could drop the payments to . . ." She continues clacking. "Three hundred dollars even."

"How long would I have to pay the loan?"

"Well, probably for fifteen years," she says.

"Ouch," I say.

"Let's get to work on a budget," she says. She gives me a handout that says "Get Back in the Black!!" with two exclamation marks.

At the top of the list is "Know Your Finances."

"I think we've covered this," she says. "Let's move on to 'Set Reasonable Financial Goals.' "

"Did I mention that I was an art major and that I am no good at math?"

Sheila doesn't say anything.

"Just looking at an Excel document makes me sweat," I say.

Sheila looks at me, expressionless, without giving me so much as a weak smile of social obligation.

I can tell this is going to be a long afternoon.

You know you're in trouble financially when even a paid credit counselor can't seem to work out a budget. Sheila has been staring at the figures on her Excel spreadsheet for the better part of a half hour and she still can't get them to work.

"How did you do this to yourself?" Sheila asks me.

"Low self-esteem," I say.

I decide that no matter how hard it is, I'm going to make a budget and stick to it this time. The last time I was responsible enough to think about a budget, I made one out and then stuck it in a desk drawer and never gave it another look again. This time, I'm serious, I think.

And because I am no longer too proud to take a job beneath me, I end up taking up offers of dog walking which come in through Mom, her coworkers, and Todd. Pretty soon I have three or four regular customers, and while it doesn't pay as well as my temp job did, it also causes less chronic depression.

With my meager cash earnings, and not paying rent for a while by laying low with Dad, and by avoiding restaurants, taxis, shoe purchases, and any new make-up, I just might get out of debt within my lifetime. I have actually learned how to save money, instead of instantly blowing it the minute it hits my hot little hands. If I've learned anything from being fired, it's that the financial experts really aren't joking about the necessity of having savings.

I now earn my money $20 at a time scooping up poop from hyperactive terriers. You don't know what sacrifice is until you have to follow around dogs with plastic bags all afternoon. I think this is what's called paying my dues.

I am making progress, albeit slowly, toward becoming a responsible adult. Kyle, I think, would be proud, even though I haven't heard from him since I saw him in my dad's kitchen. I finally work up the courage to call him. I leave a message thanking him for his help with my legal troubles and apologizing again for my bad behavior.

The phone rings almost as soon as I put it down, and I snatch it up, hoping it's Kyle. It's Steph.

"Where have you BEEN?" Steph exclaims, harshly, as if I have been deliberately avoiding her.

"It's a LONG story," I say, too weary to begin to tell it.

"Forget it. Look, something serious has happened," she says.

"Are you and Ferguson eloping?" I ask.

"This is no time to be joking," Steph chides. "Ferguson is in jail. He was arrested. This morning. At Maximum Office."

"What?" I echo, sitting up in bed.

"They think he masterminded the break-in," Steph wails.

"Ferguson couldn't mastermind an escape from a paper bag," I say.

Steph ignores me.

"He used his one call from jail to call me—isn't that romantic?" she sighs. "We've GOT to help him."

"You mean turn ourselves in?" I say.

"What are you, *crazy*?" she hisses at me. "Of course not."

"What are we supposed to do then?"

"I've already got friends working on finding him a lawyer," she says. "In the meantime, I have an idea and I need your help."

"I don't know if this is going to work," I say, skeptical.

Steph and I are sitting in my parents' living room with several dozen pieces of poster board and giant permanent markers in front of us.

"It will work," she says.

Steph's plan involves making a few dozen "Free Ferguson" signs which will be held by members of an extremely radical, anti-corporate protest group during a march outside the county jail.

"World Trade Organization protestors are championing Ferguson's cause," she tells me.

"They condone company embezzlement?"

"If it's in the name of slandering overpaid executives, then yes," she says. "I made a few calls. I think I've gotten some local media interested."

"Aren't these the same people who completely demolished Seattle?"

"Right. I'd say it's best not to mention how much you like Starbucks, Jane," Steph advises.

It takes us the better part of the afternoon to make the signs, and then when Dad sees what we're doing, Steph spends the evening convincing him that it is a good idea. Dad insists, however, that we do it during the lunch hour so Todd can be my chaperon and make sure that no drugs are involved and that we both aren't carted off to jail.

At the front of the courthouse, I discover that somehow Steph has managed to assemble fifty-odd protesters, some of whom are under the mistaken impression that Ferguson worked at the McDonald's corporate headquarters instead of Maximum Office. Others think he used to work at Starbucks.

"Whatever gets them here, I don't care," Steph says when I ask her about the deception.

The protestors are all wearing what looks to be homespun clothing—no name brands, and poor-fitting shirts. None of the women are wearing make-up of any kind, and more than a few of them have tattoos with a big X mark through WTO. They have backpacks made of hemp with bumper stickers that read "I am not a corporate slave."

"Is that a Gap shirt?" asks a woman standing next to me. She smells like an elephant.

"No," I say. Technically, it's Banana Republic. "I got it at a thrift store," I lie.

"Oh," she says, her hostility dropping four notches. "Good."

She is wearing a T-shirt with a picture of a riot-torn Seattle street on the front.

I feel like I'm an undercover cop in prison. One false move and I'm dead. I shift my hand so it's covering the Gap tag on the back of my khaki pants.

"Listen up, folks," Steph says, using a bullhorn. I have no idea where she got a bullhorn. "The local camera crews will be here any second. I want us to form two lines and be orderly. Everybody take a sign."

Todd has not yet arrived. I hope he doesn't show. His Eddie Bauer leather loafers alone might get him killed.

Steph gets on the bullhorn again.

"Now, we want to keep things peaceful here," she says. "But we also want everyone to know about the injustice of jailing a person for using nontraditional channels to protest the stranglehold corporate America has on our freedoms."

Steph is good. I had no idea she was this good.

"We're tired of being pushed around," Steph shouts.

A few other people shout back. They are getting riled up.

"We're tired of corporate America making itself rich while they make the rest of the world poor!"

"That's right, sister!" shouts a guy in the back.

It's beginning to feel like a church revival.

"Men like Ed Ferguson should be listened to—not jailed!"

"Dead right!" yells someone else.

I wonder how these people get by without having jobs. Or wearing designer labels. The woman who smells like an elephant raises both arms to cheer Steph, and shows a small forest of underarm hair growth.

"We cannot let the corporate American dictators jail a man for expressing his opinions! We must demand that our oppressors release Ferguson!"

Steph could be a cult leader. She is that good.

"Free Ferguson!" someone in the back shouts. After a few minutes, the whole crowd is chanting it. Within minutes, half of them are taking their signs into the street in front of the courthouse, totally indifferent to the cars that are slamming on brakes and laying on horns.

Instantly, a row of forty or more people link arms and span the width of the street in front of the courthouse. Steph, who is shocked, nearly drops her bullhorn. Next to me, the woman who smells like an elephant grabs my arm and attempts to pull me into traffic. I resist as much as possible and just manage to keep my toehold on the curb.

As if on cue, the local television crew arrives, cameras on and filming. Horns are blaring. Curses are flying. And then things start to really get ugly.

A shouting match begins between a FedEx truck driver and one of the protesters. The driver is shouting at one of the men wearing a "Meat Is Murder" T-shirt. One thing leads to another, and the protester spits on the FedEx driver's uniform and calls him a Nazi Fascist Oppressor, and then the shoving begins. Almost immediately, a few wild punches are thrown.

The scuffle stops only when two police officers run out from the courthouse and disentangle the two men. The officers then try to convince the protesters to back down but, significantly outnumbered and without riot gear, the officers give up and simply take away the now slightly dazed and ruffled FedEx driver, who is bleeding from the nose.

I look over and see Steph talking with the local camera crew, explaining the situation and attempting to gain spin on the story, while the rest of the protesters abruptly sit in the middle of the street—arms linked and legs crossed. They glare at the drivers and are oblivious to shouts of insults about mothers, foreign objects, and demands that we go be intimate with ourselves.

The woman who smells like an elephant takes particular offense when one of the men shouts that she should spend less time protesting and more time investing in shaving equipment for her underarms. She lunges forward, attacking the man with her "Free Ferguson" sign.

I take advantage of her distraction to drop my sign and disengage from the protesters, taking up a safer position as a spectator in the growing crowd of onlookers gaping on the sidewalk in front of the courthouse. About this time, Todd arrives, wearing a befuddled look on his face and is nearly trampled by the dozen or so riot-gear-clad policemen who come streaming out of a recently arrived police van.

Todd and I are separated by the police officers, and Todd is being pushed into the crowd of protesters.

"What the hell?" Todd yells.

The next events race by in a blur.

The police swarm the crowd, dispensing pepper spray like air freshener and throwing locked-arm protesters to the ground, fastening their arms behind their backs with plastic ties. Todd, who is still confused, is standing behind the woman who smells like an elephant. She ducks to avoid a police officer spraying mace, and Todd gets a mouthful of chemicals. Todd, sputtering, spits profusely. Unfortunately, his spit lands on the riot helmet of the police officer in front of him, and before I can even say "Run!" Todd is being spun around and his hands are being secured behind his back. He is led off to a nearby paddy wagon along with several dozen other protesters who are kicking at the legs of the riot police.

The last thing I hear from Todd before the police close the doors of the van, is: "I am a Republican, dammit!"

•   •   •

Todd handles jail remarkably well, and by well I mean he doesn't, as I expect, have a total and complete mental breakdown in which he is frozen in a silent fetal position. Losing the afternoon of work alone would usually be enough to push him over the edge, but this time he's remarkably calm. And by calm, I mean shouting profanities at me for only twenty minutes straight on the phone.

"Todd, calm down," I say. "Todd, I'm going to hang up if you don't calm down."

"IF YOU DON'T GET ME OUT OF HERE I AM GOING TO KILL YOU," he's screaming into the jail's pay phone.

"Tell him to keep calm," Steph advises me. Steph avoided being arrested, but she did get a healthy dose of pepper spray, along with the news crew. She is sitting with me on my dad's couch.

"Todd, I'm going to put Dad on the phone," I say. I hand the phone to Dad.

"Don't use that tone with me, young man," Dad barks at Todd. "We're going to do what we can to get you out."

Dad pauses.

"If you use that kind of language with me, son, I'm going to hang up the phone," Dad says.

He pauses again.

"I mean it, Todd," he says.

Then, without hesitation, Dad hangs up.

"That will teach him," Dad says.

Steph coughs. Her eyes are nearly swollen shut from

the pepper spray. She looks like she's been attacked by a swarm of bees. "We're going to be on the ten o'clock news and in the paper for sure," Steph says.

"I don't see how that is good news," Dad says.

Steph then attempts to explain the finer points of public relations and marketing to Dad. At the end of it, Dad coughs.

"Liberal yahoo rubbish," he says when Steph finishes.

Steph and I watch ourselves on the six, six-thirty, and ten o'clock news. Luckily, I am in none of the shots, but Steph is articulate and calm even when she gets jostled and pushed around by the protesters. She gives great sound-bites that land intact on the news—a thoughtful, articulate indictment of Maximum Office's treatment of its workers, and most especially the "trumped up" charges against Ferguson. She even manages to get her web site, www.freeferguson.com listed in two of the news reports.

Dad springs Todd from jail that same night. When he walks into the lobby, Todd looks disheveled, his usually pristine golf shirt collar wrinkled and askew. He is still a bit puffy from the mace.

Todd glares at me.

"I don't think I need to tell you this is all your fault," he says.

"I'm sorry," I say, but I am having trouble not laughing.

"I never expected you'd be arrested with those hippie protesters," Dad says, in a semi-teasing tone.

Todd's face turns red, and he looks like water that's about to boil.

"Don't even start with me, Dad," he says.

"It could've been worse," I say. "You could've been arrested trying to get Hillary Clinton's autograph."

"I am not speaking to you. Again. Ever," Todd tells me.

The next few days are a whirlwind of activity. Media outlets keep calling Steph, and the *Tribune* runs a series on corporate corruption and excess, featuring the Maximum Office layoffs and the protests. Some companies start canceling Maximum Office orders, fearing a reprisal. The big merger between Maximum Office and its closest competitor, Office Online, is put on indefinite hold because of bad publicity and Maximum Office's tumbling stock price. And I discover, through Steph, that there are rumors that Mike Orephus's fiancée is dumping him.

I am amazed how little I care that Mike is getting his. I think it's because Kyle has sucked all the fun out of revenge.

"Oh, and did I tell you?" Steph breathes. "Two more attorneys have offered to take Fergie's case for free."

In my parents' living room, I find Dad sitting on the sofa completely engrossed in *The View*. He abruptly changes the channel to ESPN when I walk into the living room.

"I saw what you were watching," I say.

"I don't know what you're talking about," Dad says.

There's a pause.

"You can put it back on," I say.

"OK," he says.

He flips back to ABC and *The View*. "I'm hoping watching this will help me understand your mother better," he says, rather defensively.

"You don't have to justify it to me," I say.

"By the way, Kyle called for you," Dad says.

My heart leaps. Maybe he doesn't hate me after all.

"He called? When?"

"I don't know. Yesterday. Or maybe the day before," he says.

"Dad," I say, collapsing over in an exaggerated fit of frustration. It's as if I've gone back in time and I'm fifteen again. I straighten. If I learned anything from an adolescence filled with missed phone calls and Dad's bad message-taking, it's that Dad does not respond to fits of hysterics.

"This is very important," I say, enunciating every syllable as if I were talking to a person who doesn't speak English as their first language. "Tell me *everything* he said."

Dad thinks about this a moment.

"We talked about the Cubs," Dad says.

"And *what* else?"

"What else *is* there to talk about?" Dad barks. As far as Dad's concerned, men only talk about three things: baseball, business, and lawncare.

"You don't remember when he called?"

"Maybe Monday," Dad says.

I sigh and throw up my hands. Trying to get a message from Dad is like trying to translate French backward while underwater.

"Did he sound happy or mad?" I ask.

"What kind of question is that?" Dad scoffs.

I call Kyle, but all I get is his answering machine. After three hang-ups, I remember that he has caller ID.

Credit Counselors U.S.A.
1408 Dempster St.
Evanston, IL 60611

Jane McGregor
1410 Elmwood St.
Evanston, IL 60201

May 17, 2002

Dear Ms. McGregor,

You have taken your first steps on the road to financial freedom. Congratulations!

With your new debt consolidation loan, you have consolidated your payments, won a lower interest rate, and have successfully avoided bankruptcy.

Enclosed you'll find information on our mascot, Debt-Free Stan—The Checkbook. Remember, Debt-Free Stan says, "Everybody Wins with Good Credit!"

Sincerely,
Rachel Inman
Customer Representative
Credit Counselors U.S.A.

22

My attorney, Dan Schmidt, calls to tell me he has managed to discover that the district attorney's office is not currently investigating anyone else for the Maximum Office break-in, and furthermore, because of pressure from the company (a contributor to the district attorney's campaign) the charges against Ferguson likely will soon be dropped.

Dan Schmidt also has sorted out my lease agreement, and tells me Landlord Bob is willing to forgive most of the back rent in exchange for seizing my furniture. Given that my furniture probably permanently smells like pot, thanks to Ferguson and Ron, I'm happy to oblige.

My clothes and personal items, however, must be removed immediately.

"At least this won't be on your record," Dan Schmidt

says. "If we'd gone to court and this was on your credit history, I doubt you'd be able to rent anything else again."

I am not sure whether or not this is supposed to make me feel better.

"Thanks," I say.

Mom and Dad come back with me to my apartment for one last time on Saturday to help clean out clothes and anything that isn't "furniture." Technically, they are not back together, but they have moved beyond the need to be in completely separate rooms at all times. Dad has taken this new development as a sign that reconciliation may still be a possibility.

My old apartment is a mess. Empty beer cans, broken bottles, toppled furniture and food and other stains cover the floor and walls.

"What in the world?" Mom exclaims, mouth agape.

"This apartment isn't as nice as I remember," Dad says.

It takes us a few hours to pack up everything, and most all of it fits in the back of Mom's white Volvo station wagon.

Before I leave for good, I take one last look at my trashed apartment, like Mary looking at the studio in the last episode of the *Mary Tyler Moore* show. I switch off the light and don't look back.

• • •

I'm turning the corner when I practically plow into Kyle.

"What are you doing here?" I squeak at him, holding my chest so my heart doesn't fall out.

"Todd said you'd be here," he says.

"I thought Todd wasn't speaking to me," I say.

"He isn't speaking to you, but he's speaking to me," Kyle clarifies.

"Oh," I say. I am still having trouble looking him in the eye. It takes a great amount of effort just to manage to stare at his shoelaces. I am afraid he's going to lecture me about the protests and about jail and about how it's my fault Ferguson is facing a court date.

"Jane!" shouts Dad, laying on the horn. "Get a move on!"

"One second, Dad," I shout.

"Kyle! Is that you?" Mom says, getting out of the front seat.

"Hi, Mrs. McGregor," Kyle says.

"If you two want to talk . . ." Mom's voice trails off.

I am not sure I want to be left alone with him.

"Traffic's going to be terrible if we don't leave," Dad shouts.

"I can take Jane home," Kyle says, before I can say anything.

"Sure, sure," Mom says. She actually winks at me. I turn tomato red. It takes all my force of will not to run after my parents' retreating Volvo.

"Kyle, I am so sorry I didn't trust you, and I meant

to call and tell you that, but I just, well, I don't know,"
I say.

"I think I'm the one that should be apologizing."

My head shoots up. "Why?"

"You didn't tell me about Mike," he says.

"How did you find out about Mike?" I ask.

"Dan told me."

"I thought that was supposed to be confidential," I cry.

"You really should have told me," he says. "It explains
a lot. It sounds like he took advantage of you. It's not
entirely your fault. And it's no wonder that you suspected
I might be cheating. After a relationship like that, I'd be
a little hesitant to trust again, too."

"I'm over it now," I say.

"Good," he says.

We smile at each other.

Kyle reaches out and pushes some hair out of my
eyes.

"So do you hate me or what?" he asks.

"Hate you? Why would I hate you?"

"You didn't return any of my calls. Even when I came
to your parents' house, you couldn't even look at me."

"I thought you hated me. You clearly hated me first."

"I never hated you. How could you think that? I may
not have agreed with some of your choices, but Jane, I
could never hate you. I'm crazy about you. You've got to
see that."

And at that moment, looking at Kyle's earnest face, I
believe him.

"So, what do we do now?" I ask.

"Really hot marathon sex?" he offers.

I bark a laugh. "Sounds like a good idea to me," I say.

"Maybe later we can talk about the secret wife I have in Utah," Kyle says, "and the two others in Ohio and Oregon."

"There is no part of that is funny," I say, but I'm smiling.

Sex with Kyle is, hands down, the best I've ever had, which probably isn't saying a lot (considering the likes of Ron). The addition of sex to the friendship is like discovering one of your oldest friends also happens to be fabulously wealthy. Kyle being great in bed is just one of life's unexpected bonuses.

And it has taken me awhile to realize it, but Kyle is funny and entertaining and the only other person on the planet who is as much of a smartass as I am.

And he does seem to be crazy about me for some odd reason. I can't tell why. Perhaps he's secretly turned on by my thrilling life of crime.

"I'm going to have to go back to work sometime," Kyle tells me.

We're lying in his bedroom, having just finished eating pizza straight out of the box. Kyle has taken two sick days in a row, and we haven't left his apartment during that time.

"Work is for suckers," I say, resting my head on his chest.

"I think you're on to something there," Kyle says, wrapping me up again in his arms and rolling me over so I'm under him. Not working is so much better when you have someone really sexy and funny to do it with, I decide.

A week later, my mom starts crying tears of joy when I announce over pot roast at her new apartment that Kyle and I are dating.

"Mom, we're just dating. We're not engaged," I say.

"I'm just so happy for you!" she says, squeezing me tight. She then proceeds to tell Kyle about how I'd had a crush on him for years and used to kiss his picture in the yearbook when I was seven and he was eleven. Kyle does not let me live this down for weeks afterward.

Mom announces shortly afterward that she's gotten a promotion to Director of Content, and Dad takes a job at Wrigley Field selling peanuts. Dad says he's always wanted to work at Wrigley Field. Mom claims he took on a job in concessions because he ruined all his white-collared shirts by putting them in the wash with one of his red socks.

"Your father will do anything—even work for peanuts—to get out of shopping for new clothes," Mom says.

And while the two of them are not back together, and might not ever be, I take it as a positive sign that Mom is once again at least talking about Dad. And the two of them can increasingly stay in the same room for longer and longer spells without one or the other storming out. I attribute this to Dad's growing library of self-help books.

Todd starts speaking to me a month later, and I tell him about Kyle and me being an item. I dread this moment because Todd can be overprotective at times, and he, like my dad, thinks that I am asexual and reproduce by spores.

He's not angry as I suspected he would be. He's not even surprised.

"I was wondering when you two were just going to go have sex and get it over with," he says, shrugging.

"You're not mad?" I ask.

"Why would I be mad? It's a free country."

Todd's temporary brush with the law has made him far more open-minded and magnanimous. For six full weeks he's resisted the need to give me advice, and he's even made noise about possibly quitting his job and going to law school.

"Todd, I think you're a whole new person," I say. "Pretty soon, you'll start donating money to the ACLU."

"Let's not go that far," Todd says.

Steph calls me later to tell me that Ferguson has sold his story to NBC to make into a made-for-TV movie.

"He hasn't even gone to trial yet," I say.

"He's probably going to settle the case soon," Steph

says. "Maximum Office can't handle much more bad publicity. They have a merger to think about, and all. But guess who they think is going to play him? Just guess?"

"John Goodman?" I venture.

"No! Rob Lowe!" she exclaims.

I try to imagine Rob Lowe staring at a computer with a *Lord of the Rings* screensaver and chowing down Subway sandwiches. I fail.

"I always thought he looked like Rob Lowe," Steph says. "Not to mention, I think I've found a new calling. Ferguson is hiring me to be his manager."

"What else does he have going on besides the NBC deal?"

"Well, I'm talking to Subway right now, and maybe we'll think about going on a speaking tour."

"Steph, you're insane, you know that?"

"I prefer to think of myself as inspired," she says.

Later that same week, I'm walking a golden retriever, a poodle, and a Jack Russell terrier when I nearly collide with Ron. I haven't seen him since the back of the squad car, and he looks almost dressed up, wearing pants with sewn hems, a shirt that doesn't have holes in it, and mirrored sunglasses. Even his bleached blond hair looks properly highlighted and conditioned.

"Jane, I have been looking *all over* for you," he says.

"Back away from me," I say. "I don't want to be arrested again."

"I am SO sorry about that," Ron says. "Really, I am. I feel terrible. Let me make it up to you."

Ron pulls a wad of cash from his giant pocket. He counts out ten slightly soggy $100 bills.

"I can't take your drug money," I protest, trying to put up a noble fight.

"It's not drug money, dude," he says. "It's royalty money and you earned it with your CD cover. Besides, I owe you bail money. The arrest *really* helped me start a buzz about Sink Gunk."

I forgot that jail time usually improves record sales.

Ron's band Sink Gunk, he tells me, has managed to make the Billboard Top 50 with their single, "Love Bites Like Drano," and are soon to go on a national tour, hitting twenty-five major cities.

"Wow," I say, taking the money and folding the bills into my pocket. "Nice work."

"Have you heard from Missy?" Ron asks me.

"No," I say.

"I heard from a friend of a friend that she moved to New Mexico. I think she's starting her own cult or something. A commune of some kind."

"She's probably just looking for a new way to steal money," I say.

"I think she was my soul mate," Ron sighs.

I roll my eyes.

"Look, love is blind, dude, OK?"

"Whatever," I say.

"Anyway, I also wanted to get your email address and

phone number. There's this graphic design guy who's to-tally hot for your album cover, and he wants to talk to you about some other gig."

I hug Ron.

"Hey, babe, I told you we're just friends," he says, putting up his hands.

"It's not sexual," I snap.

"Whatever you want to tell yourself, babe," he says.

To: jane@coolchick.com
From: Pierre and Friends Graphic Design
Sent: 06/01/02

Dear Jane,

I am a freelance designer who works for Millennium Records, the record company that signed Sink Gunk.

After looking at your design for Sink Gunk's album cover, I'd like you to consider the possibility of interviewing for a graphic design position I have open in my firm.

If you're interested, please fax me your resume and we can go from there.

Sincerely,
Pierre Lamont

23

There's a message on Dad's answering machine for me when I get home and I am momentarily frozen by the sound of a French accent. Thankfully, it isn't Landlord Bob, who every now and again makes an appearance in my dreams wearing his pink bathrobe.

No, this is Pierre Lamont, art director, who wants to meet me for an interview that afternoon.

When I meet Pierre Lamont I notice two things right away: his permanent five o'clock shadow and the cigarette butt hanging from his lip. Immediately, he offers me one of his unfiltered cigarettes to smoke in his office, and I think I might have found my dream boss.

"You are good with lines," he grunts. "I like a woman who knows her lines, eh?"

His accent is much softer than Landlord Bob's, and I am relieved to find that not all Frenchmen shout.

"So, you up for some work, eh?" he asks me. "We do lots of CD covers zere, and concert posters and invitations—just a little bit of everyzing. I hope you like to be creative. We need creative work zere."

I nod. So far, so good. I like the idea of working in a place where I can be creative, where I can do something more demanding than designing Post-it notes.

"So. Zere's how it works, OK? I hire you for three months. I pay you, and if I like you, you get to stay on, OK?"

As I watch, Pierre stubs out his cigarette in a pile of wrinkled up pieces of paper, completely oblivious to any fire hazards, and immediately lights up another.

"I work by French hours here, so that's thirty hours a week, no more," he says. "Overtime is American, yes? We French work smart, not hard."

I am liking him more and more already.

"If you are hired on permanently, you get insurance, 401(k), and six weeks vacation a year."

Pierre puffs on his cigarette, letting this sink in. I must look as shocked as I feel, because Pierre is quick to add, "I know vacation seems short, but after awhile, maybe we bump it up to eight weeks."

Short? Six weeks is short? My hands are shaking from sheer excitement.

"And I don't like working in August, yes? I go home to France in August."

"I'd be happy to cover then," I say.

"Cover?" Pierre coughs. Smoke comes out of his nose. "No need to cover. Office shuts down for August. But the bad thing is, you have to come to Paris for a couple of weeks so you can meet my partner."

"So, let me get this straight," I say. "If I work for you, I get to go to Paris. I get August off, and six additional weeks during the year?"

Pierre nods.

"But maybe we move that up to eight after you work here a while," he says.

I am fighting the strong urge to leap over the desk and kiss him on the lips.

"When can I start?" I ask, almost too eagerly, like the kid who always knew all the answers in class.

"Eh, whenever you'd like." He shrugs. "Two weeks? Three? I call you, yes?"

"You won't regret it," I say eagerly, like a college freshman, shaking his hand.

Two weeks later, I move out of my parents' house and into my new, smaller, more financially responsible apartment. It doesn't have its own washer and dryer. In fact, it's more of a studio than a one-bedroom, but at this point, I have no furniture to put in it, anyway.

But I don't care. If I've learned anything from the last six months, it's that you can't always control everything about your life, and that losing a job or your apartment isn't the end of the world. Life goes on, and that's a good thing.

Also, I'm trying to learn to be less critical. After all, hating things is a lot easier than admitting to what you like. And being critical of the whole world means, in most cases, being most critical of yourself. I've decided to give myself, and the world, a break for once. And no matter what, I'm never going to let work get so personal again. I've more than learned my lesson.

And, you can't keep people out forever. Eventually, one or two of them might get in and hurt you, despite all your best efforts, and this is OK, too, because it's better to put yourself out there and get hurt than to never take the chance at all.

Kyle has promised to rent a truck and take me "shopping" at the annual Clean-Up Week in Winnetka, which is when all the wealthy people put out furniture on the curb and everyone else snatches it up. It's like a flea market, only it's free, and the merchandise is all Room and Board and Restoration Hardware.

Kyle, in fact, has taken Ron's place as the perennial squatter in my new digs, but I don't mind, because Kyle insists on paying for take-out, since my new budget doesn't allow for much eating out, digital cable, or buying any new clothes, shoes, or purses until I'm sixty-five. But it's not all bad. There's Kyle to keep me entertained, and besides, not having cable gives me more time to paint, which I love. Kyle has been my major subject for

the most part, and he is now the star fixture in a new series of collage portraits I'm doing. I've even been thinking of trying to get a gallery show of my paintings, which
just goes to show that being laid off and committing felonies can really inspire a person to get motivated, to have
some real ambition.

In two months, I'm going to Paris, and Kyle has
threatened to follow me to watch me paint. He has only
one stipulation—that while I work I wear my Elvis
Costello glasses and nothing else.

Up Close and Personal With the Author

What is the inspiration for *Pink Slip Party*?

Two years ago, several friends of mine suffered through some serious layoffs, and I wanted to write a book for them. Losing your job can feel like losing your identity. One day you're a "consultant" or a "programmer" or a "publicist" and the next day, you're "someone looking for a job." It can change how you see yourself, and how other people see you. Also, I think next to love interests and friends, a job is a central focus of a twenty- or thirty-something's life.

There are a couple of instances in the book where being laid off is compared to having a bad break-up. Why do you think the two are so similar?

I think many women can take the loss of a job in the same way they take the loss of a boyfriend. You feel rejected, in the same way that you do when someone tells you they don't want to be in a relationship with you. The excuse that a layoff is not necessarily related to job performance has the same false ring that "It's not you, it's me" does. I think losing your job often feels like a personal rejection, and it makes you go through the same steps you would in recovering from a bad break-up. You will be asking yourself "why" and trying to figure out what to do next.

In the book, Jane has two personal rejections—the loss of her job and her boyfriend, who is an executive at the office where she used to work.

I think many people have experienced workplace romances. While I think most women understand the perils of dating someone at work, it's almost impossible to avoid. Work is a natural place to find romance. You spend most of your time there, and when you're there you're trying to perform at your best. It's a far less intimidating place to find romance than a local bar or online. Also, I think Jane becoming personally involved at work illustrates a common problem for women in the workplace. Women often have a hard time separating the personal from the professional. It's one reason why women take career setbacks so personally, because they've invested so much of themselves, personally and professionally, in their jobs.

Jane wasn't that thrilled with the job she lost and part of her journey through the book is to find something she finds more fulfilling. Why is this important?

As Americans, I think we relate to our jobs very differently than other people in the world. We have a famous work ethic, and we instinctively let our jobs define who we are. For most of us, work isn't just a paycheck, it's an identity. This relationship is even more complicated for workers in their twenties and thirties. We're part of a generation, I think, where many of our parents told us to do what makes us happy. This is quite a challenging task. Not only are we supposed to find work, but we're supposed to find work that's satisfying. If you can't do both, somehow you're failing. But finding what you love to do and what pays the bills aren't always going to be the same thing. Jane finds a nice balance by the end of the book, and I think it's a balance that many of us seek in our own lives.

Jane has a complicated relationship with her father. How do you think that relationship influences the way she approaches her layoff?

In Jane's family, her dad was the major breadwinner for most of her life, and her example of how a career should be managed. But his view of the workforce is a bit dated. Jane's dad is only just becoming disillusioned with corporate America, whereas Jane always doubted the sincerity of corporate management. I think they ultimately help each other come to terms with the new economy.

How much is Jane like you?

The book is not autobiographical. I never broke into a company that wronged me (although I would have liked to), but certainly there is some of me in Jane. We share a similar sense of humor and some of the same opinions, but Jane is far more confident about expressing hers publicly than I am. I'd like to have some of Jane's confidence, especially when it comes to confronting landlords.

In both of your novels, *I Do (But I Don't)* and *Pink Slip Party*, humor plays a role in your storytelling. What do you find funny and where do you get inspiration for writing humor?

Humor is a very tricky thing to write, mostly because it's nearly impossible to get two people to agree on what's funny. I find lots of things funny. I grew up in a household where there was a lot of laughter and joking around about a wide variety of things. We were the sort of family—my brother Matt and I especially—who'd mimic *Saturday Night Live* skits long after they wore out their funniness. In fact, when I was three, I retold my first knock-knock joke over and over and over again. My parents, who deserve the World's Most Patient People award, would play along every time. So, developing a sense of humor starts early. Writing funny prose is challenging and I think having a balance of different kinds of humor (from sarcasm to physical comedy) is important, but actually succeeding in making someone laugh out loud is very difficult. At times, you're going to fall flat, especially if it's your hundredth retelling of a fruit-themed knock-knock joke. But you should keep trying.

Some writers have writing schedules. Others write only when the spirit moves them. How do you write?

I try to write a little bit almost every day, even on days when I'm not feeling too inspired. I don't always manage to meet this goal. I'm as guilty as anyone at getting sucked into watching *The E! True Hollywood Story* when I really ought to be working. However, I think any little work you can do helps. Writing a novel is like running a marathon. You train for it little by little, and you only get there running one mile at a time.

Do you work from an outline? Do you have the entire story planned in advance?

I have major plot points planned, but as far as some of the details in many of the chapters, those I tend to improvise. And I've found that stories often change from initial outlines. When you get into the middle of a book, and you really feel like you know your characters even better than you did when you started, then some of the plot may seem weak or implausible. Or, you may simply become inspired to take the plot in a new direction. The great thing about fiction, and what separates it from nonfiction, is that radical changes in plot are possible and often make the story stronger.

What advice would you give to people who want to become writers?

I do believe in the adage *write what you know*. But I think what's more important is to write about what you find interesting. If you or your friends are interested in the subject and story, then chances are, other people will be, too. Books need readers, especially if you want to publish your book some day. The vast majority of writers are entertainers, and entertainers need audiences.

Turn the page for a sneak peek of

CAN'T TEACH AN OLD DEMON NEW TRICKS

by
Cara Lockwood

Coming soon from Pocket Books

One

Would you watch your wings? They're in my face," said Gabriel Too (not *the* Gabriel, archangel, but Gabriel, lower-ranking, non-archangel—thus the "too").

"Sorry," apologized Frank the New. "I'm not used to them." Frank the New scrunched his shoulders and folded in his wings so they flapped less conspicuously as they glided toward Earth.

"It takes awhile to get used to," agreed Gabriel Too, giving the new recruit a soft pat on the shoulder. "And make sure not to lose the halo. They're always slipping off. They never fit right. They should come in half sizes but they don't."

"Thanks for the advice," said Frank the New, as he adjusted his halo, which happened to be tilting a little too far to the right.

"Hang on," Gabriel Too said, holding up his hand and signaling to Frank the New that he ought to stop. "You always look both ways before crossing the jet stream." The two paused as a 777 jet cruised by. "Okay, it's safe to go."

"Thanks for the heads up." Frank the New kicked his feet out of the long hem of his robe. Frank was slight in build and much shorter than Gabriel. His white billowing robe swam on him and his ears were a little oversized, a combination that made him look not a little like Dopey the Dwarf. His small stature, however, didn't change the fact that if there were a fight at hand, he was going to run in, fists up. He had more courage than he did size.

"So when do we vanquish some demons?" Frank the New asked, rubbing his hands together in anticipation. He spoke in a clipped British accent, not unlike Anthony Hopkins. "I am very ready to trounce some evil."

"Whoa, whoa, *whoa* there, double-oh-seven," Gabriel Too said, holding up his hand. "Not so fast. I know you are a little tough guy, but we're just watchers. We watch."

"I'm sorry, but I am not a sidelines kind of fellow." Frank the New rolled up one of his blousy sleeves and sighed. "How are you supposed to fight evil in these robes?" he asked, sliding out a hand in a fake punch, only to have it covered by the cuff of his billowing white sleeve. He shook his hand loose and then grabbed the golden harp he'd slung under one arm. "And what's this for? Where's my flaming sword?"

"You don't get one. You don't fight evil. You just watch it."

Frank the New grimaced. "I'll have you know that I didn't stop the Antichrist by sitting around and watching." Frank the New was talking about a few months back when he was still an angel in training, and managed, with the help of a reluctant psychic, Constance Plyd, to stop the devil from impregnating a vapid pop princess and thereby preventing the conception of a half-demon who would've brought the end of the world. He also happened to do all this while in the body of a French bulldog, which he thought should've earned him extra points.

"You aren't in the Wrath Division, or even Messengers, who occasionally get to dust it up. We are *watchers*. We watch. Period."

"Well, then, the Big Guy made a mistake. I'm not a watcher. I'm a doer." Frank the New finished rolling up his sleeves and started popping his knuckles.

"The Big Guy doesn't make mistakes," Gabriel Too said. "Not even dinosaurs or the platypus. Which, by the way, is a sore subject with the Big Guy. Don't mention the platypus."

"I wasn't planning on it." As the two angels floated down from the sky, the earth came into view below, showing a truck stop and a highway, framed on both sides by long slopes of grass with cattle grazing.

"Hey, this place looks familiar," Frank the New said, nodding to the cows.

"It should," Gabriel Too replied, leading the pair across Route Nine and over to a small grassy subdivision. "This is Dogwood County—the place you saved from the Antichrist—am I right?"

Frank the New nodded.

Dogwood County, population 17,891, sat smack-dab in the middle of east Texas and was famous for award-winning chicken-fried steak, the largest pecan pie ever baked (weighing in at 35,000 pounds), and ground zero for the epic battle of good versus evil. Not that most of the Dogwood residents knew their quaint country home happened to be the place where angels and demons fought it out for the souls of all mankind. Only a select few knew about Dogwood's importance in the scheme of things, and God and the Devil hoped to keep it that way. They were waging a covert war that neither wanted on the front page of the *Dogwood County Times*.

The street below came into view, home to about five houses spread out over a little hilly patch and separated by the occasional grazing cow. Gabriel Too stopped above the house belonging to Rachel Farnsworth. Rachel was sound asleep in her bedroom, one foot sticking out of the covers and her arm thrown over her eyes. Her son, Cassidy, had come awake in his crib next door, and was eyeing a small wooden train engine on the floor. Both angels could see through the roof, one of many convenient angel powers, including the ability to be invisible and hear the voice of God without shattering into a million pieces.

"So what do we do now?" Frank the New asked, as the two settled onto a large branch of a nearby oak tree.

"We watch and report."

"But—correct me if I'm wrong—but God already knows what's going to happen. He doesn't need our little reports."

"Yes, God is omniscient. Or omnipotent? I always mix those up." Gabriel Too looked thoughtful. "Anyway, whatever it is, the short answer is, yes, God already knows everything but He has to give us something to do."

"So it's a test then?"

"Probably. Most everything is. God likes pop quizzes."

The two angels watched as Cassidy tried to stick his arm out of his crib to reach the little wooden train engine. After trying, and failing, to reach it, he stood on sure legs and started climbing up the crib's side, his dark brown curls bouncing as he went. In seconds, he'd jumped off the edge and landed in a pile of stuffed animals in the corner of his room. He pulled himself up to standing and then waddled over to the train, picking it up with a look of triumph in his bright brown eyes.

"This is a waste of time." Frank the New sank his chin into one hand. "I didn't almost die defeating the devil so I could be on babysitting duty."

"He's not, technically, a baby."

"Toddler-sitting then."

"No, no, no, I mean he's not technically human. He's half-demon. But he's definitely a toddler."

"Demon? How come I couldn't smell him out then?" Frank the New took a whiff of the air, but didn't smell the telltale sign of burnt popcorn—the trail most demons left behind.

"He's pretty good at camouflage. Must be one of his powers."

Frank the New smashed one fist into his palm. "Well, then, old sport, what are we waiting for? Let's send the demon tyke back to hell." He made as if he were going to march down there and swoop up the child.

"Hold on, buddy," Gabriel Too chided, grabbing Frank the New by the arm. "There is no vanquishing. There is no fighting. There isn't even any cussing. We don't lay a finger on that boy. We watch him. That's it. *Do you understand?*"

Frank the New crossed his arms across his chest and sighed. "Fine."

"We're supposed to sit here and wait and see if her husband shows up, and if he does, we're supposed to report back to Peter. It's the dad who's the full-blooded demon, and he's gone MIA. Everybody is looking for him, too. Heaven *and* hell."

"Why is he so important?"

Gabriel Too shrugged. "Dunno. Peter didn't tell us. We don't have the right kind of clearance."

"So we can't zap this kid?"

"Nope."

"Not even with holy water?"

"Not even with holy water."

"What if he runs out of the house and eats one of the neighbors?"

Gabriel Too looked down and saw Cassidy had made his way to the kitchen and was opening cabinet doors. His mother, who was still sleeping, hadn't heard his escape.

"We can't intervene," Gabriel Too explained. "You don't know the h-e-double-l we'd catch if we stuck our noses where they don't belong. We just watch and take notes." Gabriel Too waved around his legal notepad. "That's our job."

Below them, Cassidy was bouncing around the kitchen, half-leaping, half-flying from one counter to the next.

"I can't believe I got a desk job," said Frank the New with a sigh, as he took the notepad.

Two

$\mathcal{R}$achel Farnsworth was used to minor disasters. She was a mother.

What she wasn't used to was quiet.

It was the peace and quiet that broke Rachel's slumber the morning of her son Cassidy's first birthday. Her house was never peaceful or quiet.

She glanced at the clock and realized with a shock it was already eight-fifteen. Cassidy never slept this late, usually being up at six in the morning, having by then ripped up the bedding in his crib, dismantled the Winnie the Pooh mobile, and tried to climb over the rails at least three or four times, all while shrugging half out of his diaper and his pajamas. It was only then, normally, that he'd give a bloodcurdling scream loud enough to wake the neighbors, a sound as endearing as an ambulance siren that Rachel had come to think of his her own personal alarm clock. Her husband, Kevin, naturally slept through it, because he slept through everything. She glanced to Kevin's side of the bed and found it empty. He must've gone to work already.

Rachel threw off her covers and raced to Cassidy's room, only to come skidding to a stop halfway through the door. The crib was empty. Rachel's heart stopped. Her first thought was that he'd been kidnapped by some horrible predator, like the ones she always saw on TV being caught soliciting sex from twelve-year-old virgins. She shook the thought from her head and told herself not to panic. That was when she came to her senses and realized Cassidy must've jumped out of his crib, because there was a trail of rumpled clothes and toys along the floor. Rachel comforted herself with the knowledge that a predator wouldn't have bothered to stack up his alphabet blocks on his way out, so Cassidy had to have sprung himself. The little Houdini had done it again.

"Cass?" she called, trying not to sound mad, in case he might be about to stick his head in the oven. "Where are you?"

Cassidy could be anywhere. There wasn't a restraint made by man he couldn't get out of. Clothes, diapers, high chairs, even car seats were no match for the grubby, quick hands of Cassidy Henry Farnsworth. Even at the tender age of one, he'd mastered all but the most complex of latches. Last week, he even managed to open their front door and sprint out naked as a jaybird, much to the dismay of half the neighborhood. Rachel knew what the other moms said about her. That she was careless. That she didn't pay attention. But, honestly, he was simply too quick and too smart for his own good. Just last week, he unlatched his car seat. A flash of corduroy overalls in her rearview had clued her in to the fact that he was happily hopping up and down on a sack of groceries in the back-seat. That little surprise had nearly made her veer into oncoming traffic.

Plus, he always seemed quicker than he ought to be, and smarter, too. She didn't know of other babies who took their first steps at five months, for instance. The other moms never believed her, but Rachel swore he could do things he just shouldn't be able to do.

"Ma Ma!" came a muffled shout from somewhere in the vicinity of the kitchen. This was followed by a clatter that sent Rachel sprinting. She stopped at the threshold of her kitchen and her mouth fell open.

It looked like a hurricane had blown through. Cassidy had hit the pantry and raided the snack cabinet, somehow dismantling the so-called childproof lock on it. The floor was covered with spilled Goldfish, a rumpled bag of Doritos, a half dozen apple juice boxes, including one that was actually open and spilling out across her kitchen tile.

How on earth she'd slept through *this* little disaster, she had no idea.

"Cassidy Henry FARNSWORTH!" she cried, hands on hips, as she stared at the floor in dismay.

"Da! Mon!" he blurted, in an almost gleeful tone. "Da! Mon! Da! Mon! Da! Mon!"

She had no idea what he was saying, but she followed the sounds. But no matter where she looked, she couldn't find him.

"Cass? Cass!" He was here somewhere. She could hear him.

"Da Da Da DA!" he babbled. "Mon! Mon! Mon! Mon!"

Rachel realized, with a sinking feeling in her stomach, that the sound *wasn't* coming from the floor. Or anywhere near the floor, which was where her little one-year-old usually spent most of his time. It was coming from much, much higher.

And that's when a little cheddar-flavored Goldfish fell on her head from above like a little snowflake from Pepperidge Farm.

She looked up, dread in her throat, and saw Cassidy, naked as the day he was born, do a little jump that made the dark curls on his head bounce. He was balancing precariously on the top of her refrigerator, grubby hands full of cheddar-flavored fish crackers.

"DA! MON!" he cheered.

Rachel's whole body went cold. She flung up her arms, praying he stayed away from the edge long enough to get him down without a free fall. She didn't have time to wonder how he got there. She just wanted to get him down in one piece.

"Come to Mama," she commanded, hoping to keep the panic out of her voice. "Come now."

"No!" Cass shouted, gleefully. Standing up on the refrigerator, he raised his arms like he was preparing to do a swan dive onto her tile floor. Rachel grabbed one of his chunky legs and then the other, and soon she had him cradled safely in her arms.

"No climbing. *NO,*" she said. "Why do you have to scare Mama like that?" Her heart rate was slowly returning to normal, her panic draining away. Now she had the time to wonder just how Cassidy had managed to climb up on top of the counter *and* reach the top of the refrigerator. No matter how she studied the scene of the crime, she couldn't figure it out. It was like he sprouted wings and flew there. She wondered, briefly, if there was an explanation she was missing. If she hadn't birthed Cassidy herself after twenty-eight hours of labor, she just might have thought he fell from space in a meteor like Superman. The boy did things Rachel simply couldn't explain.

Also available from *USA TODAY* bestselling author

Cara Lockwood

Can't Teach an Old Demon New Tricks

Whipping up prize-winning
chicken fried steak…
Fighting demonic forces…
Saving the world.

**East Texas gal Constance Plyd
can do it all!**

Coming April 2010 from Pocket Books!